P9-DUG-855

"Are you saying that what's between us right now is all there will ever be, Spence?"

"That's exactly what I'm telling you. I've never met a woman like you, Joanne. You make me feel things I never thought I'd feel again. But that doesn't change the facts."

"What facts are those?"

"That I'll never marry again. Neither will I live with anyone."

"I don't fully understand why." She was pushing him in a direction he didn't want to go, yet she didn't care. She had to know why he was doing this.

"I promised myself I'd spend my life making up to my daughter for everything I took away from her. Anyone else has to come second."

She knew she was in dangerous territory, and she didn't give a hoot.

"She's going to want a life of her own, Spence. That's what growing up is all about, isn't it?"

He didn't answer. Just left the room.

Joanne had wanted him to stay, talk with her. But before she could say those things, he was gone.

Dear Reader,

Several years ago, a newborn disappeared from the maternity ward in the small city where I live. Until the baby was found and safely restored to its parents, there was a universal feeling of anxiety and the sense of a loving community united in a common cause.

As a parent, I could imagine what it must feel like to have a newborn abducted. As a writer, I saw the seeds of a story.

I believe dramatic situations that touch our hearts in such a fashion serve a valuable purpose. For a few hours, a few days, we become aware that despite the diversity of the faces we present to the world, within our souls is a deep unity, an instinctive understanding that there's really only one of us here, that love in all its guises is a powerful glue that can make us whole.

I hope you enjoy reading *Full Recovery,* as I've enjoyed writing it for you.

Much love,

Bobby

FULL RECOVERY
Bobby Hutchinson

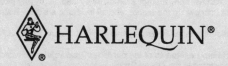

HARLEQUIN®

TORONTO · NEW YORK · LONDON
AMSTERDAM · PARIS · SYDNEY · HAMBURG
STOCKHOLM · ATHENS · TOKYO · MILAN · MADRID
PRAGUE · WARSAW · BUDAPEST · AUCKLAND

If you purchased this book without a cover you should be aware that this book is stolen property. It was reported as "unsold and destroyed" to the publisher, and neither the author nor the publisher has received any payment for this "stripped book."

ISBN 0-373-70925-0

FULL RECOVERY

Copyright © 2000 by Bobby Hutchinson.

All rights reserved. Except for use in any review, the reproduction or utilization of this work in whole or in part in any form by any electronic, mechanical or other means, now known or hereafter invented, including xerography, photocopying and recording, or in any information storage or retrieval system, is forbidden without the written permission of the publisher, Harlequin Enterprises Limited, 225 Duncan Mill Road, Don Mills, Ontario, Canada M3B 3K9.

All characters in this book have no existence outside the imagination of the author and have no relation whatsoever to anyone bearing the same name or names. They are not even distantly inspired by any individual known or unknown to the author, and all incidents are pure invention.

This edition published by arrangement with Harlequin Books S.A.

® and TM are trademarks of the publisher. Trademarks indicated with ® are registered in the United States Patent and Trademark Office, the Canadian Trade Marks Office and in other countries.

Visit us at www.eHarlequin.com

Printed in U.S.A.

For Bev, Patricia, Lois, Carol, Margot, Gail, Cathy and Kathy. *Full Recovery* is dedicated to all of you, the women who mean so much to me. During any crisis, happy or sad, you come like caring sisters bearing soup or flowers, candles or bubble bath. You offer hugs and attentive silence, into which can be spilled joy or sorrow or anything in between. I'm so blessed to have all of you in my life.

ACKNOWLEDGMENT

Gratitude, as always, to Patricia Gibson,
who always comes up with the answer to whatever.
Many thanks to Sid Harrison for advice on investigation,
and to Marci Ekland for helpful information on sexuality in
spinal cord injury. And a huge thank-you to my lawyer,
who also happens to be my beloved daughter-in-law,
Trudy Hopman Jackart. Trudy solves legal problems for
my characters and never bills me.

CHAPTER ONE

"ALPHA ONE calling Alpha two."

Spencer Mathews reached for the portable radio hooked to the regulation belt of his gray security uniform and pushed the transmitter button, wishing his partner, Murray Kellerman, would learn that hollering into the device wasn't necessary.

Murray's booming voice startled two nursing aides walking ahead of Spence down St. Joe's busy hospital corridor. They whirled around, and then, recognizing his security uniform, smiled at him and resumed their conversation.

"Alpha two, go ahead," Spence responded in a barely audible tone.

"Geronimo in fifteen. Copy on that, Alpha two?"

Geronimo was Murray's code for a coffee break. Their scheduled time in the morning was 9:45, still nearly an hour away. Spence had learned during these first three weeks on the job that Murray consistently stretched the rules to suit himself, and he suppressed a sigh.

"Affirmative in fifteen." Working with Murray

made him wonder whether letting his old friend Bud Ansell talk him into taking this job at St. Joseph's had been a smart move. Bud owned Vector Security; he'd hired Murray.

Not that Murray was a bad guy. Not at all. It was just that he was so damn...amateur.

And what the hell are you, Mathews, some sort of expert just because you spent twenty years in the RCMP? You're forty-four years old. You're damn lucky to have been offered a job that pays as well as this. The money goes a long way toward Devon's tuition and the medical bills that insurance doesn't cover.

Thinking of his daughter elicited a familiar barrage of emotions—overwhelming love, then the inevitable guilt that gnawed at his gut like an ulcer.

To have the radio immediately crackle to life again was almost a relief. This time it was the dispatcher at the switchboard, and there was an undercurrent of urgency in her even tone.

"Alpha one, Alpha two, request attendance in Emergency, *stat.* We have a J2 with a knife."

Adrenaline coursed through Spence's body. *J2* was code for a violent patient.

"Request police backup," he snapped into the receiver, and then he was racing down the corridor in the direction of the emergency ward.

He paused for an instant outside the swinging

doors, drawing a deep breath. *Not good procedural policy to burst in like the Keystone Kops, Mathews.*

Nice and easy.

Now.

He moved slowly, as unobtrusively as possible, through the doors and into the bright neon glare of the ER. A tense group of bodies near Admitting pinpointed the danger zone, and to Spence's relief, no one noticed him.

He became aware of a woman's voice, talking in a quiet, rational tone. Patients were gaping from treatment cubicles; staff were cowering against the walls; an aide was sobbing hysterically.

The center of attention was a tall, emaciated figure in dirty jeans and a torn blue tee. He looked about sixteen, with shoulder-length, greasy brown hair. His eyes were wild, nearly popping out of his skull, and he was holding a long switchblade at arm's length, waving it in erratic circles. A junkie, and totally irrational.

Spence's heart sank.

"Stay away from me, assholes." The boy giggled in a manic, choking burst, feinted at a green-gowned figure, giggled again when the person scrambled away.

"We'll get you drugs if that's what you want. You don't wish to hurt anyone, do you? We're here to help. You know you need help. Just relax, okay?"

Spence recognized the speaker and felt a surge of admiration for her. She was Dr. Joanne Duncan, senior ER physician. She was standing just out of reach of the circling knife, doing her best to hold the boy's attention and calm him down.

Spence became aware of blood on the floor beneath the boy's feet. There was a widening pool, and more was soaking the uniform of a nurse kneeling on the floor, placing a tourniquet on the upper arm of the moaning intern sprawled in front of her. A long gash had laid his right arm open from wrist to elbow.

So somebody had already been cut.

"You're in pain. We'll help you any way we can. Let's just relax..." Duncan's low, soothing tones were holding the boy's attention.

Spence was moving quickly now, already on the periphery of the group, planning his best move, when the swinging doors exploded open behind him, and Murray launched himself onto the scene.

"Everybody back. Everybody stay back now." Murray's stentorian voice echoed through the room. "Just stay back, and nobody'll get hurt."

The kid spun toward Murray, his high-pitched words running together in a terrified litany.

"Staybackfuckincopsdon'ttouchme..." The kid was swiping the ugly blade in ever-widening circles, and for a heart-stopping instant Spence was certain Dr. Duncan would be the next victim. But she moved swiftly back, and the group scattered. An intern knocked over a cart filled with basins and instruments, and the kid whirled and lunged toward him, his back to Spence for a split second. The clatter brought screams of terror from the nervous assembly.

"Don't touch me. Keep away."

Two strides, and Spence grasped the heavy three-cell flashlight at his belt. As he closed in, he yanked it out of the holder.

The kid shot toward him at the last second, but Spence was already lifting the flashlight high.

He brought the instrument down full force on the arm holding the knife. The weapon flew. The kid hollered with pain, falling to his knees and cradling his right arm.

"You broke my arm—you broke my arm!"

Too hard. You hit the kid way too hard.

With a banshee cry, Murray chose that moment to pounce on the boy. He was applying a choke hold just as two city policemen came rushing through the sliding entrance doors, guns drawn.

Within a few moments, the drug-crazed youngster was handcuffed. Dr. Duncan checked his arm and pronounced it badly bruised but not broken, then he was taken away, tears and snot mixing with the grime on his gaunt face.

Spence felt a flood of relief, along with a stab of

pity for the kid as the officers half dragged him out the doors and into a waiting squad car.

That could have been me at his age if I hadn't been lucky—if it hadn't been for Bud....

In the ER, pandemonium reigned as everyone in the immediate vicinity raced in to find out what had happened. The ER staff went into frenzied action around the injured intern, starting intravenous lines, arranging for an operating room and a plastic surgeon, lifting him onto a gurney.

Joanne Duncan supervised the process. When the gurney was pushed off toward the elevators, she came over to Spence.

''Thank you, Mr.—'' Her moss-green eyes dropped to the name tag on his lapel. ''Mr. Mathews. We're all really grateful for what you did.''

Spence could see how pale she was, and he noted that the ringless hand she used to swipe at her dramatic mop of silver-blond hair trembled more than slightly. She wasn't as much in control as her voice and manner indicated, and Spence felt a rush of empathy.

''Poor kid. I was too heavy with that flashlight.'' It was what he was thinking, and the words popped out of their own volition. His insides were shaking something fierce, and he felt icy cold. There was a burning sickness in his gut. It was a familiar feeling; he'd experienced it before, more often than he cared to remember. It was the aftereffect of physical danger.

Dr. Duncan was looking up at him, her startling green gaze direct and compassionate. "You did exactly what was needed to prevent any more injury. The boy's arm is bruised, not broken. Someone could easily have died if it hadn't been for your quick thinking." She motioned with one graceful, long-fingered hand to where Murray was standing, some distance off, loudly extolling his heroism to two young policemen who'd just arrived on the scene.

"Too bad your partner wasn't as perceptive. Or as kindhearted. What he did was totally unnecessary."

Spence looked over at Murray and ruefully shook his head. "He's young."

"And noisy." She smiled, and Spence noted that the smile catapulted her from attractive to stunning.

"There's a lot to be said for maturity," she added.

It was Spence's turn to smile. "I used to think so," he said quietly, "before I got mature myself."

She chuckled, and Spence felt ridiculously pleased. She was more relaxed now. How old would she be? There were laugh lines at the corners of her eyes, and there was that wild, rebellious mop of hair, but the silver-blond color only emphasized the youthfulness of her oval face, the amazing green of her huge eyes, which were set far apart beneath a wide forehead. He'd noticed, and admired, the slight swagger of her springy walk, the air she had of being ready for any challenge.

He'd guess her at maybe thirty-seven, thirty-eight tops. At least six years younger than he.

"Well. Thanks again, Mr. Mathews. I should go see how my intern's doing in the OR."

She hurried away, and Spence watched her go. Even in the loose hospital greens, it was obvious she was slim, long-legged, gently rounded at the hips. He hadn't really noticed women in a great while, and he smiled wryly as he turned away.

She's a doctor, head honcho here in the ER, he chided himself. *And you're a lowly security guard, Mathews. Get a grip, as Devon would say.*

"Hey, Spence, we're headin' down to the cafeteria for java. You comin'?" Murray, puffed up with the thrill of having two uniformed cops actually listen to him, strutted off down the corridor without waiting for an answer. His voice trailed behind him, hovering in the air like the pungent smell of the disinfectant a janitor was using to clean the intern's blood from the floor.

Spence had no desire to join Murray and his entourage. A vending machine stood in a corner near the front entrance, and he walked toward it, sorting coins for a container of milk. Before he reached the machine, however, the entrance doors slid open and a turbaned man raced through. He looked around frantically at the deserted Admitting desk and then grabbed hold of Spence's sleeve, his accented voice frantic and high-pitched.

"Sir, she is having the baby now, in my taxi. Please to come and help me bring her inside? *Please.* We must hurry, sir."

Spence, too, looked around for help. The staff were scattered throughout the ER, furiously busy, doing their best to treat the patients who'd been ignored during the recent crisis.

In a doorless closet beside the vending machine sat three folded wheelchairs. Spence pulled one out and flipped it open, then followed the distraught taxi driver as he careered out the door.

The outside air was spring fresh. The April morning was warm and the faint breeze miraculously carried the smell of ocean instead of the usual stench of exhaust from the busy street in front of St. Joe's. Spence filled his lungs, realizing he hadn't taken a deep breath since before the J2.

"Here, sir, over here, quickly, quickly, please." The driver pulled open the rear door of a canary-yellow taxi, talking in urgent bursts to the young woman in back. "Here we have help, miss. Now you must to go inside. Please to get out...."

The girl was young and beautiful, her lovely face drained of color, contorted with pain. She crouched on the torn seat like a little animal, moaning and shaking her head, her long auburn hair flying loose, terror blatant in huge cornflower-blue eyes. Her legs were jackknifed up against her swollen body; her feet, in high-topped sneakers, were perilously balanced wide apart on the seat in front of her. The crotch of her maternity pants was soaked, as was the seat, and the acidic smell of amniotic fluid assaulted Spence's nostrils as he leaned in toward her.

"C'mon, honey, let's get you out. Put an arm around my neck. There's a girl. What's your name?"

"Natasha…Stevens," she gasped.

She did as he instructed, and he lifted her easily, but before he could swing her into the wheelchair, she grimaced and an anguished groan came from her throat.

Spence recognized the sound. She was bearing down. He'd delivered two babies in his years on the Force, and he'd been present when Devon was born. The driver was right. They needed to hurry and get the girl inside.

Her arm tightened on his neck, and as Spence tried to place her in the chair, she started screaming. The driver had enough sense to hold the chair steady, and Spence managed to unhook her arms from his neck and get her seated.

"Hold on, Natasha. Hold on. Here we go…" He sprinted across the cement, pushing the chair ahead of him. The wide doors sighed open, and they were halfway through, when she stopped screaming and began that ominous grinding groan again.

Her head tipped back until she could see Spence, and there were urgent desperation in her eyes.

"It's—coming—I can—feel—"

For one instant, Spence longed for Murray's vocal chords. The second they were inside the door he hollered, "Help, somebody. Get over here. This girl's having a baby. We need help."

Staff stampeded toward them.

With a final protracted groan that erupted into a scream, Natasha slid out of the chair, onto the tiled floor. Spence shoved the chair aside and supported her as well as he could. She grabbed his hand and held on, her strength astonishing.

"Get her pants off. Bring a gurney. She's delivering." Dr. Duncan, snapping on a pair of gloves, knelt beside them now; one nurse removed Natasha's sneakers while another yanked maternity pants and stained pink panties down and off. A pool of blood and feces spread from under her buttocks.

"What's her name, Mathews?" Duncan was using a stethoscope on the girl's belly.

"Natasha Stevens." The girl loosened her hold on his hand for a moment, and a nurse took his place.

Spence, dazed at the speed at which things were occurring, moved out of the way.

"Pant, pant like this. Don't bear down. Don't

push. You've got to pant, Natasha,'' a nurse instructed in a loud voice.

The staff were trying to lift her to a gurney, but Natasha was sobbing and struggling.

"She's crowning," Dr. Duncan hollered. "She's crowning. Don't move her," she called out again. "Don't push. Don't push," she ordered Natasha. "You mustn't push. Pant, honey. Pant.''

Spence could see the top of a tiny head, wet and bloody, with a dark coating of matted hair, and then the entire elongated head appeared. Dr. Duncan quickly suctioned the baby's nose and mouth, supporting the head as Natasha gave a lengthy shriek, drew in a quick breath, and then, ignoring the staff's advice, gritted her teeth and bore down hard.

In the next second, the minuscule form of a baby girl, pale as alabaster, popped from Natasha's body like a cork from the neck of a wine bottle.

Dr. Duncan caught her.

Spence held his breath.

The baby choked, coughed, and a long, tense moment later the outraged squalls of a healthy newborn echoed through the ER.

CHAPTER TWO

LIKE MAGIC, the small body turned from blue-white to pink to purple as her cries strengthened. Two nursing aides clapped, and a ragged cheer sounded from other staff.

Spence couldn't stop grinning, although he could also feel tears gathering in his eyes. He had to struggle for an embarrassing moment to keep them from escaping, and his chest felt constricted.

Natasha was lifted to a gurney and the baby placed on her abdomen. Dr. Duncan cut and clamped the cord, then turned her attention to the baby, rating her on the Apgar scale at an eight, one minute after birth. Then she administered eyedrops, before letting the nurse take an identifying footprint.

The afterbirth was delivered, and then Natasha was whisked away. A nurse carried the baby, and Spence could hear the small but piercing voice fading as the group disappeared in the direction of the elevators.

Dr. Duncan stood still for a moment, staring after them, a satisfied smile on her face. "Haven't delivered a baby in a while,'' she commented to a nurse. ''It's a blessing that nature does most of the work.'' She glanced around and caught Spence watching her.

''Well, Mr. Mathews, it's been quite a morning,'' she said, still smiling. Her green eyes were sparkling.

''Any word on how the young intern's doing?'' Spence inquired.

''I'm going to check on him now. He should be out of surgery soon. Call down in half an hour or so, and I'll be able to tell you how he is.''

''I'll do that. Let's hope that's all the excitement for today,'' he responded. She rolled her eyes heavenward and nodded. ''One can only hope.''

JOANNE WATCHED as the tall security man walked toward the doors that led out of the ER. In the aftermath of the knife attack and then the emergency delivery, her adrenaline was pumping like crazy, but Mathews looked absolutely calm.

He'd been affected by the birth of the baby, though; Joanne had noticed the sheen of unshed tears in his eyes. So he had a soft heart—but he had both dignity and poise under fire, too. She admired that in a man. His strong, muscular build and flat abdomen also did justice to that crisp security uniform; so many guys got a huge gut along with maturity.

"Dr. Duncan?" Portia Bailey, the new intern, stood at Joanne's elbow, holding a chart. "Dr. Duncan, if you've got a minute?"

"Sure, Portia. What's up?"

"This is a forty-five-year-old professor from Simon Fraser University. Went to bed last night with a headache. Woke up this morning confused and disoriented. His girlfriend brought him in. He's vomiting, and he's got inflammation of the optic nerve in both eyes."

"Papilladema," Joanne translated.

Portia nodded, adding, "He's also confused and restless." She went down the extensive list of tests she'd run. "None of them was conclusive, and no focal findings. With your approval I'm gonna tap him. I'm almost certain he has meningitis. Will you observe?"

"Of course." Joanne was impressed with this young woman. Efficient and businesslike, Portia also seemed to have the sixth sense some doctors were born with—an uncanny ability that allowed them to figure out an accurate diagnosis in cases that stymied even the most experienced of physicians.

The tap was perfectly executed, and when it was over Joanne checked again on Tom Glasgow, the intern cut by the junkie. He was still in the OR. She attended to a laceration on a construction worker's head and then dealt with a drug overdose in a young woman she'd diagnosed with full-blown AIDS only a week earlier.

When a lull came, she glanced at her watch and decided to take her lunch break—she'd brought soup and a sandwich from home. She made her way to the staff lounge.

She was microwaving her soup and boiling water for a cup of tea when the intercom sounded; the female voice was unable to disguise the undercurrent of tension in her even tones.

"Code Yellow, *stat,* Maternity. Code Yellow, *stat,* Maternity. Code Yellow, *stat,* Maternity."

Joanne felt a physical jolt of shock ripple through her body. *Code Yellow, Maternity,* repeated three times, signaled that a baby was missing.

There was a strict protocol to follow, and Joanne raced out of the lunchroom. The hospital personnel she passed looked as horrified as she felt, but the excited buzz of voices gave way to silence when she began the required procedure.

All the physicians and staff had been briefed thoroughly on the hospital's Emergency Response Plan, and Joanne went over each step in her head before she instigated it.

"Jimmy, stand guard at the Burrard Street exit. Redirect everyone to the main lobby. Absolutely no one goes in or out."

Quickly, Joanne assigned staff members to the other exits, warning all of them, "If you see anyone suspicious or notice someone with a baby, don't do anything except watch. The police will be here shortly. Notify them immediately about anything you've observed.''

Restrained bedlam reigned. Nursing aides dropped things. Patients waiting for treatment became belligerent when told that no one except those requiring immediate care would be allowed in the ER until further notice. There was a growing lineup for the bank of public telephones, and staff members whispered uneasily among themselves, speculating on what might be happening. No one seemed to know anything, and rumors flew.

It seemed to Joanne to take forever, but it could only have been a few short minutes before Vancouver City Police were everywhere.

In the midst of the pandemonium, two seriously injured people arrived at the ER by ambulance—a man and woman whose car had skidded out of control and hit a telephone pole.

The paramedics who attended at the accident had called ahead with the information that the woman's injuries were not life threatening, but the man had suffered severe trauma to the head; he hadn't been wearing a seat belt and had gone through the windshield. He wasn't breathing well. The paramedics were forcing air into his mouth through an Ambubag.

Joanne and her trauma team were suited up in

protective clothing, sterile gloves and glasses, when the man was wheeled into Trauma Room one. Joanne noted that Portia Bailey was at her side. All thoughts of the emergency situation in Maternity fled as Joanne concentrated on her patient, the man from the car crash.

He had severe facial injuries, and Joanne realized immediately that intubating, which involved getting a tube down his throat and into his trachea, was out of the question. The facial injuries made it impossible to see inside his mouth. Her only other choice was to cut into his neck and place a breathing tube directly into the trachea. The procedure was called a *crike,* short for cricothyrotomy, and it wasn't an everyday occurrence in the ER, which made it an excellent teaching opportunity.

"We're looking for this small, soft area in the trachea," she said for Portia's benefit as she located it just below the Adam's apple. "First we make a vertical incision, like this—" she drew a scalpel swiftly and surely over the skin "—and then we follow with a horizontal cut into the cricothyroid membrane, insert a breathing tube into the incision like this, and attach a bag."

During the time it took Joanne and her team to complete the primary and secondary surveys of the patient, review the results of the blood tests and X rays and stabilize him for surgery, the switchboard announced a Code Yellow Complete, indicating that the hospital routine would return to normal.

But whispers spread rapidly throughout the building that the missing baby hadn't been found.

A short time later, Joanne was once again in the staff lounge, munching on her dried-out sandwich, when Jimmy, the ER clerk, stuck his head in the door.

"There's a police detective at the Admitting desk, Doc Duncan. He's been talking to all of us and now he wants to talk to you. Shall I send him in here?"

Joanne swallowed the bite of sandwich she was chewing and looked at the remainder of her lunch. She was hungry, and she'd be lucky to get another quiet time for the rest of her shift if the day continued the way it was going.

"Send him in, Jimmy." She could eat and talk at the same time.

He arrived before her tea water had a chance to boil.

"Dr. Duncan? Sgt. Gordon Zelaney, General Investigation Squad, Vancouver City Police. Mind if I sit down?"

Without waiting for an answer, he collapsed on the rump-sprung sofa. He was probably in his late forties, well over six feet, with a square, powerful body, a thinning crop of rusty-red hair and pale-blue eyes that seemed set too close together in his florid face.

"Would you like a cup of tea?" Joanne was sloshing water over an herbal tea bag in a mug.

"No, thanks. Doctor, I understand you delivered a baby this morning."

Joanne's nerves suddenly went on red alert. She set down her sandwich and swallowed hard. "Yes, I did. A lovely little girl." Her voice was thick. "What about her?" She clung to the cup of tea she'd just made, her heart starting to thunder.

Zelaney's blue eyes were studying her. "The baby's disappeared from Maternity."

Joanne's hand jerked and hot tea spilled across the table. "*She's* the baby who disappeared?" Her voice reflected her shock.

She'd delivered the Stevens girl—Joanne glanced up at the clock—less than four hours earlier. It hardly seemed possible that the infant was missing.

"The mother apparently assumed the medical staff had the child. About half an hour went by before the code was called. The entire hospital's been thoroughly searched. There's absolutely no trace of her."

"My God." Joanne remembered the tiny, flailing limbs, the swirls of dark hair on the small skull, the vulnerability of new life. "How can I help?"

"Up on Maternity they told us there's a new banding policy in place. Each newborn is banded with a security bracelet that sets off an alarm if the baby is removed from the unit.''

Joanne's heart thumped even harder, and a sudden icy dread came over her. She knew about the banding policy. She'd read the instructions and seen the bracelets that had been sent down to the ER several weeks ago. But this morning, following the incident with the druggie, she'd forgotten all about those bands. She'd forgotten them until this very moment, in fact.

"Did you by any chance use a security band on the Stevens baby, Dr. Duncan?"

Zelaney was looking at her intently, and it was obvious to Joanne that he already knew the answer.

CHAPTER THREE

SLOWLY JOANNE shook her head. "I forgot." Her voice was thin, and she had to swallow before she could continue.

"My God, I forgot to band her." She felt sick. "There was a stabbing in the ER this morning. One of my interns—" She stopped abruptly. That was absolutely no excuse. "It's my fault," she whispered. "It's totally my fault."

Zelaney sighed. "Don't be too hard on yourself, Doctor. Someone should have checked for the band when the baby arrived in Maternity, but apparently they had some emergency up there, as well. Could you tell me about the baby's birth?"

It was hard to talk. Her throat kept closing up. The ramifications of her negligence were enormous, and it was all she could do to keep her voice steady as she related every detail of the baby's precipitate arrival.

Zelaney asked questions, writing down her answers in a small black notebook balanced on his knees. "Who was around at that time? Did you notice anyone at all who didn't seem to belong here?''

Joanne searched her memory, then shook her head. ''There was a security guard from the hospital staff. I think he was the one who brought the girl in from the taxi. He was in Emerg because of the stabbing we'd just had. His name is...'' Her mind was suddenly blank. She could see the guard's strong, handsome face vividly, but it took a long moment before his name came to her. ''Mathews. His name is Mathews. Spencer Mathews.''

''Spence Mathews?'' Zelaney's pale eyebrows shot up. ''I know Spence. We used to work together sometimes. I'd heard he was on Security here.''

''He's a policeman?''

''Retired Royal Canadian Mounted Police.'' He scribbled something down, put his notebook in the pocket of his sport coat and then stood up. ''Thanks for your help, Doctor. If you can think of anything else, anything at all, give me a call.'' He handed her a card with his name and number.

After he left, Joanne sat motionless, her thoughts a turmoil of self-blame and regret. Sure, she knew that mistakes were human. One of the first things a good doctor picked up was that when mistakes happened, you learned from them, did your best not to repeat them, forgave yourself and went on with business.

She'd made many mistakes during her years as

a physician, few of which had been serious. None had ever resulted in the loss of life. Now, because of her carelessness a baby was lost.

Questions began to come to her, things she should have asked Zelaney, things she *would* have asked if her brain had been working. Exactly how had the abduction occurred? Babies roomed in with their mothers; she knew that. So where was Ms. Stevens when the child disappeared?

Joanne had heard about newborns being stolen from hospitals, but she'd never paid much attention; hadn't thought she would ever be involved with that sort of thing.

She seemed to remember there was a time frame during which the police were most likely to recover a baby, but she couldn't recall what it was. Newborns changed so quickly. After a few weeks it might be almost impossible even for their own mothers to recognize them.

"Oh, please, please," she moaned, resting her face in her hands in entreaty. *Please let the police find that baby girl soon. Please let her be fine. Don't let anything horrible happen to her.*

"Dr. Duncan, we've got a multiple GSW. ETA, seven." The nurse stuck her head in the door and then was gone.

Multiple gunshot wounds, arriving in seven minutes.

Joanne lurched to her feet. One good thing about

the ER. You never had much time to feel sorry for yourself. It was the reason she'd taken this job in the first place, the reason she went on with it, year after year. She swept her uneaten sandwich into the trash, rinsed her teacup and hurried out, forcing her mind to concentrate on the problem at hand.

The gunshot victim was in his early twenties, and he was DOA—dead on arrival. It was that kind of day. Joanne sighed to herself as she pronounced the victim dead and filled in the necessary papers. She never got used to verifying the end of a life. She never failed to wonder what that life might have held or contributed had it continued.

During the next few hours, details of the baby's abduction spread through St. Joe's like an airborne virus, and it seemed to Joanne that everyone she spoke to had some new information. The question was whether that information was accurate. Joanne listened, trying to put together the most consistent account.

When Natasha Stevens had left the ER, she'd been wheeled to Maternity, where the entire staff were in a flurry because one of the doctor's wives was in labor, giving birth to triplets. Natasha was put in a private room. Her baby was checked over by Bernie Trent, a neonatal specialist, pronounced healthy and placed in a glass bassinet by the mother's bedside.

Almost immediately, Natasha visited the bathroom, and when she came out her baby was gone. Assuming a staff member had taken her for another medical procedure, Natasha wasn't concerned at first. But when forty minutes passed and the baby was still not back, Natasha called a nurse, who notified security right away. All hospital exits were immediately sealed, but an intensive search of the entire hospital and a roadblock of the downtown area yielded no trace of the baby or her abductor.

Joanne felt physically ill as the hours of her shift dragged on. She had to use every ounce of discipline she possessed to apply herself to the patients who presented at Emerg that afternoon. By the time her shift ended at three, bone-deep weariness and a pervading sense of doom surrounded her like a cloak.

She was relieved to be able to leave the hospital and reclaim her small, practical car from the doctors' lot.

Driving through heavy afternoon traffic, she went over every detail of the baby's delivery, and remembered the exact instant the tiny blue-white girl shot out of her mother's body and into Joanne's hands. She could see the mass of wet, dark hair, could hear that first wavering cry.

She didn't want to hear it, and reached over quickly to turn on the car's stereo player, then slip in a CD by a popular female vocalist. The raw, edgy lyrics distracted her, and Joanne relaxed a little.

But that evening, when her solitary meal was eaten and the few dishes had been loaded into the dishwasher, she found herself pacing from one end of her spacious living room to the other. She finally stopped by the gas fireplace and glared at the photo of Henry she'd set there.

They'd met in medical school and been married fifteen years when he died of congenital heart failure.

"I shouldn't have let you convince me that having kids wasn't a good idea," she accused in a loud voice that startled her with its vehemence and its anger. "I should have insisted, and if you still didn't agree, I should have tricked you, Henry Duncan."

That wasn't the first time the thought had crossed her mind. But it was the first time she'd said it aloud, and to him.

To his picture, Joanne corrected. And what did it matter what she said to his picture? She should have said it when he was alive, when he was there to listen and respond.

"I am so lonely tonight my whole body hurts," she went on belligerently, still talking out loud. "And I've got no one to speak to, to confide in."

That wasn't strictly true. Her parents were long dead, but she had friends she could call. Tonight, though, she longed for what she didn't have—a lover, a husband, someone who loved her unconditionally, someone she wouldn't have to make explanations or excuses to because he'd just know that whatever the circumstances today, Joanne Duncan had done her best. He'd know because he knew her through and through.

As Henry never had. In so many ways, her marriage had been superficial. She'd made many concessions. But she hadn't realized that until long after Henry was dead—until distance and time gave her the perspective to examine their relationship honestly.

She'd done what she thought was her best with Henry and her marriage, just as she had today with the baby.

She walked to the windows and drew back the vertical blinds that masked the magnificent view of Vancouver's inner harbor—the view that had convinced her to buy this particular apartment after Henry had died and she'd sold the house.

The moon was full. A million lights twinkled in the darkness, and beyond them, out on the inlet, the huge cruise ship she'd seen earlier in the day slowly and regally made its way out to the open ocean. She'd never been on a cruise. Henry hadn't ever wanted to go, and she'd never insisted.

Somewhere down there, Joanne mused as her heart twisted, was a fragile little girl, not even a day old. Did she even have a name? Was anyone caring for her, or... She shuddered and closed the blinds, then turned back to the warm, plum-colored room, with its framed Gauguin prints and soft, cushy purple furniture. She'd chosen everything in this apartment—the lush, goose-down pillows, the muted oriental rugs, reveling in the sensuality of color and style that suited her. For the first time in her life, she'd created a nest that was truly her own, a reflection of *her* tastes and preferences. But to-night, she couldn't find comfort or peace in any of it.

Working in the ER, Joanne had seen every hor-rifying kind of human neglect and inhuman cruelty inflicted on children. She couldn't let herself think for a moment that the Stevens baby might be suf-fering, or she'd lose her reason.

She'd have a hot bath; she'd play music that soothed her; she'd have a glass of white wine and go to bed and sleep. Morning came early. Her eight-hour shift in the ER began at seven. Tomorrow was another day; tomorrow they'd likely find the miss-ing baby, and all her fears would be for nothing.

SPENCE ARRIVED HOME that afternoon after his shift at St. Joe's to find that his mother, Lillian, had made his favorite dinner; thick stew over mashed potatoes; salad; and her special fresh biscuits. Lillian only cooked when she felt like it, and Spence was always grateful when she did.

She sat to his right at the small dining table, Devon to his left. His daughter had inherited his blue eyes and the cleft in his chin, but that was as far as the physical resemblance went, Spence reflected. Devon had his mother's dramatic high cheekbones and strong, handsome bone structure, the same long, straight, raven-black hair Lillian used to have; his mother's hair now was striped with white along both temples, and she kept it short.

Spence often teased the two of them about having some unknown Native ancestor. Both women were tall, almost six feet; not thin, but not heavy, either. They even had the same proud way of walking, shoulders back, stride certain.

Devon didn't walk that way anymore.

"You're getting tanned already, Dev," he commented, thinking how lovely she was with her dusky skin and black braid. "Lucky you got the expensive skin that tans easily; instead of this cheap stuff of mine."

It was an old and weary joke. His mother said he was like her Nordic ancestors, but Spence suspected he'd taken after the father he'd never known. His fair skin burned long before it tanned.

The shopworn words were all he could come up with tonight. His mind was distracted by the dramatic happenings of the day, and he couldn't seem to turn it off.

He'd been late getting home, having spent more than an hour in the hospital administrative offices, answering questions from the brass about what steps Security had taken immediately following the baby's disappearance. The hospital was already getting heat over their handling of the kidnapping, and they naturally wanted to be prepared with answers.

"Gramma drove me down to the beach this afternoon. We sat on a log and watched the tide come in."

Devon toyed with her fork and then added in a rush, "I really want to learn to drive myself, Dad. It's not fair to Gramma to have to chauffeur me everywhere. I'm nineteen years old. I feel like a total jerk having her baby-sit me."

The argument was becoming a familiar one, and one that never failed to upset him. Spence sighed, and his gaze slipped automatically from his daughter's face to the sturdy cane propped next to her chair. "You've only been out of the wheelchair a few months, Dev," he reminded her gently. "Give it some time. Wait until you're stronger. We'll see in the fall."

"In the *fall?*" Devon echoed incredulously. "Dad, maybe you haven't noticed, but it's barely *spring*. It's only *April,* for heaven's sake. I want to be totally independent by this summer." Her blue eyes shot sparks at him. "So my right leg doesn't work too good. I could learn to use hand controls. Lot's of disabled people drive cars with hand controls, Dad."

He winced. Thinking of Devon as disabled still sent an agonizing jolt of guilt and shame and denial straight to his soul, like an arrow hitting a bull's-eye.

"We'll see, honey." It was his standard evasive answer.

"Gramma says she'll teach me how to drive if you won't." Devon's tone was rebellious. "I can't believe that someone who roars around on a motorcycle would consider driving a car dangerous, whether it's hand controlled or not."

Spence glanced at his mother, noticing the stiffness of her expression, the heightened color in her cheeks. He knew how unfair it was to put her in the middle of these arguments with Devon. Lillian had moved in to take care of his daughter, and her presence had been a godsend. He didn't want to make her uncomfortable this way. He just didn't know how to avoid it.

"I said I'd help you learn only if your father agreed, sweetheart," Lillian corrected Devon. "And you both understand the dinner table isn't the place to discuss this," she added firmly. "Spence, what's this about a baby being taken from the hospital today? The news was on the car radio when we were driving home."

Grateful for a reprieve from the driving controversy, Spence described in detail his role in the baby's birth, adding, "I was on my lunch break when the call came on my pager that a baby was missing. There's a strict procedure we follow. My job was to monitor the surveillance cameras while other personnel secured the exits. City police arrived within minutes and took over, but they were too late. The baby was long gone."

"But surely someone noticed something." Lillian's normally cheerful face was somber. "I've heard you say more than once that a large part of investigating was just getting people to remember what they saw or heard."

"That's true." Spence had spent a number of years in the investigative branch of the RCMP. "A nurse in Maternity this morning did notice a young woman with cameras and a large leather bag slung over her shoulder. She just assumed the woman was a photographer taking pictures of newborns. That seems to be the only lead the cops have. Last I heard, no one had made any ransom demands or anything. That could still happen, but the mother is young and unmarried, so it seems pretty unlikely."

Lillian shook her head. "I'm so sorry for the staff in Maternity. Every single nurse who was on shift at the time must feel horribly responsible. Nurses always do when something like this happens.''

''Were any babies taken when you worked in the hospital, Gramma?'' Devon had become interested in the conversation and seemed to have forgotten her fixation with learning to drive.

''We never had a baby abducted in any of the hospitals I worked in. On a couple of occasions we did misplace a patient, but only temporarily.'' She smiled at Devon and then turned to Spence. ''What are the chances of getting this baby back?''

It was a question he'd naturally been pondering all afternoon. ''The first twenty-four hours are crucial. That's the optimal window for recovery. After that, the trail gets cold and chances go down drastically.'' His eyes met his mother's, and he saw she was thinking along the same lines. Who had taken this baby mattered a great deal; most often in cases such as this it was a crazed woman longing for a child of her own. If so, the baby might have a reasonable chance of being well cared for and found.

Same thing if the abduction was a straight kidnapping for money, which seemed highly unlikely in this instance: the Stevens girl was apparently a single parent, and certainly not wealthy.

Other possibilities hardly bore considering: sex-crazed perverts, child porn rings—his years on the Force had taught Spence that the depths of man's degradation were bottomless.

"Let's go watch the early news and see if there're any updates," he suggested. "The dishes will keep for a while. We'll get to them later." He and Devon cleaned up on the rare occasions Lillian cooked.

They moved into the study and Lillian sat on the worn tweed sofa. Spence waited. He'd learned that Devon's limp always indicated his daughter's well-being; it grew more pronounced in direct proportion to how tired or upset she was.

Tonight it was only moderate. Spence offered a hand, which Devon refused. When she was settled, Spence sat down and switched on the television.

"...Police are extending their search for the new-born baby who was abducted this morning from St. Joseph's Hospital. We take you now to Hillary Stone."

A smartly dressed young woman standing just outside the ER entrance at St. Joe's motioned dramatically behind her. "Just inside these automatic doors, a young and promising actress named Natasha Stevens delivered her first child this morning—a healthy baby girl. Mother and baby were taken to the maternity ward. Despite a newly installed security system, the baby disappeared without a trace within two hours of her birth. Ms. Stevens is a single parent, and I spoke with her this afternoon as she left the hospital."

An image of Natasha Stevens, sitting in a wheelchair, filled the screen.

"Wow, she's drop-dead gorgeous," Devon breathed.

The assessment was accurate, Spence realized.

Even fresh from childbirth and with tears streaming down her cheeks, Natasha Stevens was startlingly beautiful. Her lashes were long and thick, her luxurious auburn hair looked attractively tousled, and her voice as she stumbled over her words was husky, making her heartrending plea all the more touching.

"Please, please, whoever you are, bring my baby back to me," she begged. "I only got to ho-hold her once, and I'm so scared for her. I—I can't stand to stay in this place without her." Her face crumpled, and she sobbed again, then visibly pulled herself together. "She's—she's so little. Please take good care of her and bring her back to me safe. Her name is…Abigail. It…it was my mother's name." Natasha's head dropped and she covered her face with her hands as the camera switched back to the announcer.

"Poor little soul," Lillian murmured. "She's only a child herself. I wonder if she has anyone at home to take care of her tonight."

"I doubt it. She came to the hospital in a cab this morning, and she was alone." Spence felt his own throat constrict with emotion, and both Lillian and Devon wiped tears from their eyes as the news report continued.

"Constable Terry Flett of the Vancouver City Police Investigation Squad had this to say about the situation."

Terry Flett was fresh-faced, female and appealingly slim in her uniform. She was also well spoken, with a forthright manner, which was obviously why she'd been assigned the role of spokesperson. She reiterated that the police were doing all they could to locate the missing baby. She asked anyone with information about a young woman carrying camera equipment in the vicinity of the hospital that morning to please come forward, and stated that anyone with information that might prove helpful to authorities could phone the number now flashing on the television screen. "Officers will be available to take your calls," she promised.

"We will be bringing you hourly updates on this story," the news anchor reported somberly. "Please stay tuned."

Spence switched off the television and got to his feet. He felt restless, edgy, anxious.

"I feel so sorry for that Stevens girl," Devon remarked. "She doesn't look much older than me." She turned to Spence. "So how would your team have investigated a thing like this when you were in the RCMP, Dad?"

With uncanny accuracy, she'd zeroed on

Spence's thoughts. He'd been mentally going over the investigation ever since he'd heard about the abduction.

But he'd left all that behind him when he'd quit the Force four years ago. He'd deliberately sought out jobs far removed from criminal investigation, working on construction in the summer, selling and repairing motorcycles at a friend's shop in the winter, until Bud had talked him into this job with Vector.

And now this particular situation had involved him in a personal way. He could see in his mind's eye how Natasha Stevens had crouched on the seat of that taxicab this morning; he could hear the grinding sound she'd made as her labor intensified. His right hand still ached a little from the frantic grip with which she'd held it, as she'd lain helpless on the floor of the ER. And most troubling of all, he could envision that tiny newborn girl and recall her first wavering cries.

Into his mind, too, came the image of Joanne Duncan, and the tender expression on her face as she cradled the baby before handing her to the nurse—

"Dad? How will they go about finding this baby?"

Spence dragged his thoughts back, focused on his daughter's question, did his best to answer it.

"Well, there's a team approach in an investigation of this sort. Because of the urgency, a large number of people will be working the case,'' he explained. ''I expect RCMP investigators will have been called in to help City police. They'll have set up checkpoints at all the U.S. border crossings and at the airport, as well as roadblocks on all the major highways leading out of the city. Every single staff member in Maternity will be interviewed, and everyone in Emergency, as well, seeing that the baby was delivered down there. And investigators will check on every mother who might have lost a baby recently.''

''But what would *you* do, Dad?'' With extreme difficulty, Devon struggled to her feet and balanced herself on her cane, pointedly ignoring the hand Spence extended.

Watching her struggle just to sit down or get up wrenched his heart, but she'd lashed out at him too many times already about helping her. She insisted on doing it herself, even though lifting her up and easing her down was a simple matter for him.

''I guess I'd talk to people at the hospital,'' he mused aloud. ''In fact, I'd talk to every last living soul who was around there today. And I'd find out everything I could about Ms. Natasha Stevens, in the hope that somewhere I'd discover clues as to how and why this particular baby was taken.'' He knew that investigators would be searching out every detail of Natasha's life, locating the father of the baby, interviewing Natasha's relatives, friends, acquaintances. Relatives were always the first and most likely suspects.

Still talking about the baby, he and Devon cleared the table and loaded the dishwasher.

Lillian left for her yoga class, and once the dishes were done, Devon headed for her room.

"I've got a biology exam tomorrow. I've gotta study."

"You should have said something, honey. I'd have cleaned up myself."

She gave him an exasperated look. "I want to do as much as I can for myself, Dad. Most of the people in my classes at university have part-time jobs. They live in the dorm. They get their own meals and keep their own rooms clean. Compared with them, I'm totally useless." She became angry. "I don't need you fussing over me every minute. Can't you get that through your head?" She turned awkwardly and made her way down the hallway to the large room Spence had converted for her when she'd come home from the rehab center.

Devon had still been in a wheelchair then, and he'd widened doorways, built a ramp outside the front door. He'd insulated the sunporch and, with Lillian's help, turned it into a spacious and cheerful bedroom.

Devon went in now and slammed the door, hard enough to shake the windows.

CHAPTER FOUR

SPENCE, HANDS LOW on his hips, stood and stared at the closed door for a moment. At last he shook his head in exasperation.

He turned and made his way back to the study and the television, using the remote to click from one channel to the next without registering anything that was on.

There were times, like right now, when helpless anger at his daughter flared inside him, bright and hot. He had to stop himself from bellowing at her, reminding her that he was only trying to help, that she *needed* help, for God's sweet sake, that… Anger faded to disheartenment, and he switched off the sound on the TV and, with a sigh, let his head flop back against the brown tweed.

He wanted to remind her that he loved her, that he'd do anything in his power to make her life easier. That he'd gladly give his own life if he could undo the accident that had injured her hip, taken away her mobility, stolen her carefree spirit, destroyed her dreams. That he knew it was his fault and his alone that she was crippled, and that he'd

never forgive himself for it. In one instant of negligence, one moment of blind rage, he'd changed
her life forever.

It had been four years now, but the accident and
its horrific aftermath were like deep ruts in his
mind, places his thoughts went to automatically,
like a tongue to a tooth that ached—and the resulting emotional pain seemed physical in its intensity.

It robbed him of sleep; it made his gut churn; it
was a place he hated visiting over and over again.
His brain knew he needed to put the event behind
him, but his heart still hadn't found a way to do
that.

He wrestled now with the painful memories, trying to concentrate on something—anything—that
would distract him.

He turned the sound back on just in time to catch
another news flash about the Stevens baby.

"...Still no trace of the newborn who disappeared shortly after her birth this morning from St.
Joseph's Hospital. Authorities will be working
throughout the night in an effort to find the baby."
The clip of Natasha Stevens pleading for the return
of her child ran next, and Spence watched it again.

The phone rang, and he picked it up just in time
to hear Devon giggle and a deep male voice say
something Spence didn't catch. He hung up
quickly, pleased that Dev was making friends again,

curious who this young man was. Dev hadn't mentioned him or brought him home to meet her family.

In that way, too, as in most others, the accident had changed Devon.

Spence thought about what she'd been like as a little girl—an outgoing, bubbly child who attracted other children. During the years before he and Helen had divorced, his daughter had always been at the center of a giggling group of small girls.

After Helen moved to Calgary with their daughter, Spence would fly Devon to Vancouver for the summer to stay with him, and within hours the house would be filled with her noisy friends.

Following the accident, friends in Calgary and in Vancouver had visited a lot, but as the months of rehab wore on, Devon had gradually severed her relationships with them. She told Spence it was because they had nothing in common anymore; her entire life had changed. But she hadn't made new friends, and her aloneness added to Spence's overwhelming sense of guilt.

When the phone rang again, half an hour later, Spence didn't pick up, assuming that it was for Devon once more. But a few moments later she hollered down the hall that the call was for him, and he lifted the receiver.

"Spence, it's Bud." Bud Ansell was an old friend, and at the moment he was also Spence's boss. Spence had phoned him from the hospital earlier that day to tell him about the missing baby and to fill him in on the actions his security force had taken.

"I've just had a reporter from the *Star* on the blower, asking who was on duty when the kid disappeared today. I gave him your name. I wanted you to know what to expect when he calls. I'd rather have you talking to the media than Kellerman. His mouth and his brain are on independent tracks."

"Okay, Bud." The *Vancouver Star* was the largest morning paper in the city.

"Hell of a thing to have happen. I saw the mother on the tube. Doesn't look old enough to even be in high school, never mind have a kid. Older I get, the younger you young people look. Why the hell is that?"

Spence smiled. "Same thing's happening to me lately. I must be catching up to you."

Bud gave his gravelly laugh, and suddenly it took Spence back to boyhood days, when he'd wake in the morning and hear Lillian and Bud laughing together over coffee, down on the porch below his bedroom window.

They'd had a long relationship when Spence was a boy, and although it had ended many years ago, Bud obviously still carried a torch for Lillian.

"You got what—two more day shifts before your

break?'' Bud was saying. "How about we grab breakfast on your days off?''

"Sounds good." It did. The older man was as close as Spence had ever come to having a father. He'd taught Spence about fishing and football and motorcycles. He was a retired Vancouver policeman, and it was Bud who'd encouraged Spence to go into the RCMP.

"Everybody okay at your place? How's Lillian?''

"Mom's at yoga. Devon's cramming for an exam.''

"Yoga, huh? Maybe I oughta take something like that—get the kinks out. Where's the class held?''

"Every Tuesday and Thursday evening at seven, down on Arbutus, in the community center at Forty-First.''

Spence had to grin. Bud wasn't very subtle. Spence wondered if he'd get a tongue-lashing from Lillian for having divulged this.

"Maybe I'll wander down there one evening. Good luck with the reporter. At least you've done media interviews enough times to know how to handle them.''

"I suppose. I'm pretty rusty, though." Spence had been in the line of fire with the media more than once during his years as an investigator, but that seemed long ago and far away now. "I'll call you and let you know how it goes."

They said good-night, and Spence hung up. He sat staring into space, wondering not for the first time what had really happened between Lillian and Bud. He'd asked his mother once, years ago.

"Bud?" Lillian had shrugged. "Oh, I wanted to get married and he didn't. Then when he'd changed his mind I'd already married Willis."

Willis Lamotta had been Spence's stepfather from the time Spence was twelve until he'd turned sixteen—when Willis and Lillian had finally divorced. Spence had long ago gotten over wanting to kill Lamotta, but he figured he still wouldn't mind planting a fist in Willis's beefy face for the rotten way he'd treated his mother and him.

Spence hadn't let Lillian get away with her evasive answer that day. "So how come you and Bud didn't pick up together after Willis left?"

"Oh, Bud was married to Marlene by then."

"They didn't stay married, Ma. There's been lots of time since to get going with Bud again. I always figured you two would end up together."

Lillian had given him a long, level glance from those inscrutable hazel eyes. "You figured wrong" was all she would say. If she didn't want to talk about something, there was no way Spence had ever discovered to make her.

So he'd asked Bud the same question a short time later. What had happened between Lillian and him?

Ansell's wide mouth had curved down and his brown spaniel eyes, usually so direct, had avoided Spence's gaze. He gave a sigh that seemed to originate in his toes. "Ah, Lil was smart and stubborn, and I was just a dumb young cop. We had a falling-out. It was my fault. By the time I figured it all out, it was too late. Irreconcilable differences—isn't that how the saying goes?"

Spence had waited for the rest of the explanation, but Bud never said another word. And now neither Lillian nor Bud was young anymore; his mother was sixty-five, Bud sixty-seven. It didn't look as if they'd ever get together.

Well, like mother, like son, Spence told himself. He was alone, and he planned to stay that way.

Before the accident, he'd gone through a string of relationships, none of them serious, all of them in the interest of a good time. Afterward, he hadn't dated once. His entire focus had been, and still was, his daughter.

Inexplicably, the image of Dr. Duncan popped into his head. She didn't wear any rings, but that didn't mean she was single. Did she have kids? Did she have a husband waiting when she got off shift? He decided she probably did; she was far too vivacious and pretty to be unattached.

He wished he knew someone he could ask about

her—just out of curiosity, of course. Murray would know—he knew all the hospital gossip—but Spence would never ask his loudmouthed partner. Murray would read things into the question that weren't true.

Besides, what was the point of knowing? He had no intention of getting involved with anyone, even if she was free, even if there weren't that wide social gap that yawned between a security guard and a doctor. His life now was his family, his daughter.

For one single instant, however, he let himself fantasize. He saw Joanne Duncan in his mind's eye; he heard her husky voice in his ear, he imagined how it would feel to hold her...

BEING HELD IN THE NIGHT was what she missed most.

At 12 a.m., Joanne was still awake, eyes wide-open and burning with fatigue, as she envisioned the band that should have been snapped onto the tiny wrist, unable to stop castigating herself for her carelessness.

By 1:30, she felt as if she'd never sleep again, and for the first time in months, she gave in and swallowed two of the pills she'd last used in the painful months after Henry's death. As the drugs began to work, she floated, dreaming of what it would be like to be held...

CHAPTER FIVE

"MR. MATHEWS?"

Spence turned around, knowing exactly who was standing behind him in the cafeteria lineup.

"Hello, Dr. Duncan." It was barely noon. The cafeteria wasn't busy quite yet.

She smiled up at him. He could see faint lines of strain around her eyes and mouth, as if she hadn't slept well the night before. He could sympathize. He hadn't, either, but lying awake during the long night hours was no longer an unusual occurrence for him: an unbroken night's sleep was rare.

"Could I talk to you for a few minutes?" She had a bowl of chicken noodle soup and a bagel on her tray, along with a cup of tea.

"Of course." He gestured to the cashier, indicating both trays, and paid the tab.

"I didn't mean for you to buy me lunch."

"Speeds things up," he said with a smile, allowing her to lead the way to a table by the window.

"Thank you."

They sat. Spence opened a container of cream

and stirred it into his coffee, and she undid a package of crackers and took one out.

"They haven't found her yet."

There was no need to explain who she was talking about; the topic on everyone's mind and lips was the missing baby.

Spence shook his head. "Not many leads, I guess."

More than twenty-four hours had gone by, and he understood only too well that with each hour that passed, the chances of recovery grew less. "The police are working around the clock."

"I've just spent over an hour with the hospital administration. They wanted to know everything about the baby's delivery."

"Yeah. I spent forty minutes myself being grilled by them earlier today." He sympathized with her. Nerves were on edge, and the interview hadn't been an easy one.

"Also, a Sgt. Zelaney came to see me yesterday," she said. "He asked me a lot of questions because the baby was born in the ER, and when I mentioned that you'd been there when it occurred, he said he knew you."

Spence nodded again, wondering where this was going. "That's right. Zelaney and I sometimes collaborated on investigations."

"He said you'd been in the RCMP. That you worked on criminal investigations."

"I did." Spence ignored his food—a plate of macaroni and cheese—and instead watched her face. He saw anxiety in her lovely green eyes, and he sensed she needed something from him. He grew tense, wondering what it was, anxious that it might be something he was incapable of giving. He had a deep, instinctive, yet inexplicable desire to do whatever he could for this woman.

Her voice became hesitant. "I wondered—I wondered if maybe, if perhaps— Have you heard anything more today, anything at all, about the search for the baby?"

Spence shook his head. "Sorry, I haven't. I'm not really involved in the case, so I'm very much out of the loop. Like I said, the security staff were all questioned again this morning by the hospital administration on procedure, how we reacted when the Code Yellow came. But as far as the actual investigation is concerned, I'm as much in the dark as you are."

"I see." She toyed with her bagel, tearing bits off but not eating them. She stared blindly down at her soup, and Spence couldn't help but notice how long her eyelashes were, how soft and curly, not gummed up with too much makeup.

"This whole thing has you spooked, Doctor?"

She looked up, straight into his eyes, and the anguish in her gaze shocked him. "I made an unforgivable mistake yesterday, Mr. Mathews. As you probably know, a couple of weeks ago the hospital instituted a new security policy for newborns. A band should have been put on the baby's wrist immediately after she was born.''

He nodded. He'd heard the criticisms about the band not being in place.

She drew in a quivering breath. ''I didn't do it. I forgot. I had the bands right there in the ER. I'd read the directive. And still I forgot.''

''You had a lot on your mind yesterday morning. That kid with the knife, your intern getting cut, the baby coming along right after. Don't be hard on yourself.'' He leaned toward her, understanding far too well how she was feeling. ''We all make mistakes, believe me.''

''But there's no way around the fact that this— this tragedy— It's my fault.'' There was raw agony in her voice, and her mouth trembled. ''I couldn't sleep last night until I took meds. I feel sick, realizing that I could have prevented this. I prayed that the baby would be found by morning, that she'd be in her mother's arms once more. But that didn't happen, and I don't know what to do.'' Her tone became passionate. ''Believe me, I'd do anything in my power to get that baby back safe and sound, Mr. Mathews.''

''Spencer. Spence for short, okay?''

She nodded. ''Spence. Spence, you're an investigator…?''

"*Was.* I'm not any longer." He'd emphasized the past deliberately, to see how she'd react. "I'm just a security guard, Doctor." A note of sarcasm tinged his voice. "Very low on the totem pole here at St. Joe's."

She ignored that. "My name's Joanne." She offered him something that passed as a smile. "Correct me if I'm wrong, but isn't being a policeman something like being a doctor? Once you take on the role, it's yours till you die."

There was more truth to what she said than he cared to admit. "I quit the Force four years ago," he acknowledged in a firm voice. Why couldn't he just leave it at that? He never explained to people, so why did he want to do it now?

"There was a car accident." His voice was clipped, and she was paying close attention, her green eyes on his face. He looked away, out the window, staring blindly at the traffic on the side street. "I was driving my daughter, Devon, and my ex-wife, Helen, to the airport. They were living in Calgary at the time. Devon was fifteen. Helen and I were fighting. We did that a lot. I was furious with her over something. A truck broadsided us at an intersection. I never even saw it. Hit the passenger side. Helen was killed instantly. My daughter's hip was smashed. For a long time it looked as if she'd never walk again. She does now, but the months of rehab were a long haul. She was in a wheelchair at first. She's progressed to using just a cane, but she's always gonna limp.''

"You weren't injured?'' Her voice was matter-of-fact, and he appreciated it. He despised sympathy; he'd have gotten up and walked away without another word if she'd shown pity.

"Not a scratch.'' He knew he sounded bitter. It was a thing that galled him.

She nodded. "Odd how that happens. We get it quite often in the ER.''

Some of the tension seemed to seep out of him, leaving him more relaxed. "So you see,'' he went on in a controlled voice, "I know how you feel. About the baby, about forgetting about that band, about feeling responsible.''

"Yes. Yes, I can see that you do.'' She glanced up as a woman's voice on the intercom calmly said, "Dr. Duncan, to Emergency, please. Dr. Duncan, to Emergency, *stat*.''

She stood up. "Sorry, but I've gotta go. I really need to talk to you. Could we meet later? My shift is over at three. How about yours?''

"Four.'' He thought quickly, came to a decision. He'd rather meet her away from the hospital, where gossip ran rampant. "There's a coffee shop a couple blocks down from here, in the lobby of the Ramada. Want to meet me there, a few minutes past four?''

"I'll be waiting. Thanks, Mr.— Thanks, um,

Spence.'' She gave a shy little nod and then picked up her untouched food, dumped it in the garbage and hurried off.

Spence forked up a mouthful of his macaroni. It was cold and it smelled stale. He glanced at his watch. He still had fifteen minutes left on his lunch break, and he was hungry.

He dumped the macaroni in the trash and went back to the counter, where he bought an egg sandwich and another cup of coffee.

He ate absently, his mind on the conversation he'd just had with Dr....with Joanne. She'd said to call her Joanne, and that pleased him. Not hard to figure out what she wanted, though. It would be something to do with getting involved in this abduction case. And as much as he liked her, as much as he wished he could help her, he'd have to tell her it wasn't going to happen.

Investigating crime was a part of his life that he'd put behind him, and he didn't feel any desire to reopen it. Not even for Joanne Duncan.

THE AFTERNOON WAS BUSY, and Joanne was grateful. She had little time to think, and although she was exhausted, the steady stream of patients through the ER demanded her full attention. At the end of her shift, she took time for a quick shower, hoping the hot water would revive her, reduce the bags under her eyes, before she met Spencer Mathews. Letting the water pour over her, she thought of what she wanted him to do…needed him to do. She had to help in the search for the baby, and she didn't know how. But he did.

She was waiting in a booth at the back of the coffee shop when he walked in. He was late; it was a quarter to five, and she'd decided that she wouldn't wait much longer.

For an instant she didn't recognize him out of his security uniform. He was wearing snug jeans and a brown leather jacket over a black tee. His thick fair hair was mussed, and he looked younger, more carefree.

He was a very attractive man, and she was aware of him on a visceral level.

"Joanne, sorry you had to wait for me. We have to brief the incoming shift before we can go off duty, and they were late. They'd had another meeting with Admin." He smiled at her, slipped off his jacket and slid into the seat across from hers. He ordered coffee when the waitress appeared.

There was an awkward silence for a few moments. Fatigued and depressed, Joanne was no longer as determined as she had been earlier that day. She didn't want to jump right in to what she had to say to him, and she fished for a neutral subject, but he spoke before she could come up with one.

"Do you have kids, Joanne?" He was stirring

cream into his coffee. His bare arm was muscular and brown, dusted with golden hair, his hands big and strong-looking. He wore no rings, and his watch was utilitarian—plain faced with a brown leather strap. She thought of his hands touching her, and was shocked at her body's immediate response.

"No, I don't have a family. My husband died five years ago. He had a genetic heart problem. We decided it wasn't wise to have children."

"Well, you're still young. If you want them, you can have them."

"I doubt it." She'd considered that more than a few times in the past five years. She gave him the answer she'd arrived at. "I'm forty-one. That's a bit too late to start. Especially as a single parent."

He didn't comment, and she added, "How old were you when your daughter was born, Spence?"

"Twenty-five." His forehead creased in a frown. "Damn, it's hard to believe I was ever twenty-five. Seems like a lifetime ago."

"For me, too. I was an intern at that age. I wouldn't go through that again for anything."

"I guess it's pretty rough being an intern. When I'm on duty at the hospital at night, I see them getting called at all hours, staggering down the corridors half-dead from lack of sleep. What made you decide on emergency medicine?"

Joanne smiled. "My mom and dad were both university English professors. I was an only child.

I grew up in a household where everything was always quiet. Decisions were based on reason and restraint and rational discussion. Nothing in our house ever happened that wasn't planned. I guess I grew up longing for a little excitement, and when I did my rotation in the ER as an intern, I knew it was where I belonged, although it took me years to finally make up my mind. I'm an adrenaline junkie. All of us are who work in the ER.''

"I guess you'd have to be, dealing with one disaster after another.''

She gave him a quizzical look. "But aren't cops the same—craving the rush of adventure, the variety that each day brings? Isn't that why you became a policeman, Spence?''

He smiled at her. "Nope. Not because of adrenaline. I generated enough of that in my teens to last a lifetime. I was your typical rebel without a cause until I was sixteen, getting myself into trouble with the law. I'd have ended up in jail eventually if a policeman hadn't taken me under his wing. I smartened up because of him, and it was natural to want to follow in his footsteps.''

"You enjoyed your work as a policeman, then?''

"I did.'' A shadow crossed his face. "But I reached a point where I didn't feel I was suited for the job anymore.''

"Because of the accident?'' She remembered exactly what he'd told her earlier that day, about feeling responsible for his daughter's injury.

"Yeah." He nodded and took a gulp of his coffee. "I couldn't shake the conviction that I wasn't morally qualified to do the job. Couldn't get past it. So I resigned."

"But it wasn't your fault. You said the truck broadsided you, that you didn't even see it coming."

A muscle in his jaw clenched, and she noticed the sudden tension in his face. "That's right as far as it goes. But I *should* have seen it coming, don't you understand? I wasn't paying attention the way I should have been. I was too busy fighting with Helen. If I'd been alert, it wouldn't have happened."

She thought he was being much too hard on himself, and she said so, adding, "There weren't any charges against you, were there?" She knew the system well from working in the ER. The police would have investigated the accident thoroughly, would have conducted a formal inquiry.

"No charges, no. The truck driver didn't have a license, and his blood-alcohol was well over the limit."

He leaned forward, looking straight into her eyes, his voice low and rough-edged. "But that doesn't make a hell of a lot of difference. What matters is whether I *feel* responsible. And I do." He held her gaze, his blue eyes compelling. "Just as you do about the Stevens baby, Joanne. I can assure you till we both lose our teeth that you weren't responsible for that baby disappearing, but it won't change the way you feel, will it."

Here was the crux of the matter, the real reason she'd wanted to talk to him. Or at least part of the reason.

"No, it won't change how I feel," she whispered. The coffee suddenly tasted like acid, and she set her cup down.

"Please, will you help me, Spence?" Her voice grew louder, higher. "I have to do something. I'm going nuts just listening to reports that say the police have no new leads."

She heard the note of desperation in her own voice; she knew she sounded shrill. She didn't care. All that mattered was that he heard, and understood, and gave her some direction. "You and I were both in the hospital the day it happened. You're an investigator. You must know of something, anything, that I could do to help find her."

He didn't answer, and the silence dragged on and on.

"Spence?" She needed him.

"Yeah. I know how bad you feel. I know how desperate you are." His voice took on a harsher note. "I also know you're asking me to get involved, and I can't do that, Joanne. Investigating's not my job anymore. Besides, the police are following up on every angle—you can bet on it. And I don't have access to their information." He paused a few seconds, then told her, as he had Lillian and Devon, "I do know that abductions of this sort are often the result of obsession, usually on the part of women plagued by infertility or miscarriage. The cases aren't as common in Canada as they are in the U.S., but in the past couple of years there've been several instances of babies taken from hospitals in various provinces. The recovery rate is good. Most kidnappings are solved with no harm to the infants. But there's always a small percentage that remain unsolved. The optimal time for recovery is the first few hours. After that, the chances drop significantly."

"You've researched this." It wasn't a question.

"A little." He didn't say how, and she didn't ask.

"So what can I do?"

"Not much. Keep your ears open, I guess."

She frowned at him. "What do you mean?"

"I know the staff in Maternity have been instructed not to talk to anyone except the authorities. But you might by chance hear some detail, some bit of information, that could be valuable. Sometimes the smallest thing becomes significant."

"And if I should hear something, who would I tell? You've just said that you won't be involved.

I'd feel silly running to the police with trivial gossip.'' A note of accusation laced her voice. She'd allowed herself to hope for more from him.

Once more, he was silent for some time. At last, he sighed and gave her a wry grin. "Okay, you might as well tell me. At least I know who'd be able to use any information you get, and I can pass it along.'' He thought for a moment and then said, "Do you have access to hospital records?"

She nodded. If she couldn't access certain files, she knew that Jimmy, the clerk in ER, would for her.

"It might be helpful to find out everything you can about Natasha Stevens. Again, I'm certain the police already checked her admission records, but it never hurts to double-check in case something was overlooked.''

"I'll do that. Anything else?"

"Yeah. Have lunch with me tomorrow?"

There was challenge in his eyes and his voice, and she sensed his words were impetuous.

"Of course.'' She felt ridiculously pleased and relieved that he'd asked. "My break is supposed to be at 11:30, but it'll depend on what's going on in the ER.''

"I'll call you just past eleven, see if you're clear. How's that?"

"Fine.'' Joanne knew that having lunch with him had a lot to do with the baby's abduction. But it also had a little to do with the attraction between them. The pull was certainly there for her, like a magnetic charge. And now she was reasonably certain he felt it, too.

"You can fill me in then on whatever you come up with."

She smiled at him and nodded. "Absolutely. And, Spence...?"

He didn't speak. Instead he lifted a quizzical eyebrow.

"Thanks. For listening, for your suggestions. And for being open with me about what happened to you. It helps."

He held her gaze for several long seconds and then he got to his feet and slipped his arms into his jacket. "Hafta go. I'm gonna be late for dinner, and my mother will take a wide strip off my hide."

Joanne, too, got to her feet. He reached for her jacket and held it for her as she slipped her arms into the sleeves. "You live with your mother?" The question was out before she could stop it.

"Yeah. She moved in when Devon came home from the hospital. She's a nurse, retired. How about you, Joanne? Your parents around?"

"They died just after I graduated medical school, within a few months of each other."

Spence waited politely as she walked to the counter, but before she could take her wallet from her bag, he paid.

"You're making a habit of paying my bills. Thanks again, Spence. Tomorrow, lunch is on me."

"We'll see about that." He held the door and she went outside. "Where are you parked?"

"I walked. I left my car in the hospital lot. It seemed easier than finding a spot around here," she explained, adding, "Besides, I needed the fresh air."

A powerful black motorcycle sat parked at the curb a few car lengths from the coffee shop. To Joanne's amazement, Spence ambled over to it and unhooked a helmet from the back of the seat. He grinned at the stunned surprise on her face, reached into the bike's carrier, extracted a spare helmet identical to his and held it out to her.

"Put this on. I'll give you a lift back to get your car." His eyes were twinkling, and in a teasing voice he added, "Not scared, are you, Doc? This is just another way of spiking adrenaline."

She hesitated, but not for long. She'd never ridden on a motorcycle, and this might be the only opportunity she'd ever get. She thrust vivid images of the ER and gory accidents out of her conscious mind.

"Of course I'm not scared." She was, a little, though. She took the helmet, aware of his large and slightly rough fingers grazing her chin as he helped her strap it in place.

"Trust me, I'm a safe and careful driver," he

assured her with a wink. Then he straddled the bike, balancing it and indicating the pegs for her feet. Gingerly, she climbed on behind him, glad she was wearing pants instead of a skirt, wondering what to do with her handbag—and in an instant the motor roared to life. She hastily looped her bag around her neck and across her chest and wrapped her arms around him, shocked at the warmth and hardness of his torso, the enforced intimacy of the seating as he pulled smoothly into traffic.

Joanne's fatigue and low spirits seemed to blow away with the breeze that caressed her face as the bike accelerated, slowed at the light, took off again with a surge of power.

"You okay?" Spence asked over his shoulder.

She felt herself grinning idiotically. "Fine," she called, holding on for dear life and barely suppressing a scream as they rounded a corner and the bike tilted.

She realized he was taking a very circuitous route back to St. Joe's, and she didn't care; in fact, she was delighted as they wound their way down to the ocean, maneuvered along narrow busy streets, then sped up as they entered the winding road that bordered the seawall and led in a huge circle around the point of land that formed Stanley Park.

It was like…flying. It was seductive and wild and aggressive and physical, and she loved it. She clung to Spence's midriff, absorbing his body heat, getting used to the dance of cornering, allowing her body to effortlessly flow with his.

Several times she laughed aloud with sheer exuberance when the road was free of traffic and the powerful bike growled and shot ahead with dizzying speed.

All too soon, they were back at St. Joe's. Spence stopped outside the parking garage, and Joanne climbed off, legs trembling slightly. He propped the bike on a kickstand, swung a long, denim-clad leg over the seat, then unhooked her helmet and lifted it off gently. He ruffled her hair with his hand, and her scalp tingled at his touch.

"I loved the ride, Spence." She couldn't seem to stop smiling, and her blood was coursing through her veins.

"You're a natural. You have a feel for it. We'll go on a longer ride one day soon, if you like," he promised.

"I'd like—a lot." She held out a hand, and he took it, holding it a bit longer than she expected. His palm was calloused.

"Thank you so much, Spence. I feel better. The ride was therapeutic. See you at lunch tomorrow?"

He nodded, still holding her hand. She looked at him and wondered what it would be like to kiss him. The thought made her blush, and she hastily slid her hand out of his grasp and started fishing in her bag for her car keys.

He waited until she'd found them, and then followed her to where she'd parked her car, chivalrously making certain that she was safely inside with the motor running before he gave her a mock salute and walked away. She watched him, his stride easy and powerful, until he rounded a cement column and disappeared from her sight.

Only then did she back the car out of her spot. Without conscious thought, she followed the Exit arrows that led to the side street behind the hospital. She felt younger somehow, more vibrant and alive than she'd felt for—how long? Days? Weeks? Could it be years, even? It was a good feeling, a euphoric feeling.

She turned on the radio and heard a somber male news announcer say there were still no new developments in the abduction of Baby Stevens.

Joanne waited for the sickness to start again in her belly, for the guilt and tension and fear to settle over her like a huge dark cloud—and they did, but the feelings were more muted than before.

Spencer Mathews had given her a gift, a few precious moments of lighthearted fun and fantasy in the midst of a dark reality. That evening, as she opened a tin of soup and toasted stale bread for her solitary dinner, vowing that tomorrow, for sure, she'd go to the market for salad greens and fruit and staples, she thought of Spence, re-creating the ride in her mind and anticipating their lunch the following day.

CHAPTER SIX

LILLIAN MATHEWS RAN for a lot of reasons.

The exercise kept her sixty-five-year-old body reasonably slender and toned. She also felt, although there were no medical data to confirm it, that running warded off arthritis and other nasty aging conditions, all of which she'd avoided developing. Besides, the fresh air cleared her brain; the routine got her up early each morning and out of the house, away from the tensions of her family.

Her preparations this morning were automatic, the result of long habit; she'd started running in her late forties, and now it was like brushing her teeth—a function so natural she didn't think about it at all.

Spence and Devon kept buying her fleecy jogging suits in Easter-egg colors, but she considered the suits far too luxurious for running. Instead, she wore the same washed-out, comfortable cotton apparel she'd worn for years: thermal underwear bottoms with rugby shorts pulled over them, a long-sleeved tee under a green kangaroo top with the hood cut off and gaily striped slouch socks. Her runners had a hole right where the bunion on her left foot rubbed. She considered herself the token bag lady of the jogging community.

After closing the door softly behind her—Spence had left for work half an hour before, but Devon was still asleep—Lillian set off down the street, greeting Mr. Swain as she did every morning. He walked his wife's poodle.

"Looks like rain," he said, even though the sky was denim-blue. He said the same thing every morning. Mr. Swain never admitted to good weather.

Lillian drew in lungfuls of air and started to run, very slowly at first, then speeding up as her body warmed and her breathing deepened.

She passed the long avenues of cedars, the mildewed old houses scattered among the newly constructed ones, but she didn't see them. She was thinking about Spencer.

It hurt her to admit it, but he was damaged, in some deep, seemingly irreparable way. He'd been like that since the accident. Lillian had assumed that time would heal him, as it did most things, yet it wasn't happening.

When she'd given up her comfortable apartment to move into Spencer's house and care for Devon, Lillian had figured it would only be for a year or so, until Devon adjusted to her physical condition and was strong enough to get through her days on her own.

That was two-and-a-half years ago, and although Devon was doing quite well now, Spencer wasn't. He hadn't moved on with his life, and, what was worse, he blocked Devon when she tried to get on with hers.

Now Devon was in love, with a man Lillian suspected Spencer wouldn't approve of. Devon had confided in Lillian, knowing her grandmother wouldn't betray her confidence, but it put Lillian in an awkward position. She hated being caught between the two people she loved most in the world, and lately it was happening more and more often.

How ironic and sad, Lillian mused as she huffed up a small hill and down the other side, that she and her son had each had just one child.

It was too late for her, but if Spencer would marry again, he was still young enough to father a couple more kids. That would take the pressure off Devon…and it would also set Lillian free to live her own life.

That thought led straight to Bud Ansell.

He'd turned up at her yoga class, of all places. And he'd registered, which was akin to having Hulk Hogan study ballet. Lillian chuckled at the memory of Bud, portly and stiff, earnestly doing his awkward version of the sun salutation, sweat dripping off his nose, belly hanging.

When last night's class ended, he'd asked if she'd have coffee with him, adding quickly that he wanted to talk to her about Spence. He knew her well; he knew she wouldn't refuse if it was about her son. Had the subject been her and Bud—well, she was still undecided about that. She'd told him often enough that there was no point getting into it until her family situation got straightened out.

Not that Bud ever gave up. He had a one-track mind. Lillian would never tell him so, but it thrilled the feminine side of her to know that he cared enough to do such ridiculous things as join a yoga class just to spend time with her.

"I want Spence to take over the company, Lil," Bud had announced when they were settled into a booth at the small coffee shop on the corner. "I'm almost seventy. It's past time for me to step down, start taking life a bit easier."

Bud had left the police force ten years earlier and started Vector, the security company that now had the reputation of being the best in the Lower Mainland.

"But the boy won't even listen when I bring it up. He's wasted working as a security guard at St. Joe's. Not that I'm not grateful to have him working for me, but him doin' shifts at the hospital is like hitching a racehorse to a cart."

Lillian couldn't help but think of the irony of

sitting here with Bud and talking about Spencer as if the two of them were his parents.

"I can't change his mind, Bud. I can't get him to see reason these days. He just goes quiet and won't say anything."

Bud shook his head. "It's a damn waste of great talent. He was the finest investigator the RCMP had. I can understand him needing time out after what happened. I can even see him not wanting to spend his entire life on police work. God knows, I'm the first to admit it's tough and soul-destroying. But by now he oughta be movin' ahead, finding another use for his ability. If not Vector, then something else." He'd slumped back in the seat and had heaved a sigh.

"I'm gonna give him an ultimatum, Lil. Three months to make up his mind. There's this guy from Calgary interested in buying me out. I can't keep him hanging forever."

"And what'll you do without the business?"

He'd cast a long look her way. "Spence isn't the only one who's stuck, Lil. I'm giving you three months, as well. I'm buying a condo in Hawaii, and I'm gonna live there. You know how I feel. You know what I want."

She did know. *Three months.* She just wasn't sure she could leave old fears behind and walk into the sunset with him.

Sunset, hell. There were still sunrises to consider.

She was sweating now, and she'd reached the street that marked her turning point. She ran a short distance down it and then headed for home, still thinking about Bud.

Did she love him enough to forgive and forget, once and for all? She stopped running a block from the house and walked, pondering what Bud had said.

She hadn't realized it until he'd pointed it out last night, and she hated to admit it even now, but maybe Bud was right. Maybe she was just as stuck as Spencer. Maybe she ought to examine herself a little more and her son a little less.

"SPENCE, HOW'S IT GOIN'? Good to see you."

"And you, Gord." Spence shook the meaty paw Zelaney stuck out.

"How's Devon doing?"

Zelaney had been a faithful friend both before and after Spence left the Force. He'd visited Devon in the rehab hospital more than once.

"She's out of the wheelchair, walking with a cane. Hell of an effort for her, but the docs say it'll get easier as time goes on."

"That's great news, Spence. Great news." Gordon's face split in a delighted grin. After a minute he said, "You gotta minute?"

It was eight-thirty in the morning. Spence's shift

was only half an hour old, so going to the coffee shop was out of the question. He explained that.

"Is there somewhere around here we can talk private?"

Spence nodded and led the way into a supply room not much larger than a broom closet. Zelaney glanced around and shut the door behind them.

"This baby abduction," he began. "Between you and me and the gatepost, the case is a bastard, Spence. It's a real coincidence having you workin' here just when it happened."

"I talked to one of your guys, told him exactly what had gone down that morning," Spence said. "I wasn't a hell of a lot of help. I wasn't anywhere near Maternity when the baby was taken. I monitored the security cameras afterward, but the perp was long gone by then."

Zelaney nodded. "Maybe you could keep your ear to the ground for me. I'd sure appreciate any tips you might pick up. We've got zilch to go on."

"What about relatives?"

Zelaney shook his head. "Apart from the baby's mother, *nada,* not around here anyhow. Stevens has one sister, down in Seattle. We ruled her out. She was working at the time. Got little kids of her own. The mother's dead. Father died when Natasha and her sister were kids."

"The baby's father?"

Zelaney shook his head. "Not on the scene.

Can't find him. Stevens won't even give us a name. Says that the guy dumped her before she even knew she was pregnant. He has no idea the baby is his. She sort of insinuates he's married, but she won't come out and confirm it.''

''Think that's the straight goods? He'd have motive if he wanted the kid.''

Zelaney shrugged. ''I'd say she's telling the truth. I did suggest a lie detector test, but she went ballistic. You saw this morning's headlines—'Kidnap Mom Probed By Police'? We were receivin' nasty calls before I even arrived at work today.''

Spence had read the piece. ''What about her? She's really got the press on her side. How much is legit and how much is contrived?''

Zelaney shook his head. ''No motive that I can see. Stevens had arranged a private adoption for the baby—a couple named Dirk and Betsy Halstead. They live in Richmond. Real straight-up couple, financially sound. He's a lawyer. She's an artist. They covered Stevens's expenses all during the pregnancy. They'd agreed to pay her a hefty lump sum when the baby came. We checked them out pretty thoroughly. They're on the level. They're real torn up over the whole deal. Stevens really needed the money they were gonna give her. She's not exactly living in the lap of luxury. Losing that money's gotta be a blow to her. And she's also half out of her head over the abduction. Deciding to give the kid up was tough enough, but to have it stolen out of the hospital—'' Zelaney sighed.

"I feel for her. Abduction is every parent's worst nightmare. I don't think she's got anything to do with it, but we tapped her phone just as a precaution.''

"And?''

"Nothing so far.''

Spence thought for a moment. "There's been nothing on the news about her giving up the baby for adoption.''

"She and the Halsteads mutually agreed not to make that public. They're private people and they don't want the publicity that would result. It was a smart decision, if you ask me. I wonder how long it'll be, though, before some wiseass journalist finds out about it.''

"So you figure the abduction was haphazard? Some nuttso who knew his or her way around the hospital and took advantage of what was going on that morning?''

"Looks like it. Best we can figure, it was a young woman, probably wearing a wig and phony glasses, carrying a camera, with a sports bag over her shoulder plenty big enough to stick a newborn into. Nobody twigged for at least a half-hour that the kid was gone, so she had plenty of time to get away. I've got guys checking on every woman who lost a baby in the past six months, in case one of them went cuckoo and took the kid, but so far no luck. It's a hell of a job. Lower Mainland's a big assignment.''

"How would she have known that this particular baby didn't have a security band?" That had bothered Spence from the beginning.

Zelaney shrugged. "You got me. All I can figure is she had to be familiar with the hospital routine at St. Joe's, knowledgeable enough to spot an opportunity and snatch it. We're checking background on every single employee in Maternity, and we're trying to trace whoever was fired there the past year. Could be somebody like that, who went crazy and decided to take the kid.''

Spence nodded. "It could also be cleaning staff, lab techs, X ray guys—anybody who had reason to be on the maternity floor.''

Zelaney rolled his eyes. "A zillion people, more or less, in a hospital this size. You see why we're having problems.'' Zelaney sent Spence a beseeching look. "If you could see your way clear to giving me a hand on this, I'd appreciate it, buddy.''

Spence opened his mouth to tell Zelaney that was out of the question, since he wasn't an investigator anymore, and a vivid image of Joanne Duncan flashed before his eyes.

She'd asked him to do exactly the same thing.

As he had so often during the past couple of days

and nights, Spence remembered the tiny baby girl, the fragility of her curled-up newborn body, the forlorn sound of her first cry. The memory haunted him.

"Okay," he sighed. "Okay, I don't know what I can do, but I'll give it a shot." He could see that Gordon was surprised; in spite of his plea and their friendship, he'd expected Spence to refuse, as Spence had several times in the past two years for other cases.

"Super. Thanks, Spence."

"Anything your boys are holding back?" There was usually some detail that the police wouldn't release to the media, some tiny fact that only the abductor would know. It was valuable in ruling out the confessors, the crazy people who, guilty over God only knows what, called and insisted they'd committed the crime.

"The baby was wearing a little knitted red toque. The nurse put it on her after the specialist examined her. It wasn't anywhere we could see. Not much, but it's all we got."

"Did the hospital switchboard register any calls to or from the mother's room before the baby disappeared?"

"Nope. There're a couple of pay phones in the hallway outside Maternity. We're checking on calls made from them. So far nothing. And, of course,

Stevens could have had a cell. She says not. We're investigating.''

The door to the supply room burst open and a nursing aide hurried through. She stopped short at the sight of Spence and Zelaney.

''Sorry,'' she said with a knowing grin. ''I didn't realize this was occupied. You boys oughta put a sign on the door.''

''We're just leaving.'' Outside in the hallway Spence paused. ''I'll be in touch, Gord.''

Zelaney was frowning, looking over his shoulder at the supply room. ''You don't figure she thought we were...''

Spence kept a straight face and nodded. ''Yeah, I'm sure she did. Happens all the time around here.''

''C-ripes, Spence. You be sure and set her right, okay?'' Zelaney's florid cheeks were nearly purple, his expression horrified.

Spence was enjoying himself. ''The more you deny a thing, the guiltier you sound, Gord. You know how that goes.''

Zelaney swore, and he was still muttering as he got on the elevator.

Spence, still grinning, continued his work, strolling through the hospital, aware of the sounds and smells surrounding him, the murmured conversations of patients, the soft laughter and hurried greetings of nurses changing shifts at the stations, the bleary blood-red eyes of a weary intern as he staggered out of the cubicle where he'd been stealing sleep.

A subtle aura clung to the corridors. It was an invisible residue of terrible fear and despair—of hope—powerful ghosts of emotion left behind by the battered tide of humanity that flowed in and, with luck, out again, through the many doors of St. Joseph's. It clung to his uniform, too, like a cobweb, and Spence thought about Joanne and wondered how she dealt with it.

And then he thought about how he was looking forward to lunch a little too much for comfort.

SHE HURRIED into the cafeteria at exactly eleven-thirty. He'd called her earlier, as he'd promised, and she'd said in a formal voice that although they'd had a busy morning, things were relatively quiet now and she could keep their appointment.

He'd noticed she was careful not to label their get-together a date.

She'd taken off her lab coat, and was wearing a soft lilac top and a gray cotton skirt that emphasized her narrow waist and slender hips. Her silver-blond hair was shining and intriguingly tousled. A becoming blush colored her smooth cheeks, but he didn't think it was from makeup, because she had barely even a trace of lipstick on her full mouth.

"Trust me to choose lunch for you, Joanne?"

When she hesitated and then nodded, he gestured at a table in a small alcove that was fairly private. "Snag that for us, and I'll be along in a second."

He bought two plates of the day's special—stir-fry over rice—and added coffee for himself and the herbal tea he'd noticed she favored. After plunking two huge oatmeal cookies and a handful of napkins on top, he carefully carried the load to where she was sitting and divided the food between them.

"This was supposed to be my treat." She smiled up at him.

"You can buy when we go to that expensive French restaurant, how's that."

He saw the idea pleased her. He'd been joking, but he filed the thought under *Maybes*.

"It's a deal, Spence." She studied her plate. "This looks good. I'm really hungry."

"Me, too." He wasn't, but he wanted to put her at ease, so he ate in silence for a few moments, covertly watching as she swiftly and efficiently dispensed with her food.

She caught him staring, flushed and set her fork down.

"Sorry. Everyone in the ER eats as if it's a last meal. We hardly ever get to finish anything unless we're quick about it." Her eyes danced, and he could see a mischievous humor he hadn't known was hiding in her. "You can dress us up, but you can't take us out anywhere civilized," she warned, then snapped her fingers and pretended chagrin. "Darn, there goes the French restaurant."

"Your visual effect is enough to get you by." The compliment was easy; he liked the way she ducked her head and turned pink again.

When she glanced up, her eyes were somber and she'd lowered her voice, so he had to lean closer in order to hear. He caught a whiff of her perfume, light and grassy.

"I checked the hospital admission records on Natasha Stevens," she began, then repeated exactly what Spence had just heard from Zelaney—that no father was noted on the form; that Marilyn Rogers, a sister with a street address in Seattle, was named as next of kin.

"I also talked to a friend in Maternity. Natasha wasn't up there long enough before the baby's disappearance for the nursing staff to form any opinion of her. And afterward, of course, she was naturally hysterical and angry."

"Were any of the cleaning staff in her room before the baby disappeared?"

"The girl on shift then is on her day off right now. She'll be back tomorrow. I'll see if I can get her to tell me anything. Everyone's paranoid about talking. Administration has sent out a directive warning that if anyone speaks to the media or gossips at all about this situation, it'll mean instant dismissal."

Spence grinned. "Well, there go our jobs. What'll you do when they fire you?"

She pretended to take the question seriously. "Oh, I always thought I'd like to run a restaurant," she said after a minute. "It's people oriented, the tools are similar to the ones we use in the ER, there's a lot of pressure to juggle everything at once and not kill anybody. Heck, it's probably a lot like emergency medicine—a major crisis a minute, staff who have to work as a unit. It could be challenging, particularly when you consider that I don't cook."

He laughed. "That might be a slight problem, all right. Although you could always hire someone."

"I've considered that without having a restaurant. How about you, Spence?" She tilted her head and gave him a mischievous smile. "What'll you do when you get fired?"

"Oh, that's easy. I'll drop out, like they used to say in the sixties. Climb on my Harley and just drive across North America. Stop in little towns that I fancy. Get a job now and then pumping gas or washing cars." He sat back in his seat and crossed his feet under the table. "Make sure I follow the sun, so when winter comes I'm in Mexico or South America." He hadn't indulged in a flight of fancy in a long time. He liked the feeling it gave him, and he went on. "Sleep under the stars. Fish when I want to."

"Come by my restaurant when you're in town. I owe you more than a few lunches."

They grinned at each other, delighted with their fantasies, forgetful of where they were.

Reluctantly, he drew them back to reality. "Just so you aren't too guilty about snooping around, I told Zelaney I'd be part of the investigation."

She blew out a long breath. "Spence, I'm so glad. I don't know why, but I feel relieved."

"Don't get your hopes up, because I really don't know whether I can help, Joanne."

She nodded. "I understand that. It just makes a difference that you'll try." She took one of the cookies and broke it in half, handed a portion to Spence and bit into hers with relish.

"I love cookies." She filled her cup with tea and sipped it, then munched away. "Mmm, oatmeal with chocolate chips."

There was a cookie crumb on her chin. Without thinking, Spence reached across the small table and brushed it off with his thumb.

She started, and then glanced around to see if anyone had noticed. He cursed himself for being foolish and thoughtless. The hospital cafeteria was full of her co-workers; she was a prominent figure at St. Joe's; he'd embarrassed her.

"Sorry." He felt like a dolt. "Won't happen again."

"Spence, please." Impulsively, she took his

hand in hers and held it for a long moment, forcing herself to look straight into his eyes.

"I'm a bit shy is all. Don't take it the wrong way." She let his hand go, but gave it an intimate little squeeze before she released it. Deliberately, she changed the subject.

"How long have you ridden a motorcycle?"

"Since I was seventeen." He relaxed again, although he was aware that he'd have to leave in a few moments or Murray would burst through the door trumpeting the fact that Spence was infringing on his lunch break.

"Did you buy a bike at that age?" She sounded sincerely interested.

"Yeah, I did. I worked hard for the money." She was so easy to talk to. "I'd been going through my punk stage—ended up in juvenile hall a couple of times, played hooky, nearly got myself expelled from school." Bud had bailed him out each time. "I finally landed in serious trouble over a stolen car. Bud Ansell, the policeman I mentioned, offered to be responsible for me, and the judge dismissed the charges, but he gave me the tongue-lashing of my young life. So did Bud. He finagled me a job nights and weekends stocking shelves in a supermarket. Told me it would give me a taste of what kind of jobs a guy with no education could expect to have. It took me a year of hard saving to buy that beat-up old Harley.'' Bud had gotten it for him cheap, at a police auction.

"And you stayed in school."

"Yeah, the cans of peas did their job, all right." He glanced at his watch. "I hafta go. We stagger our lunch breaks, and mine's over. How about we meet here again tomorrow, and you can tell me about *your* misspent youth?"

She nodded without hesitation. "Barring disasters in the ER, same time?"

"Same time." He loaded the residue from their lunch on the tray and handed his uneaten cookie across to her, then he gave her a small salute. "Hope your afternoon goes well."

"And yours. 'Bye, Spence."

Once he'd returned the tray, he paused at the door and turned back to her. She smiled at him and waved.

It pleased him that she was looking.

CHAPTER SEVEN

JOANNE LINGERED over her tea, enjoying Spence's cookie. This was the first day since the abduction that food tasted good to her again. It was ridiculous, but she felt that she was finally *doing* something, helping in some small way to get baby Abigail Stevens back where she belonged—in the arms of her poor young mother.

She was well aware that the reason for her good spirits was Spence. Knowing he was involved in the investigation gave her a feeling of confidence that the very best resources were now being used in the search for the baby.

As she had many times, she thought of the motorcycle ride he'd taken her on yesterday—the unaccustomed wildness and the sense of utter freedom she'd had clinging to his back, tilting this way and that, trusting him to steer them safely through the traffic.

Something about Spence instilled in her a total trust, allowing her to relax in his presence.

And something about him made her female hormones kick into overdrive each time she was near him. His thumb on her skin when he'd brushed it across her chin had sent a sensual thrill so intense shooting through her that she'd looked around, afraid the powerful sensation would be somehow visible to everyone in the cafeteria—like a red light flashing out of the top of her head.

Did he feel it, too? He looked at her with those deep-set, blue-as-liquid-crystal eyes, and she thought she saw in them a reflection of what she was feeling, but she wasn't sure. He paid her compliments about her appearance, as he had today, but he was a courtly man, with impeccable manners. Maybe he was just being polite.

How could she tell for sure? She wasn't practiced at this game; she never had been. She'd never wanted to be, till now.

"Dr. Duncan?"

Lost in thought, Joanne took a moment to respond.

"Oh, hi, Portia." Her intern stood beside the table, a loaded tray balanced against her flat stomach.

"Mind if I sit here?"

"Not at all. I'm just leaving."

"Oh." Disappointment colored the young woman's tone. "It's quiet in the ER. I thought I could maybe buy you a cup of tea or something. I'd like to talk for a minute, if you can spare the time."

"Okay, Portia." Her bladder was going to have

a busy afternoon, but Joanne couldn't refuse. "I'll just get a refill."

"Let me." Portia took the pot and filled it with hot water, then added another herbal tea bag. She sat back down and began stirring her soup to cool it.

"Anything going down in the ER?"

"We just had a domestic. *He* complained that *she* never did housework, so *she* hit *him* over the head with a rolling pin."

"Fractured skull?"

"Nope, nothing but a bump the size of a baseball. He refuses to press charges. Says he was out of line."

"If the wife has a rolling pin she can locate just like that, she's probably a cook instead of a cleaner. I don't think I even own one."

"Me, either." They both giggled.

"Did the bike messenger with the fractured wrist go back to work like he said?"

Portia nodded and tasted her soup. "The instant we had him splinted, he signed out. Insisted he had urgent stuff to deliver and he could do it just as well with one hand."

Joanne shrugged. "Next thing, we'll have him back with a fractured leg or two."

"That little kid who was hit by the car was admitted. I went up to Peds with him. Cute little guy."

"Did they ever get hold of his mother?"

Portia shook her head. "She was supposed to be volunteering at the art gallery, but nobody there knew where she was. Said it wasn't her day to come in. My guess is, she's probably having an affair with some high roller. The kid says his dad's in Japan on some business deal. The nanny's here, but she looks all of sixteen and she barely speaks English. She's so hysterical I felt like giving her meds. The chauffeur has the day off. God only knows where the cook is. Real lucky little overprivileged kid, huh?" Portia's cultured voice dripped with sarcasm. "He gets bonked by a car and there's nobody but another scared kid around to care."

"So apart from poor little rich kids and rolling pins, are you enjoying your rotation in the ER?" Joanne finished off the cookie Spence had handed her. So it was probably loaded with sugar and fat. What the heck. No point in wasting it, and she'd likely need the energy before the day was over.

"That's what I wanted to talk to you about," Portia said, crumbling a packet of crackers into her soup. "I think I'd like to do emergency medicine. Specialize, I mean. I just wondered what it's like over the long haul. You know, for a woman?"

Joanne grinned. She knew exactly what Portia was talking about. "You mean when some green young cop thinks the clerk is the physician because he's a man and you and I are nurses because we're women?'' It had happened the first week Portia was on ER; it was a recurring thing that Joanne had become accustomed to.

''Yeah. That and lots of other stuff.''

''Well, ER medicine is still only fifteen-percent female. It's heartening to see bright young women choosing it as their specialty.''

''So you'd say it's a good career choice?''

Portia's gray eyes were fixed intently on Joanne's face. Her gaze was disconcerting. It made Joanne feel that the other woman could see right into her head. She considered the question and then shrugged. ''That depends on what you want out of life. If it's money and status, you're barking up the wrong tree.''

Portia shook her head. ''Money's not an issue. I grew up like that little kid who got hit by the car. I've got a trust fund that'll see me through.''

''Then—''

Joanne was interrupted by the intercom. ''Dr. Duncan, report to the ER. Dr. Duncan, report to the ER.''

''Duty calls. Gotta go.'' She noted the disappointment on Portia's face. ''When are you off duty? I mean, a full day off?''

''Thursday.''

''I'm done at three that day. We could go for a walk or something, if you want. But I know what it's like when you're an intern—off time is precious—so don't feel…''

Portia shook her head. "I'd like that—a lot. Thanks, Dr. Duncan."

"Joanne."

"Joanne. Thanks, Joanne." Portia beamed, and Joanne was smiling, too, as she hurried back to work.

She burst through the doors to the ER, surprised to find that the waiting area wasn't overflowing with bodies as she'd anticipated.

"What's up, Jimmy?" Joanne hurried over to the clerk, and he gestured at a short, round man in a dark suit and a tan overcoat near the automatic doors at the ER entrance.

"That guy says he has to see you. Claims it's urgent."

Joanne walked over. "I'm Joanne Duncan. How may I help you?" She smiled.

"Dr. Joanne Duncan?" He read off her home address and telephone number, and Joanne frowned, wondering what it was all about.

"Yes."

"Here you go, Doctor." He slapped a fat white envelope in her hand and, without another word, turned and left the building.

With a terrible feeling of foreboding, Joanne slowly opened the envelope. Inside were several closely typed pages.

Joanne skimmed the first page and felt her legs go gelatinous.

In a seemingly endless list of names that included the hospital administrator, the chief of staff, the head of Maternity and a dozen nurses, her own name stood out like a beacon, and it was immediately apparent to her what this was about.

The man was a process server. She, along with everyone else named on the sheet, was being sued for negligence, for an unspecified amount, for relief, the words said, of monetary and nonmonetary damages as well as emotional damages to Ms. Natasha Stevens through the abduction of her newborn daughter.

Joanne's hands began to tremble, and she had to swallow hard to keep from vomiting up her lunch.

CHAPTER EIGHT

JOANNE WASN'T SURPRISED when she was called up to the office of the hospital president, Martin Chalk, just before her shift ended that afternoon.

She was surprised to find that she was the only one there. She'd naively expected that every person named in the suit would be present; she'd thought it would be supportive to talk about this shocking turn of events with everyone.

But just Chalk and a lawyer named Abrams, a tall dour man with a bald head and dead-fish eyes, waited for her in Chalk's office.

Once again, she was asked to relate in specific detail the circumstances surrounding the delivery of the Stevens baby. And she did—feeling more and more irritated, more and more like a criminal on trial, as Chalk and Abrams listened and meticulously questioned her about every single aspect of the event.

"I totally forgot about the security band," Joanne stated baldly. "I feel absolutely terrible about it, but there's nothing I can do now to change it."

"It's a bad business all around." Chalk shook his head. "Your failure to band the baby has placed the hospital in a difficult legal position."

"It's not as if I did it deliberately," Joanne snapped. "I'm human. Humans make mistakes." She was sick to death of feeling defensive.

Abrams nodded somberly. "Unfortunately, that mistake has affected the entire hospital. As I'm sure you're aware, Doctor, you are not legally an employee of St. Joseph's. Physicians are considered independent and self-employed, so you will not be included in any defense the hospital's lawyers mount. I strongly suggest you find an excellent lawyer, Doctor. If you don't know one, I'd be pleased to suggest someone knowledgeable in this area of litigation."

Joanne looked into his emotionless eyes. "Are you suggesting that the *hospital* could find me personally responsible for what happened? That the *hospital's* stance might well be to make me a scapegoat in this whole thing, Mr. Abrams?"

"Not at all, Doctor. Not at all." It was Martin Chalk who answered, his voice hearty. "We're all in this together. Saul is merely explaining your legal position."

Joanne was trembling by the time the session ended, although she did her best to conceal it under a brave facade. In spite of Chalk's reassurances, she had the distinct impression that Abrams would sacrifice her without a moment's hesitation if it meant getting the hospital off the hook.

Feeling slightly nauseated, she retrieved her raincoat and handbag from her locker in the staff lounge and headed out to the parking garage.

"Joanne, wait up a minute."

She was so distracted that she didn't even see Spence until he spoke. He was near the hospital exit, lounging against a cement pillar.

He came over to her, and she instantly felt an overwhelming urge to blurt out everything that had just happened.

He spoke first. "I thought maybe you'd like to come for a ride on the bike. It's stopped raining, and we're actually gonna have a sunset."

"Now?" Her brain was sluggish, stuck back in Chalk's office.

"The sunset?" He grinned, teasing her. "I don't think for a couple of hours, but I could try to speed it up if that's what your heart desires."

She had to smile. "Idiot. I meant the bike ride." She was wearing a khaki skirt, comfortable for work but not suited to straddling a bike seat. "I'd love to come, but I need to change into jeans."

"No problem. I'll pick you up at home, if you give me your address."

"It's just off Davie, an apartment building, maybe ten minutes away."

He repeated the address and waited until she

found her keys, then took them from her and opened her car door. He closed it after her and gave that little salute she was becoming accustomed to.

When she got to her building he was at the door. Somehow her spirits had lifted during the short drive home from the hospital. She smiled at him, and during the ride up in the elevator they talked about where they'd go on the bike, instead of what was happening at the hospital.

"Come in, Spence. Make yourself at home while I change." Joanne was suddenly conscious of his seeing her private space. She wished she'd cleared away the cereal boxes and dirty dishes on the kitchen counter, wished this had been the day for her weekly cleaning service so there wouldn't be dust on the dining room table, or papers and magazines scattered on the floor beside the couch.

"Nice," he said. "Looks like you."

"Messy?"

"Classy. Sexy."

When she came out of the bedroom a few moments later in her jeans and sweater, wearing a pair of brown leather boots she'd impulsively bought years ago and then never worn, he was outside on the roomy terrace.

"What a view." He gestured down at the park, at the view of the North Shore mountains. "The city's an interesting place to live, Joanne. I have a house in Kitsilano. It's a good area, but we sure don't get this view.''

''I used to live in a quiet, secluded neighborhood near the university. When my husband died, I sold the house and bought this. I wanted to hear sirens at night and see freighters on the inlet and be able to walk along the seawall.''

''You chose well.''

For some reason his approval brought tears to her eyes. So many of the friends she and Henry had were horrified at her decision to sell the spacious, stately old home she'd lived in for so long. They'd visited her here once or twice, mostly, she suspected, just to assure themselves she'd made a mistake. Not one of them had ever said she'd chosen well, and it felt wonderful to be applauded.

''You look like a proper biker chick,'' he remarked with an appreciative grin as he eyed her clothing.

''And you look dangerous in that black leather jacket,'' she retorted.

He laughed. ''As long as we look the part, let's ride before the sky clouds over again. Or the motorcycle cops figure out we're imposters.''

Joanne grabbed a sturdy windbreaker, and they left the apartment. This time, she knew how to fasten the helmet and climb on behind him. She knew how to help him balance the bike, then pull her feet up and rest them on the foot pegs as they roared away from the curb.

"Do you have to be back at any special time, Joanne?"

"For work in the morning," she called out, and then couldn't believe she'd said it.

But he just laughed. "I'll do my best. I thought we'd head across the Lion's Gate and follow the road along to Whistler. Sound okay to you?"

"Sounds fine." Joanne felt excited. Her co-workers talked constantly about Whistler, a popular ski and resort area north of Vancouver, but she'd never been there. Henry hadn't been the sort to just go for a drive; he'd preferred to spend weekends and holidays at home, strolling around the university, seeing foreign films at the local theater, visiting libraries or museums. Once every couple of years they'd fly back to visit his relatives in Maine, but that was the extent of their travels.

The afternoon traffic was heavy, and getting across the bridge took some time, but then the highway broadened and they gained speed. The scenery was soon breathtaking—vistas of ocean bordered by high rock walls, the road a challenging series of twists and turns that Spence attacked aggressively.

Snuggled against him, with the wind whistling around them, Joanne didn't try to talk. Instead, she gave herself up to the stomach-tilting delight of leaning into curves, the unique sensation of relying on someone else to make every decision.

He obviously knew the route well, because he pulled off the highway at one point and drove along a curving narrow road to a playing field where a rugby game was in progress. A small concession there offered strong coffee and large newspaper containers of fries—greasy, salty, delicious.

They carried the snack over to a wooden picnic table.

"D'you come here often, Spence?"

"Not often enough, and not lately. I used to coach junior rugby. I haven't for a few years now." He looked past her, to the playing field. "I also used to ride the bike a lot more than I do now. Last couple of years I've mostly used it just as transportation to and from work. I've missed longer rides."

"I can understand why. It really blows all your worries away." She realized she hadn't even thought about the lawsuit once since she'd climbed on the bike.

"I'm getting sued, Spence." She blurted out the news, but the prospect didn't seem as immediate or as desperate here in this cheerful place.

He raised an eyebrow and swallowed a mouthful of fries. "How's that?"

"I got the notice today. A lawyer acting for Natasha Stevens names me and half the hospital staff, everybody who even remotely had anything to do with the baby or with her. However, the lawyer for the hospital informed me that I can't be defended by the hospital. I have to find my own lawyer." She repeated what Abrams had told her, along with her suspicions about his putting the legal responsibility on her if he could.

"Of course I knew that was the legal situation with my job, but I never gave it much thought before. You just do your work and don't think much about legalities."

She drank her coffee, grateful for its warmth. "The awful thing, the part that makes me feel sick, is that not once did Abrams mention the baby or say he was concerned about her safe recovery. All he and Chalk talked about was the hospital's liability."

Spence didn't sound taken aback at the news. "That figures. You know a good lawyer?"

"I'm gonna call the Canadian Medical Physicians' Association. A lawyer from that organization gave a talk to doctors a few months ago. He'd been a doctor himself before he went into law. I liked him."

"Call him right away. I suppose I shouldn't be surprised that Stevens would go this route, but I am. She got on the bandwagon pretty fast. It's been less than a week."

Joanne couldn't find it in her heart to resent Stevens, in spite of the problems the girl was creating. "Some smart lawyer probably got hold of her. She's not in any emotional shape to be making decisions."

Spence considered that. "And yet she is making them. Pretty big ones, too, if she's suing the hospital. You'd think she'd be more interested in the investigation than in a lawsuit."

"It's human nature," Joanne said. "People get money and love all mixed up, don't you think, Spence? They mistake one for the other. They figure one is a substitute for the other." She told him about the little boy in the ER who'd been hit by a car, how his parents had provided everything material and yet weren't available when the kid most needed them. "So I can see where Natasha Stevens is coming from. She's desperate."

"You could be right." He gestured at her coffee. "Want a refill before we take off?"

"Nope, this was great."

And so was being on the bike again. For the next hour, Joanne clung to Spence's back, comfortable now with the enforced physical intimacy, loving the wind on her face, the swoops and dizzying corners, the way other bikers saluted as if she and Spence belonged, with them, to a select club.

Spence slowed when they reached the village of Whistler. It wasn't ski season, yet cars crowded the parking lot of the huge hotel and the sidewalks were filled with people; the resort was obviously an all-season destination.

Spence drove off the highway and into the town. They slowly explored the narrow streets until they reached a European-looking café. He pulled to the curb and helped Joanne off. Her legs were rubbery, and she stumbled. He slid an arm around her waist, holding her steady.

"You're weak with hunger," he teased. "Feel like some dinner? It's not French, but it's close geographically."

"I'm starving," she confessed. "How's that possible? I ate all those fries just a little while ago."

"Riding a bike does that to you. It's the fresh air and the fear of imminent death. C'mon."

She was very conscious that he kept his arm around her as they went inside. The café was decorated like a Swiss chalet, and in moments they were seated in a padded booth by a deep window that commanded a view of the mountains.

"Won't your family worry when you're not there for dinner?" Joanne remembered a remark he'd made about his mother being displeased if he was late.

"Nobody home tonight. Devon's working late at the university library, and Mom's eating with her yoga group."

"I've always wanted to do yoga." Joanne studied the menu, thinking that if her appetite stayed at this level, she'd soon have to become a lifetime member of Eaters Anonymous, never mind take up yoga. Could riding on the back of a bike really be considered aerobic exercise?

The hell with it. She ordered a meal that began with cream soup, progressed to thick stew with the best cheesy potatoes she'd ever eaten and finished with apple torte smothered in a rich almond sauce.

She ate every morsel and then slumped back into the cushions. "Is there an award here for gluttony? Because I've just won it."

Spence laughed. "More coffee?"

"I couldn't hold another ounce of anything."

"Then we'd probably best be starting back, before it gets dark."

He paid the bill, and returned to the bike.

The sun had set and the spring evening was soft and warm. Entirely content, Joanne let her body rest more fully against Spence moving with him as if they were one unit while he maneuvered the bike through the village and back to the highway.

Despite the physical intimacy, riding pinion allowed uninterrupted time to reflect, and her mind roved over the occurrences of the past week. It seemed to her that the events surrounding the baby's birth had changed her life in ways she could never have imagined one short week before. As she did each time she remembered baby Abigail, she sent a fervent prayer heavenward for the infant's safety.

A week ago, Joanne mused as the wind rushed past, she would never in her wildest dreams have thought she'd be racing through the twilight on the back of a bike, clinging to this big, capable man.

The lawsuit she was facing, the guilt she felt about the baby, the everyday stress of her demanding job—all were still there in the nether regions of her mind, but this little interval had lessened their effect.

Spence knew that. He understood how freeing it was to fly along on a powerful machine. The time stolen from ordinary life was his gift to her, Joanne concluded, his way of helping her through a dark period in her life. She was grateful to him.

But was it only gratitude? Her arms encircled his strong torso, and once in a while he took a hand off the controls and gave her fingers a reassuring squeeze. Her breast, belly, abdomen, thighs—all were pressed intimately against him, and there was no mistaking the sexual response she felt. Did he feel it, too?

They'd been flying along, but now Spence was slowing, steering the bike off the highway, along a rutted path that opened to a small camping spot with a panoramic view through the pine trees of the ocean and the evening sky.

When they stopped, he propped the bike on the

kickstand and helped her off, then looped her fingers through his and led her to a spot at the very edge of the cliff that fell away sharply to the water far below.

"I camped here once. Woke up at sunrise, and the eagles were diving for fish down there. Sometimes when I can't sleep I remember that morning, how peaceful the world was as I sat here with a cup of coffee I'd brewed over a campfire, having nowhere I had to be at any certain time, nothing desperately wrong with my life." His deep voice was soft. Joanne looked up at him, to find his rugged features bathed in the diffuse light.

They stood for a moment, and it seemed entirely natural when he drew her into his arms.

"Do you mind if I kiss you, Joanne?"

The request was so quaint and formal, it touched her heart.

"I'd like that," she whispered.

He tipped her head back, and then his lips touched hers, feathering at first, tasting, growing subtly bolder.

She tilted her head, accommodating him, and the kiss intensified. He used his tongue to open her mouth farther. One hand cupped her neck erotically, then slid up to the back of her head, fingers spread wide, threading through her hair. The other hand slid down and drew her hips sharply against him, so that she was aware of his body pressing against hers, his smell enveloping her, leather and denim and fresh air, with a delicious undertone of something musky and male.

She was woozy with sensation, with aching lust that caught her totally by surprise. She wrapped her arms around him and clung, drowning in the powerful feelings of desperate need that pooled in her belly.

She shivered and moved her pelvis against him, and he growled deep in his throat. This unexpected sense of feminine power, the knowledge that he was every bit as aroused as she, was utterly intoxicating. Her breath was coming in short gasps, and her hands ached to touch his skin. She reached a hand up and stroked his cheek, feeling the warmth of skin, the roughness of beard.

"I've thought about kissing you so many times." His voice was hoarse.

"Me, too. Oh, me, too, Spence."

"Now that we've started I don't want to stop, but we're gonna have to get moving." There was palpable regret in his tone. His blue eyes were hooded, his jaw tense with desire. "It'll be dark before long. I want to have you home before it gets late and cold."

She tried to move away, but he stopped her, drawing her close again, kissing her with a ferocity that made her feel she was drowning.

Her legs were still trembling when he half lifted

her onto the bike. He got on, too. Now she had no hesitation, no reticence about encircling him with her arms and holding tight. He reached back and touched her thigh, then drew her arms even tighter as they roared down the highway.

Joanne couldn't help but wonder what would happen when they reached her apartment. Would he come up with her, make love to her? She wanted him.

But when they arrived at her building, he walked her to the door and pressed a gentle kiss on her lips.

"I have to get home. I'll see you tomorrow at lunch. Be sure to call that lawyer, won't you?"

With one swift, unsatisfying kiss, he moved back. He gave her that distinctive little salute of his, then waited until she was safely in the building before he mounted the bike and rode off, leaving her windblown, exhilarated, chilled to the bone and yet burning inside, frustrated, aching for him.

CHAPTER NINE

SPENCE CURSED HIMSELF for every kind of a fool as he tore along quiet back streets and up alleyways to avoid traffic.

He remembered a line from *Zorba the Greek:* *"There is one sin God will not forgive,"* Zorba told the young professor. *"If a woman calls a man to her bed and the man does not go. I know because a wise old Turk told me."*

Zorba and the wise old Turk would be more than disgusted with him tonight, Spence mused. Well, they couldn't be more disgusted than he was with himself.

Why hadn't he taken the key from her, let her lead the way up to that seductive female nest she'd created for herself? At this moment he could be undressing her slowly, the lights low and the curtains drawn tight.

The images made him grit his teeth against the need in his groin. She'd felt so soft; she was so beautifully warm and fragile and feminine. Her lovely mouth, swollen and moist and parted; her involuntary movements; her rapid breathing—all had signaled that she wanted him. There was no mistaking it.

And when he left her at the door, her eyes had telegraphed confusion and hurt, even with her chin high, even as she thanked him politely for the ride and the dinner.

As for him, he craved her with an urgency that had been missing from his life for longer than he cared to remember. So why wasn't he back there making hot love to her, the way they both wanted?

For the past four years he'd been celibate. He'd ruthlessly subdued the raging need that had driven him when he was younger, when sex was a delicious game to be savored.

Tonight, he longed for the closeness, the satisfaction that came with sexual fulfillment, but some demon held him back. He told himself that the difference in their positions at St. Joseph's had something to do with it, but he knew that wasn't strictly true.

Joanne was vulnerable, and he didn't want to hurt her. Yet he knew that this, too, was mostly a self-serving lie.

He even tried to convince himself he'd left because he had no condoms, but there was a drugstore on the corner of her street.

The bare truth was that making love to her would force open a part of him that he'd carefully locked away, the part that embodied trust and faith and belief in a future, belief in himself, confidence that he wouldn't hurt someone he loved—and he couldn't do it.

Savagely, he shifted gears and leaped away from a stop sign, recklessly accelerated past a police car, all but daring the uniformed man behind the wheel to turn on the siren and ticket him. Nothing happened, and after a moment Spence came to his senses and slowed down.

He figured maybe he could still walk away from her forever, if only he didn't have to see her all the time.

But he'd promised to help her, and he was a man who took promises very seriously indeed, which was why he was so reluctant to make them.

Despite his casual tone regarding the lawsuit, Spence had no illusions about the danger Joanne was in. He knew from his years as a policeman how businesses operated, how seldom they had any concern whatsoever for anything beyond their spreadsheets. And he knew that St. Joe's was a business.

The missing baby was a massive worry to them, a public relations disaster, because it could negatively affect public opinion, which, of course, had a direct effect on government funding. If they had a choice between saving their own asses and protecting Dr. Duncan, it didn't take a genius to figure out what they'd choose.

He pulled the bike into the garage, aware that the

house was dark and empty. As he made his way
through the connecting door he scowled.

It was after ten, for cripes' sake.

Where was his mother? Even more disturbing,
where was Devon?

IT WAS HER FIRST TIME, and Devon was scared to
death.

Fortunately, she'd been able to whisper that fact
to Eric, and she'd had to giggle when he rolled his
eyes at her and pulled a face.

''Seems to me I'm the one who oughta be terrified. We're relying on my equipment here, and
that's anything but a sure deal. Leave the worrying
to me, why don't you. All I want is for you to enjoy
this.''

They were naked, on his bed in the dorm. His
roommate was gone for the night, and although rau-
cous sounds from the other rooms filtered through
the paper-thin walls, a feeling of privacy existed
here on the narrow bed with the door firmly locked.
Overhead was the bar that Eric used to hoist himself
up so he could maneuver in and out of his chair,
which was parked close to the side of the bed.

She could feel the bulging muscles in his arms
flex and relax as he drew her still closer to him.
His handsome face was now against her bare shoulder, his breath sweet, his lips hot and arousing on
her skin.

It comforted her, though it shouldn't have, to know that Eric, at least, had done this before. He'd told her he'd had several serious relationships before the diving accident that damaged his spinal cord seven years earlier, and he'd had two sexual partners since. He'd been honest with Devon, and she appreciated it, even though she couldn't help feeling a little jealous of those other women.

He'd gone to great lengths to explain that sex was different for him now, that erections weren't always certain. There were techniques he used to sustain them that men who weren't spinal-cord-injured didn't have to rely on. He'd shown her the constrictor bands he placed at the base of his penis once he attained an erection, and he'd mentioned the various options that were available—vacuum devices, injectable medications, oral medications. He preferred the bands because they were noninvasive, but if the time came when they didn't work, he had other choices.

"You are so totally beautiful." He kissed her—deep, hot kisses that sent waves of sensation to her breasts, to the spot between her legs where his fingers were rubbing in a knowing rhythm that made her toes curl and her breathing unsteady.

Ever since her injury, she'd wondered what it would be like to undress in front of a guy, let him see the precise pattern of her interlocking scars, let him look at and touch the ugliness of her disfigured hip.

She'd thought for a long time that she'd just never allow herself to get into that space, that it would just be too gross, that she'd have to shove her fantasies about love and happily-ever-after into the garbage along with her dreams of teaching phys ed. Who wanted to have some man get physically sick at the sight of your naked body?

With any other guy, she might not have dared, but Eric understood. He knew what it was like to have had a perfect body you never appreciated enough until it was damaged irreparably. They'd talked about it, the way they talked about everything.

He knew how it felt to struggle with the daily routines everyone else took for granted, like getting out of bed, making it to the bathroom in the night, dressing. She'd told him how her limp grew much worse when she was tired or upset, how much effort it took to control it and how embarrassed she felt when she couldn't.

He understood. He knew.

And so did she. Eric was the one she'd been waiting for, the one she could trust with her heart and soul, and with her damaged body. His love went far beyond words.

Still, it had taken every ounce of courage she possessed to strip her jeans and panties off, to let him look at her. She'd stood as if at a doctor's exam, turning slowly so he could see the damage once and for all.

He'd pulled her down beside him. He'd kissed her. He'd told her how strong and beautiful she was, how he loved the length of her legs, the shape of her breasts, the softness of her skin, her perfume. He'd traced every single scar with his lips and had said that he loved them, too, because they were part of her. He'd told her she was gorgeous, a beautiful, sensual woman whom he desired. And she could tell by his voice and his eyes and, yes, by his erection, that he really meant it.

The band was in place.

He was kissing her breasts, sucking hard, touching her in a way that made her forget everything except the pleasure building in her belly. And then, just when she began to explode, he half lifted her up, showing her how to straddle him, how to guide him inside her.

And together, they learned how to fly.

SPENCE WAS WAITING, seated at the same table they'd shared before, when Joanne strode into the cafeteria just before noon. She plunked a ready-made sandwich and a salad on her tray and hurried over to sit with him.

"Hi, Spence." She looked into his eyes, searching for some reflection of what was foremost in her mind: the vivid image of the kiss they'd shared on that cliff yesterday afternoon, the disappointment she hadn't been able to hide when he left her.

"How are you, Joanne?"

He wanted her. It was there in the caressing tone of his voice, the way his eyes lingered on her lips.

"I'm okay, thanks." She smiled and unwrapped her sandwich, satisfied by what she saw, eager to tell him what she had learned.

"I just had a talk with the girl from the cleaning staff who was on duty when the baby disappeared. She's very young. She hasn't been in Canada long. Her English isn't that good. She was really nervous about saying anything to me, but when I explained that I'd delivered the baby, she relaxed a little. Her name's Rohenna Khan, and she was cleaning the bathroom in Natasha's room when they brought her up from Emerg."

"And what was her impression of Ms. Stevens? Did she say?"

Joanne frowned. "She didn't like her much. She said Natasha swore at her, told her to get the hell out of the room, used a nasty racial epithet."

"Was the baby there at that point?"

Joanne shook her head. "Rohenna didn't see the baby. Abigail must still have been with the neonatal specialist. Rohenna gathered up her cleaning stuff and hurried out. She said Natasha seemed nervous and really bad-tempered."

"Kinda strange behavior for a mother who's just delivered a healthy little baby, don't you think?"

"It does appear out of character."

Spence didn't reply. Instead, he unfolded a stack of magazines and newspapers he'd set on the empty chair beside him. Natasha's picture was on every front page, every glossy cover. "Look at this. She's got more ink than the queen did on her last visit. I guess this is what happens when you're young and photogenic," he commented. "She's being interviewed on the national news tonight, as well."

"Maybe some good will come of this, after all," Joanne said thoughtfully. "Natasha wants to be an actress. This amount of media coverage has to be good for her career." She bit into her sandwich. "I can't help but think about the baby, Spence. Where she is, whether she's safe and warm and being fed properly. Whether she's even…even alive."

She lost her appetite and set her sandwich down. "The baby seems to get forgotten in the midst of all the hype in the papers, and yet, small as she is, she's the central figure."

"That's—" Spence started to reply, then stopped.

Puzzled, Joanne gazed at him.

He was smiling over her shoulder, and she turned to see who'd caught his attention.

A tall, older woman with perfect posture and dramatic black-and-white hair was making her way across the crowded cafeteria to their table.

Spence got to his feet and pulled out a chair.

"Hello, Mom." Affection and pleasure were evident in his tone. "This is a nice surprise. What brings you here?"

The woman smiled at Spence and then nodded in a friendly way to Joanne.

"I had a dental appointment just across the street, so I thought I'd see if you had time for coffee, Spencer. I was about to have them page you, but I decided to check here first, given it's lunchtime."

She slipped off her denim jacket and hung it on the chair back. She was wearing a smart, calf-length denim skirt that matched the jacket, and a rose-colored T-shirt.

Joanne was struck by how attractive the woman was. The resemblance between her and Spence was easy to pinpoint. Their coloring was drastically different, but they had the same shape to their faces, the same quiet dignity in their manner.

"I'm probably interrupting, but I won't apologize," Lillian said. "I need a reward after an hour in the dentist's chair, being poked and prodded and scraped." When she smiled, her teeth were strong and very white against her dusky skin.

"Mom, this is Dr. Joanne Duncan. She's the head honcho in the ER. Joanne, my mother, Lillian."

"I'm so pleased to meet you." Joanne smiled and extended her hand. Lillian's was lean and strong, like the rest of her.

"My pleasure." The wide-set coal-black eyes studied Joanne for a moment. "You're the doctor who delivered the Stevens baby. I remember Spencer telling us that night."

"Yes, I am." Joanne felt the usual sinking in her gut. "She was—" She corrected herself firmly. "She's the sweetest baby. She had all this thick dark hair. It looked long enough to braid."

"I'm sure they'll find her soon." Lillian was reassuring and positive, as if she knew exactly how Joanne felt about the abduction. "The culprit is usually some poor woman who can't have a baby of her own, and of course a woman like that takes wonderful care of the child."

"I hope so much that's true in this case."

"Oh, I'm certain it is." Lillian turned to Spence. "Could you get me some food, Spencer, please? Soup and an egg sandwich, something soft and comforting. My mouth feels as though they used a sander on it, but I'm hungry. I didn't eat this morning. There wasn't time after my run."

"You're a runner? No wonder you look so great," Joanne said, as Spence went to get a tray. The compliment was absolutely sincere. Joanne thought Lillian was strikingly attractive and young-looking.

"Thank you. It keeps me feeling good, which is why I keep on doing it. Lord knows, there're lots of mornings I'd sooner give in to getting old and just stay in bed."

Lillian glanced around and changed the subject. "They've really made improvements here since my day. This place was half the size, and the coffee always tasted burned."

"You worked at St. Joe's?"

"Eight years, before I retired. I was an OR nurse."

"I did a residency in general surgery before I could specialize in ER medicine," Joanne confided. "I've got the utmost respect for the nurses in the operating room. On at least one occasion when I was a green intern, they saved my career with discreet suggestions."

Lillian gave an appreciative nod. "It's addictive, the same way I suppose ER medicine is. I missed it when I retired."

Spence was back with a loaded tray. He set soup, a sandwich and a container of vanilla yogurt in front of his mother.

"Thanks, Spencer, that's perfect." The look Lillian gave her son spoke volumes to Joanne about their relationship. Thinking to give them some time alone together, she began piling her trash on her tray. "I should get back," she said, but Spence reached over and laid a restraining hand on her arm.

"You just got here. Finish your lunch and talk to us, at least until your fans on the intercom decide they can't live without you."

"Please, do stay," Lillian added. "I get so lonesome for shoptalk. Tell me about any interesting cases you've treated this morning."

"None this morning, but we had a dandy two days ago." Joanne sat back and related the story of the two-year-old boy who'd been brought in with the bottom section of a large nail sticking right out of the top of his head.

"His dad was fixing the basement stairs, and he hadn't bent the end of the nail over. The kid went underneath the staircase and stood up, impaling himself on the nail. A fireman managed to saw the end off so they could bring the little guy in. He's fine. They took the nail out in the OR, but first we did a CT scan, and by some miracle the nail hadn't punctured any critical area of the brain. He's going home today. There wasn't even much swelling."

"Kids are absolutely amazing, aren't they? Too bad we don't keep those recuperative powers. Do you have a family, Joanne?"

"No, I don't, unfortunately." She explained about Henry's congenital illness, adding that she was now a widow.

Spence watched and listened quietly, Joanne noted, and then a glance at the clock told her it really was time for her to get back.

"It was great meeting you, Lillian."

"You, too." Lillian grasped Joanne's hand in hers. "Why don't you come for dinner tonight, meet my granddaughter. I'm making stuffed salmon. There'll be plenty of food."

The impromptu invitation took Joanne completely by surprise, and when she glanced at Spence, the expression on his face told her he was as caught off guard as she.

"Oh, I don't think—" Joanne began to refuse, but Spence interrupted.

"If Mom's cooking, you really ought to take advantage of it," he urged Joanne with a wink. "She's good at it, but she doesn't do it very often. You might not get another chance like this for several years."

"Nonsense, Spencer," Lillian chided. "I distinctly remember roasting a turkey last Christmas. That wasn't that long ago." She turned to Joanne. "Do come. If you do I'll stretch my cooking skills to the limit and make an apple pie for dessert."

Again Joanne glanced at Spence, trying to gauge how he felt about having her intrude on his private life this way, but he seemed pleased. He was grinning at her. "You have to come, now that there's an apple pie hanging in the balance. This only happens when the moon's in Sagittarius and there's an eclipse."

"Six o'clock," Lillian said firmly. "Spencer can give you directions."

"All right, then. I'd love to. Thanks for asking me."

"You're welcome to bring a friend, if you like."

Behind Lillian's back, Spence rolled his eyes heavenward and held up his hands helplessly at his mother's none-too-subtle probing, and Joanne suppressed a giggle.

"No, thanks, Lillian. I live alone."

"See you at six, then." Lillian's wide smile came and went. The mischievous twinkle in her fathomless dark eyes convinced Joanne she knew exactly what Spence had been doing. "And we don't dress for dinner, so be comfortable."

Joanne went back to work eagerly anticipating the evening.

WHEN JOANNE WAS GONE, Lillian turned to Spence.

"I hope you don't mind, Spencer. I really like her."

She did, but it wasn't the only reason she'd invited Joanne. Devon had asked that morning if she could bring Eric to dinner, and of course Lillian had agreed. But she'd anxiously wondered what Spence's reaction would be to the young man. When it came to his daughter these days, there was no predicting how he'd react. And as far as Lillian

knew, he wasn't even aware Devon had a boyfriend.

"I'm glad you asked her, Mom."

Lillian only hoped he'd still feel that way after
Eric appeared. Spence would be the perfect host
under any other circumstances, but she'd seen
Devon and Eric together. It was impossible to mistake the fire that burned between them. The air
fairly sizzled with sexual tension, and Lillian had
noted how they couldn't keep their eyes or their
hands off each other. She suspected their friendship
had progressed far beyond the casual stage, and
Spencer was astute about such things. He'd know
in the first five seconds that Devon and Eric were
lovers, and Lillian didn't think he'd be overjoyed.

So it had seemed a sort of miracle to find Spencer
having lunch with a beautiful single woman—a
woman who, if her lovely green eyes told the truth,
cared more than a little about Lillian's difficult son.

And what about Spencer? Lillian mused. How
did he feel about Joanne?

She'd watched his face, listened to his voice, for
some sign. But when he wanted to, he could hide
his feelings all too well, although Lillian had caught
the way his eyes followed Joanne out of the room.

*Please, God, let this be someone he'll fall in love
with,* she prayed fervently. *You and I both know
that love is the best cure for this load he's been
carrying too long. And it would make my life and*

Devon's so much easier. It would be an altruistic gesture on Your part, God. And we'd be so grateful.

"Anything you want me to pick up for this dinner party you're throwing, Mom?"

"Some wine would be nice."

For me, for purely medicinal purposes, to drink while I slave in the damn kitchen, Lillian added silently. *And also to buoy me up in case this whole thing backfires.*

Spence was giving her a considering look.

"Anybody else coming, Mom? Just so I know how much wine we need," he added with a sly grin.

Here was her chance to prepare the ground. "Devon's asked a friend from university, a boy named Eric Palmer."

Spence smiled with pleasure. "That's wonderful. It's good she's making friends. I've worried about her being lonely."

Hold that thought, Spencer.

"And I thought I'd ask Bud." She hadn't thought any such thing until this very moment. "That is, if you don't object to having your boss for dinner?" Might as well line up the troops. She could count on Bud to keep the conversation going; he was gifted that way. She remembered Bud's ultimatum to her. Three months wasn't very long, and time was passing.

Spence's approval was heartwarming. "I could

probably manage to suffer through having Bud. We were supposed to go out for breakfast this week, but I took these extra shifts.''

''Perfect. I'll find a phone and call him right now. You know his work number, right?''

Spence rhymed it off, and Lillian copied it down on a paper napkin.

The evening would be interesting—for a whole lot of different reasons.

CHAPTER TEN

AT HALF PAST SIX, Joanne pulled her car up in front of the cozy gray stucco house with the green roof. It was one of the original old two-story homes common in this upscale neighborhood on Vancouver's west side.

The front garden had a lilac tree in full bloom, and in the flower bed beside the house daffodils blossomed. Spence's house looked comfortable, well cared for and quietly prosperous.

She'd fussed over what to wear, what to bring, and now she had another moment of gut-wrenching uncertainty. Were her tan silk slacks and black sweater appropriate? Was the immense bouquet of fresh spring flowers too gaudy?

Sheesh. Get on with it, Duncan.

She marched up the walk and rang the doorbell, noting the wheelchair ramp installed next to the steps.

From inside, she heard a female voice carol "I'll get it" a second before the door opened. A tall young woman with Spence's blue eyes and Lillian's cheekbones smiled at her. She was lovely, with her grandmother's dusky skin and inky hair. She was in jeans and a cherry-red tee, and as she moved back and gestured to Joanne to come in, it was obvious that walking took an enormous effort. Her body contorted and straightened again with each step.

"Hi, you must be Dr. Duncan. I'm Devon. How d'you do?"

"Hi, Devon, it's great to meet you. And please, call me 'Joanne.'" She went inside, awkwardly clutching the bouquet.

"Those flowers are fantastic. Gramma's gonna love 'em." Mischief sparkled in Devon's eyes. "Unless you brought 'em for Dad..."

"I was thinking more of Lillian, but if Spence's feelings will be hurt, I'll give them to him, instead," Joanne improvised, grinning at Devon. "It's your decision. You know him better than I do."

Devon pretended to consider the suggestion. "He's pretty tough. You're probably okay." She gestured down the hall. "Dad and Gram are in the kitchen—some sort of emergency with the oven. Just put your jacket on the coat tree there."

Devon neatly slammed the door using the tip of her cane, but while Joanne was hanging up her coat, the doorbell rang again. Devon opened it eagerly.

Joanne watched as a young man in a wheelchair

smiled up at the girl and Devon's entire face lit up as if a flashbulb had gone off inside her.

"Hey, Eric, good to see you. Come on in."

"That's a killer ramp." He wheeled inside. His eyes lingered on Devon before he nodded at Joanne. He had a bottle of wine balanced on his knees.

"Dad built the ramp when I was in my chair. He fixed the whole first floor so it's crip friendly. Wide doorways, bathroom enlarged, the whole nine yards," she quipped, and she and Eric grinned at each other.

After a moment Devon realized she hadn't introduced Joanne. "Oh, you guys, I'm sorry, rotten manners. Joanne Duncan, Eric Palmer. She's a doc over at St. Joe's Emergency. He's a third-year math and science major at UBC."

"Glad to meet you, Joanne." Eric stuck out a hand. He was an extremely good-looking young man, with curly blond hair, strongly drawn features and well-developed upper-body muscles under his blue chambray shirt and sport jacket. There was a sense of energy about him, and his smile was sunny. He was very adept with his wheelchair, and Joanne guessed that he'd been using it for a long time.

"Why don't you two come in the living room. I'll just see how the oven thing's progressing." Devon, a little flustered now, indicated a large, pleasantly untidy room.

After a moment's hesitation, Joanne set the flowers down on the coffee table. Eric wheeled himself over and placed the wine beside them, then parked his chair near the sofa, where Joanne chose to sit.

"So what do you plan to do when you finish university, Eric?" Such an uninspired beginning, Joanne reflected. But they had to start somewhere.

"Medical research," he said with no hesitation. "Some fascinating stuff going on with genetics. I've been working part-time for Bio Labs during school, and there's a chance they'll hire me full-time. I'd love to get into genetic research, and I've applied for scholarships. But if they don't come through, I'll take any job that'll pay the rent."

"Do you live alone?"

"I have a roommate in the dorm at UBC. I've lived away from home since I graduated high school. There are seven of us kids, and my folks have a small house. My dad's a bus driver for the city."

So his parents weren't at all well off. Getting a university education couldn't have been easy for him.

"Mom still fusses about me living away. She brings over care packages of cookies and homemade bread."

"She sounds like the ideal mother hardly anyone has these days."

His smile was charming, wide and proud. "Yeah,

she is. And Dad's great, too. I'm really lucky. I've got super parents."

And they have a fine son, Joanne concluded.

"Did you ever give any thought to being an MD, Eric?" With math and science majors, it would have been a logical choice.

"Yeah, I did, but the simple fact is that it takes too long before you start earning any money. How about you? You enjoy your job, Doctor?"

"Totally." Joanne was about to elaborate, when Lillian came hurrying in.

"Joanne, Eric, forgive me for not being at the door when you arrived." She swept up the floral bouquet and buried her nose in it. "Devon told me about these. They're spectacular. Joanne, thank you so much. And Eric, how thoughtful to bring wine. I'll just take these in the kitchen and get some glasses." She picked up the wine, still talking. "Wouldn't you know. The element or something blew on the oven, and of course I didn't notice until half an hour ago, so dinner's going to be delayed a little bit, but that's okay because Bud had a meeting. He's going to be a little late, anyway."

Lillian was jabbering. She was nervous, Joanne realized. It was surprising, because Spence's mother didn't seem to be the type of woman who got rattled easily. "Can I do anything to help, Lillian?"

"Nothing at all. Spencer's just finishing up. He'll

be here in a—oh, there you are." Lillian turned as Spence hurried into the room.

"Hi, Joanne." But Spence wasn't watching her as he spoke. Instead, he was staring at Eric, an unreadable expression on his face. A long, awkward moment passed before he tore his eyes away from the young man to give his mother an equally unreadable look.

"Spencer, this is Eric Palmer, Devon's friend."

Again, Joanne detected nervousness in Lillian's tone.

"How do you do, sir." Eric rolled over and extended his hand, and Spence seemed to collect himself. He shook Eric's hand, smiled and welcomed him, just as Devon came back into the room.

Devon made her way to an armchair, balanced carefully for a moment and was about to collapse into it, when Spence rushed over. He took her cane from her, before supporting her arm and easing her down as if she were made of porcelain.

"Thanks, Dad."

Despite Devon's politeness, it was evident to Joanne that Devon would have been happier doing things by herself. The girl's tanned face was flushed, her eyes rebellious, and she avoided looking at Spence.

Instead, she waggled her fingers at Eric. "Sit beside me," she invited.

He rolled his chair next to her, and with a defiant

glance at her father, Devon deliberately took Eric's hand and threaded her fingers through his.

Spence's face reddened, although he pretended not to notice. He sat down on the sofa beside Joanne, giving her a poor facsimile of his usual easy smile. "So did you have a busy afternoon, Doc?"

Joanne shook her head. "An older gentleman who tried skateboarding broke his arm, a girl fell off her platform shoes and tore the ligaments in one ankle and a baby ate underarm deodorant. It was a boring afternoon."

Everyone laughed, as she'd intended, but then an awkward silence fell.

"That's a beautiful chess set," Eric remarked, motioning to the ornately carved figures set out on a shelf of the bookcase in the corner. "Do you play, sir?"

He directed the question at Spence.

"I used to, with my grandfather," Spence replied. "That was his set. I haven't played in years. I tried to teach Devon, but it wasn't her game."

"It's one of my favorites," Eric admitted. "Maybe we could play sometime."

Spence nodded, but all too obviously wasn't enthusiastic about the idea.

Lillian had taken the flowers and the wine into the kitchen, and Joanne was relieved when she came back with a tray holding the opened wine bottle, stemmed glasses and an assortment of hot hors d'oeuvres.

Spence was pouring the wine when the doorbell sounded. In a few moments Lillian introduced the new arrival—Bud Ansell.

There was an easygoing, Old World charm about Bud, and in a few moments he had them all chuckling as he related a far-fetched, funny story about his attempts at playing golf.

His arrival, and the wine, eased the peculiar tension that had been evident earlier, and by the time Lillian called them to the table to serve perfectly cooked salmon, steamed asparagus and tiny buttery potatoes, Joanne had relaxed and was enjoying both the food and the company. She was seated between Bud and Spence. Under the cover of the tablecloth, he surprised her by reaching over and squeezing her hand for an instant.

The intimate acknowledgment said that he was glad she was there, and it thrilled her and made it easy to join in the casual conversation that ebbed and flowed while the meal progressed.

"So, young fellow," Bud said in a matter-of-fact way to Eric, as Lillian served apple pie and coffee. "How did you end up in that chair?"

Joanne had wondered about that all evening, and she admired Bud for his honesty and openness.

"I was a swimmer," Eric said. "I dove into a friend's pool seven years ago, when I was seventeen. I misjudged the depth, hit the bottom and fractured my spinal column. I was really lucky, because it was only a T10 so I have the use of my arms.''

''Eric's a wheelchair athlete,'' Devon announced proudly. ''He won the Vancouver Marathon last year in the wheelchair division.''

''I wondered how you got those great biceps, son,'' Bud commented with a grin. ''You have to train a lot?''

''Some,'' Eric admitted. ''I usually go to the gym after classes every day for an hour or two.''

''Don't you need a special kind of chair for competition?''

Joanne was fascinated, and she listened closely as he explained the differences in wheelchairs and how wheelchairs were made. She'd done a portion of her internship in a rehab hospital, and she knew exactly how difficult everyday living was for the physically challenged. The fact that Eric carried a full class load, worked a part-time job and also trained for athletic events told her how much grit and determination he had.

Spence was silent as Bud and Eric chatted about sports and police work. Joanne noted that Spence's eyes were often on his daughter, but Devon avoided looking at him.

Inevitably, the conversation turned to the abduction, and as usual when the subject of the missing baby came up, Joanne lost any desire for food.

"The police don't appear to have much to go on," Lillian remarked. "I've been watching the news during the day, and there's always something about the mother. The press must be absolutely hounding her. A lot of the interviews happen outside her apartment. I'm surprised she doesn't tell reporters to get lost. But she doesn't. She's always willing to talk to them. She seems such an agreeable girl."

Lillian frowned. "Although it's eerie, watching her. It's almost as if she has a script. She says the same thing every single time. Her voice always quavers on the same phrases and then she cries. I'd be inclined to get good and mad and holler a little, or refuse outright to talk to the reporters if it upset me that much." Lillian shook her head. "And how she manages always to be so well-groomed and have her hair and makeup perfect is beyond me. I could never pull that off, especially not if I was half nuts over losing my baby."

"She's an actress, Gramma." Devon said. "It's her job to look good. Putting on makeup and doing her hair are probably things she does automatically."

"The cops always completely check out the parents and close relatives in kidnapping situations," Bud commented. "I'm sure they're keeping a keen eye on her. Don't you think so, Spence?"

Joanne glanced at Spence. She was thinking

about Rohenna Khan, the girl who'd cleaned Natasha's hospital room. Natasha hadn't been amiable with her, if Rohenna was to be believed. And what reason would the girl have to lie?

"I'm sure they've dug into her background pretty thoroughly," Spence said slowly. "They'd have to consider motive if they thought she had anything to do with the abduction."

"If you were investigating it, Dad, would you be suspicious of the mother?" It was the first time this evening Devon had spoken directly to her father, and Joanne heard the special tender note in his voice when he answered her.

"Let's just say I'd keep an open mind, Dev. I wouldn't rule out anything until it was proven beyond a doubt."

The conversation moved to other subjects. Bud was obviously very fond of Devon, and he asked her about her university courses. She explained that she was planning to teach English and history at the secondary school level.

Joanne liked Spence's daughter. She was cheerful and quick-witted, and she seemed to have come to terms with her disability. There certainly wasn't any indication of self-pity; if anything, she tried to minimize the fact that she had trouble walking.

And it was so touchingly evident that she was crazy in love with Eric. Each time she looked at him, her features softened and a small, involuntary smile played across her pretty face.

Eric was harder to read, but how could he not care for Devon? He doubtlessly hadn't met Spence until tonight, and Joanne was certain that accounted for some of his reticence. Spence was very polite to Eric, but there was no mistaking the fact that his politeness had no warmth to it.

By contrast, Bud and Spence clearly had a long history together, and their affection for each other showed.

Joanne wondered uneasily if Spence was the controlling sort of parent who automatically resented anyone his child fell in love with; he didn't appear to have that sort of personality, but perhaps she just didn't know him well enough.

When the meal ended, Lillian led the way into the living room, but Joanne noticed that Spence had begun clearing the table, so she offered to help.

"The rule around here is that the person who cooks doesn't have to clean up," he explained, as she carried a stack of plates into the kitchen. He added ruefully, "I oughta insist you go and sit with the others, but I'll cravenly accept any help I can get at this rotten job." He began rinsing dishes under the tap.

Joanne opened the dishwasher, and was surprised to find it empty except for the remains of the salmon, wrapped in aluminum foil and resting on the top shelf.

"I should have warned you," Spence said with a grin. "The element on the oven packed it in, so Mom put the fish through two cycles in the dishwasher in order to cook it. She probably stuck the leftovers in there to keep warm and forgot them. She'd read somewhere about using the dishwasher for cooking fish. Lucky thing the pie was already baked before the oven gave out."

"Your mother's an ingenious lady." Spence lifted out the fish, and Joanne loaded the dishwasher as he put a fresh pot of coffee on to drip. He filled the sink with hot soapy water and began to scrub pots and pans.

"It's beginning to look as if they might not find the baby, isn't it, Spence." That particular fear gnawed at her day and night, no matter what else she was doing, and she felt a comfort in expressing this to him, despite the despair in the pit of her stomach.

"Hard to say." He used a plastic scrubber on a stubborn stain in a saucepan, then glanced over at her.

Her desolate expression must have given her away, because he added quickly, "Don't lose hope, Joanne." He was quiet a few moments, and then he added in a soft voice, obviously intended only for her ears, "I'm no miracle worker, but because

I was there when she arrived in the world, I've got a very personal interest in finding our little Ms. Stevens.''

He finished the last pot and let his breath out in a *whoosh* of relief. ''That's it. We're outta here as soon as I wipe down the countertops and the stove.'' He set to it, and Joanne hung up the wet towels and did her best at finding where the pots lived.

''You working this weekend?''

''No, I'm off. It's my long break. I don't go back until Tuesday.''

''Me, too. I took some extra shifts so I could book off longer. Want to come for a bike ride?'' He tossed the invitation over his shoulder as he cleaned off the stove.

''Yes, please. I'm getting addicted to riding on your motorcycle.''

Or was she getting addicted to the driver? That thought sent a bolt of uncertainty through her, and for an instant she reconsidered. Maybe she should get out of this now, before her feelings turned into... She braced her back against the cupboard and looked at Spence's broad shoulders and narrow hips.

Maybe it was already too late.

''Good.'' He sounded pleased. ''I thought we'd take a ride down to Seattle. If the weather's okay, of course.''

"Seattle?" Her voice revealed her surprise. It was a long ride—at least four or five hours, even by car.

"Yeah. I'd like to see this sister of Natasha's, ask her a few questions."

"But I thought the police already talked to her." It had been reported on a newscast, within hours of the abduction.

"Probably a wild-goose chase, but I'd like to see her anyhow. You game to come along?"

"Absolutely."

"Good. We'll leave really early Saturday morning, return that night."

She swallowed her disappointment. She'd sort of hoped it would be an overnight trip.

He finished the stove and turned, almost colliding with her. Impulsively, he put his hands on her shoulders and pulled her close for an impromptu hug, just as Lillian walked into the kitchen.

"So this is what the help get up to without supervision." Lillian gave them a wicked grin.

Spence didn't rush the hug. He held Joanne several moments before he let her go, and when she glanced over at Lillian, Joanne thought Spence's mother looked delighted.

"Eric's leaving, Spencer. He's waiting to say good-night to you."

"I'll be right there."

"I have to be on my way, too," Joanne said.

"Thank you so much for inviting me, Lillian. I had a wonderful time. The dinner, the conversation—everything was so enjoyable."

Lillian beamed at her. "I had fun, once the cooking was under control. We'll do it again soon." She gazed past Joanne and scowled at the stove. "I'll order in pizza or burgers, though, instead of worrying about that dumb damn oven."

"I can't believe you cooked the fish in the dishwasher. It was perfectly done."

"Desperation, my dear, desperation."

"I'm ordering a new stove tomorrow," Spence promised.

Lillian rolled her eyes. "Not on my account, I hope. In case it's escaped your notice, Spencer, cooking's not exactly my favorite pastime."

"Mine, either," Joanne confessed. "Although it's a shame, because I do love to eat."

"Me, too, but that's why there're restaurants," Lillian said. "For women like us. All we need are men with deep pockets who'll accommodate our eccentricities." She laughed, a rich deep gurgle, and Joanne joined her.

Spence caught Joanne's eye and winked, and she remembered their conversation about what they'd do if they were fired; she remembered saying she'd run a restaurant.

At the door, Eric was waiting, Devon by his side.

"Thank you for a great evening, sir," he said to Spence.

Spence wished him a polite, but decidedly cool, good-night, and there was obvious reluctance when Eric offered a handshake.

"I'll walk you out to your van," Devon said.

By the time Joanne had also wished everyone good-night and made her way out to her car, Devon still hadn't returned.

The inside of the battered blue van parked a short distance from her car was dark, but when Joanne pulled out to drive away, her headlights illuminated the young people in the front seat, locked in an embrace.

Devon was so young, so passionate, so obviously in love. Joanne's heart went out to the young woman, and with the upsurge of emotion came a feeling of bitter nostalgia and regret.

There'd never been a time in her life when she'd loved with total abandon, Joanne reflected sadly. She'd never been rebellious as a teen; the unspoken rule in her parents' genteel child-rearing program was that she was expected to get a good education, decide early on a career, pursue it with diligence. She'd done exactly as they'd expected, and she'd even married a man similar to her father. The only way she'd ever rebelled was by choosing emergency medicine.

She thought of the lost baby, of Natasha Stevens

and the lawsuit. She thought of Spence and the trip to Seattle this weekend.

If the opportunity presented itself, did she have the courage and the good sense to follow her heart instead of her head a second time in her life?

CHAPTER ELEVEN

THE FOLLOWING DAY was Thursday. When her shift was over, Joanne drove to the parking lot in Stanley Park where she and Portia had agreed to meet.

Portia was waiting.

"I could have picked you up, but I was scared to stick my face inside the doors of the ER in case somebody gave me a job," Portia said. She appeared very different out of her customary scrub suit. She was wearing tailored gray slacks and a matching fitted jacket, which, judging from the fabric and exquisite cut, undoubtedly sported an exclusive designer label. Her dramatically short, spiky black hair and her subtle makeup underscored the unusual angles of her face.

"Nobody would recognize you. You look more like a fashion model today than an intern," Joanne said.

"This is my 'doing lunch with Mother' costume," Portia replied, and Joanne remembered what Portia had said about having grown up in a wealthy environment.

"She likes to go to Lumière, and today's her birthday, so we did it in style."

"I'll say. I love that suit. You sure you want to be seen with me?" Joanne teased. She had on her usual work uniform of khaki pants and plain white tee, and had added a casual denim jacket against the damp air.

"We can always go to a boutique and get you something more stylish for doing the seawall," Portia joked. "Do you feel like a long walk? If not, we could just sit somewhere."

Joanne shook her head. "Exercise, absolutely. It's a gorgeous day." She breathed in the fresh air and waved at a gaggle of geese that came waddling over to see if the two women had anything edible.

"So how old is your mom today?" Joanne knew Portia was twenty-five.

"Forty-six. Of course, she'd strangle me for telling you. She delights in thinking that everyone mistakes us for sisters. She hasn't quite gotten around to asking me to call her 'Lydia,' but I expect she will before many more years go by." Portia yawned. "And if I don't start getting more sleep, people are gonna start thinking I'm *her* mother, perish the thought."

Joanne was laughing as they set off at a brisk pace.

"I've always loved the seawall," Portia declared. "I used to come down here sometimes with my father when I was very little, before he and Mom divorced. I remember him buying me fish and chips from a concession in the park. I must only have been three or four.''

"Do you still see him?''

"Once in every great long while. He moved to Switzerland. I'd spend summer holidays with him. But then he remarried, and his wife and I didn't get on very well—so I stopped going. She and I were almost the same age. I think it bothered her,'' Portia added.

"Did your mom remarry?''

"Lord, yes. Three more times. All losers, all wealthy. She's between husbands now. I expect she'll find another before long. She's the type of woman who doesn't feel complete without a man.'' Portia shook her head and grimaced. "Considering that Mom's a psychic, you'd think she could get a better handle on the kind of guy she ought to marry, but it's like she's blind to her own stuff.''

"Your mom's a psychic?'' Joanne was fascinated.

"Yeah, it runs in our family.''

"I never thought of psychic ability as an inheritable trait, like blue eyes or brown hair.''

"It is with us. It comes out in different ways. My grandmother could tell what people's futures were gonna be. My mother's better at finding stuff that's lost. Me, I just see auras.''

"Auras?"

"Yeah, colors around people. Different colors mean different things."

"Is that what makes it easier for you to diagnose certain people?"

Portia shrugged. "I guess so. I can't always tell exactly what's wrong, though. That's where medical science comes in. Using blood tests and CT scans to zero in on the actual problem is the other half of the equation. I don't think about diagnosing much. I just do it."

"However you manage it, you have an incredible gift for making accurate diagnoses." Joanne side-stepped goose droppings and then asked, "Do you, um, feel that what you and your mother have is sort of a gift from God?"

Portia shook her head. "Nope, not at all. I think it's more like having six toes—a nuisance thing you're just born with. It's sort of a wiring aberration in our brains."

Joanne hesitated, then couldn't resist asking. "So you see colors around everyone? Even me?"

Portia gave her a sidewise look. "Yeah, I do. If I sort of tune in to it. I can shut it off if I want."

"Tune in, then, and tell me what mine are like."

"They change all the time, depending on what's going on with you." Portia narrowed her eyes and seemed to look through and past Joanne. "You always have a fair amount of white, mixed with a blue-green. That generally means a person who's detached, compassionate, has lots of energy. There's been quite a bit of red lately, which shows passion or maybe anger. And some huge specks of brown, which indicate that you're very worried about something just now. It's like you're in muddy water, not able to see what you're searching for.''

"That's true." Portia's assessment was accurate, but not proof of anything except acute observational ability. After all, the young woman worked closely with her, Joanne reasoned. She'd had ample opportunity to figure out Joanne's moods. And these days everyone was tense because of the abduction and the investigation. Everybody in the ER knew Joanne felt responsible.

Portia guessed her thoughts. "You're worried about the missing baby, right?"

"Yeah." Joanne pulled her jacket tighter around her, suddenly aware of a chill breeze. "I'm close to obsessed about her," she admitted. "Of course, you know about the security band that I should have put on her and didn't."

Portia nodded. "I asked Mom about the baby right after it happened. She had the impression the little girl was okay, being cared for. At least, Mom felt she was at that point." There was confidence in Portia's tone, and Joanne felt irrationally hopeful—and then sheepish at her own gullibility.

Again, Portia sensed what Joanne was thinking.

"Mom's a total flake when it comes to the men in her life, but as far as other stuff goes, she's reliable. She's quite famous in certain circles. She's helped the police in England and France track down missing people, even stolen goods. The last case she worked on was in Spain—that kidnapping one, the diplomat who was found locked in the trunk of his car, barely alive? Mom got the license number and location of the car, and the cops rescued him within hours."

"Why don't the police here ask her to assist in the Stevens case?"

"Who knows." Portia shrugged. "It depends on who's running the investigation, I guess. So much of police work is scientific, and what Mom does seems impossible, even silly to someone who relies only on facts and concrete evidence. And she's not gonna go and volunteer her services. She did that once, and they just put her down as a nutcase."

"But she *would* help if she was asked?"

"Of course she would. If she was around, that is. She travels a lot. She's leaving tomorrow for Mexico. We have a place in Cozumel."

Joanne felt a sense of extreme urgency, as if a subtle but important symptom in a patient's diagnosis were being overlooked. "Before she goes, Portia, would you please ask her for me if she has any idea where the police should look for this baby?"

"Sure, I'll call her tonight. But in order to get an accurate reading, she usually needs something that belongs to the person, something worn or treasured or touched."

Joanne's heart sank. There was nothing whatsoever that belonged to the baby. The little girl hadn't had time to gather a single possession or make a mark on her world in any way before she disappeared.

Joanne said so to Portia.

"I doubt Mom'll be able to see anything with nothing to use for impressions. I have to tell you this stuff isn't always clear-cut, anyway. It's seldom like, go to this house on this street," Portia added apologetically. "Mom sees pictures, isolated pictures that aren't necessarily linked to anything else."

Joanne didn't have any idea how it worked, or even *if* it worked. She only knew that she was in favor of chancing anything that helped to find the baby.

But if there was no hope of Lydia helping, then best to forget it. Joanne tried to put that out of her mind and overcome her sense of disappointment by focusing on the young woman striding along at her side.

"Did you grow up here in Vancouver, Portia?"

Portia shook her head. "I was here off and on, not for any length of time. I didn't spend very long in any one school when I was a kid. Mom kept marrying and divorcing, and we moved all the time. When it came time for high school, she was married to an American. The marriage actually lasted all during my high school years. I graduated in San Diego and I went to UCLA for a couple of years before I decided on medicine. I transferred to the University of British Columbia because the guy I was in love with at the time was from Vancouver.''

"Good solid reason—one I understand very well," Joanne commented wryly. "I really wanted to do my residency in Montreal, but my husband had just gotten a job at a hospital in Edmonton, so that's where I went, too.''

She hadn't thought about that in a long while. How many other times in her marriage had she denied her desires to accommodate Henry?

"Your husband was a doctor?''

"A surgeon. He died five years ago.''

"But you're so young to be a widow. Was he a lot older than you?''

Joanne shook her head. "He was just forty-one at the time. Five years older than me. Congenital heart failure.''

"Was it hard being married to a doctor?'' Portia put an apologetic hand on Joanne's arm and quickly added, "I'm sorry for being so nosy. Please don't feel you have to tell me these things. It's just that all my romantic relationships have been with doctors, and none of them has worked out.''

''I don't mind talking about it at all.'' Joanne was trying to figure out how to answer Portia's question. ''At the time, I didn't think both of us being in medicine caused us any problems,'' she said slowly. ''Now that I look back, I realize that I was far too accommodating in my marriage. I lived the sort of life Henry wanted, which ironically was the very type my parents had lived—quiet, refined, always in impeccable taste. The only thing I ever did that Henry completely disapproved of was become an ER physician.''

How peculiar, Joanne thought, to see these things clearly now, and not to have been aware of them during all the years of her marriage. ''I guess ER medicine was my one and only big rebellion,'' she admitted.

''Was it worth it?''

''Totally.'' There was no hesitation whatsoever in Joanne's voice. ''Right from the beginning, I loved my work in the ER. At first, I told myself that was because it allowed a certain amount of order in my working life. As you know, shifts in the ER are straightforward. You don't get called out in the middle of the night if you're not scheduled to work.''

''Yeah, I've considered that. It's a big plus. There aren't that many areas of medicine where you can rely on a day off actually being a day off, unless you go into dermatology.''

Joanne agreed, adding, ''I soon found I thrived on the variety, the challenge, the opportunity to treat a range of medical problems. Plus I wasn't too interested in seeing the same patients over and over again, although, as you know, we do have a few in Emerg who become regulars.''

Portia rolled her eyes. ''Like Little Abner.''

''Yeah, like Abner.'' He was a street person, a dwarf who happened to come into Emerg the first week Portia was there. He fell for her hard, and since then he'd appeared every second week with some minor trumped-up complaint or other. He refused to let any other doctor treat him, which had naturally earned Portia the nickname Daisy Mae.

''So do you feel I'd do okay as an ER physician, Joanne? Your honest opinion here. I should warn you that I can tell by your colors whether you're lying.''

Joanne laughed, pretending to think over the question. She didn't have to; she'd known from the beginning of Portia's time in the ER that the younger woman had all the makings of a first-class ER doctor.

''You just *might* have what it takes, with a lot of hard work on certain personality traits,'' she teased. ''Let's see, you're calm under pressure, but you form inappropriate attachments to patients. You're quick thinking, but you apparently don't always follow the scientific method. You're not too emotional on the surface, but patients fall hopelessly in love with you, which is a major disadvantage. But all in all, yeah, I feel you'd have a faint chance of being an adrenaline junkie along with the rest of us, if you decide that's the way you want to go.''

Portia threw back her head and laughed. ''And for that enthusiastic and extravagant assessment, Dr. Duncan, I'll buy you dinner, as long as you agree to fish and chips,'' she declared. ''Here's the concession that makes the best fries you've ever eaten.''

They ordered and took the delicious-smelling plates over to a picnic table. Portia had gathered up containers of ketchup and vinegar, and they doused the fries in both.

''You're right. These are great,'' Joanne concurred. ''I'm becoming an expert at fries. This is the second time this week I've gorged on them. My hips are expanding even as we speak.'' She had a vivid image of Spence buying her fries at the roadside stand.

''Lots of nutrition in potatoes,'' Portia stated, forking up a mouthful of fish, then sending the conversation off in yet another direction. ''So you've been a widow for five years. Do you ever think about marrying again?''

Joanne felt her neck and cheeks color as she silently admitted that she'd had more than a few secret fantasies about Spence.

"I'm not sure how I feel about that," she said carefully. "It would have to be someone really special."

Spence *was* special. He was also emotionally unavailable, she reminded herself firmly. And where did she get off thinking about marrying someone who'd barely kissed her?

Well, more than barely. Thoroughly. But he'd hurried away when there had been an opportunity for more, hadn't he?

"How about you, Portia? Have you ever been married?"

Turning the question around was lots safer.

"Nope. I was in love once. That guy I mentioned who was the reason I came to Vancouver to study medicine. That's enough for me. It ended badly, and I never want to feel like that again, so I've avoided getting involved with anyone else. Besides, when you choose medicine as a career, there's not much time or space for a man in your life, especially when you're an intern."

Joanne nodded agreement. "Later on, though, it slows down somewhat. It can get lonely, especially if you don't have much family. Your co-workers tend to be your friends. There's not a lot of time and energy left after work to socialize."

"I'm lucky with family," Portia said. "I have

one sister, and also four half brothers from Mom's other marriages.''

Joanne was surprised. ''I don't know why, but I assumed for some reason you were an only child. Are you close to your sister and brothers?''

Portia nodded. ''Very. My sister's mentally challenged. She's in a group home here in Vancouver. I see her as often as I can. My brothers are younger. Two are in university in England and the other two are working for their respective fathers, one in Los Angeles and one in Alaska, so I don't get to see them as often as I'd like.'' Portia sighed. ''Mom means well, but she's restless. She can't stay in one place for long. She's always flying off somewhere. And the men she married were high-powered business types who didn't spend much time at home, either. I was the eldest, so I felt responsible, especially for my little sister but also for the boys when they came along. We pretty much had to rely on one another. The parents were absentee caregivers, big time.''

''That had to be hard on you.''

Portia gave a nonchalant shrug, but her gray eyes were sad. ''I guess it was valuable in certain ways. It sure kept me from jumping into an early marriage and having seven kids. I had a fair idea what child rearing was like, and it wasn't something I wanted to do again for a good long while.''

They finished their meal and began to wander,

more slowly now, back to where they'd left the cars. A sense of camaraderie had sprung up between them, a warmth and ease that Joanne savored. She really liked Portia.

"I'll call you as soon as I talk to Mom about the baby," Portia promised once they entered the parking lot.

"Thanks. And also for my dinner. I really enjoyed it. The walk, as well."

"Let's do it again. Maybe we can make it a regular event. I'll check the board and see when I'm off next." She hesitated. "I don't suppose you'd like to come for lunch sometime with my sister. Not Lumière, I'd better warn you. I take her to a fast food place every other week or so. It's the big deal in her life."

Portia opened the door of her car and then stopped. She trotted over just as Joanne was starting to back out.

Joanne braked and rolled down the window.

"What about the baby's footprint? Wouldn't that have to be on file at the hospital?" Portia crouched on her heels, her face level with the open car window. "I just thought that if there was a footprint, my mom could use it to link in to the baby."

Joanne stared at the other woman. "Of course. Of course there's a footprint. The nurse took it while I was doing the Apgar." That irrational hope she'd felt earlier came rushing back. "I'll track it down in the morning. D'you think your mom might be able to come in and look at it? I can't really remove it from the file.''

"I'll ask her.'' She got to her feet and then seemed to hesitate.

"Joanne?''

"Yeah?''

"This guy you're in love with? Just give him lots of time and space. He'll come around.'' Portia turned and walked over to her car, climbed in and drove off without a backward glance.

Joanne sat stunned, with the car motor idling.

She thought back over the entire conversation she'd had with Portia. She was absolutely certain that she hadn't even hinted at a relationship, much less said anything about being in love. *She* wasn't even sure yet that was the right word for what she felt about Spence.

So how could Portia possibly know?

CHAPTER TWELVE

THE QUESTION still niggled as she climbed on the back of Spence's bike at seven on Saturday morning. Were her feelings written on her forehead in ink that was invisible only to her?

Spence stowed her small backpack in the saddlebag on the side of the bike. She'd brought an extra layer of warm clothes, a sweater, a tee, a spare pair of leggings, as well as a rainproof jacket and hood just in case the weather reversed itself; the early-morning skies were clear, but that could change quickly. Joanne didn't exactly fancy spending hours soaking wet and cold.

"All set?" He helped her on with her helmet, his fingers brushing her cheek not altogether accidentally, and then he swiftly strapped his own helmet in place and balanced the bike for her to get on. Once she was comfortable, he gunned the motor, and they swung away from the curb.

There was no traffic, and the streets were easy to navigate; soon they were out on the open road. When they reached the U.S. border crossing, the friendly Customs official smiled and wished them a safe and pleasant trip.

"We'll stop in Bellingham for coffee," Spence promised. Half an hour later, Joanne was glad to get off when he pulled up in front of a sandwich shop.

"Stiff?"

"Oh, heavens no. Whatever gave you that idea?"

He took her helmet from her and laughed as she tottered, knees locked, toward the door of the café.

It was quiet inside, and the smell of fresh cinnamon buns was irresistible. Spence got them each one of the huge delicacies, and they sat at a table by the window. The sun streamed in, and rock music played from a radio behind the counter.

Spence's gray-blond hair was mussed from the helmet, and the wind had already turned his skin a ruddy shade that made his eyes look even bluer than usual.

Joanne studied him, and at last he raised an eyebrow at her. "What? Do I have a gob of icing stuck to my chin?"

"I'm just thinking what a handsome man you are." As soon as she'd blurted out the words, her own audacity shocked her, but his wide smile and the expression in his eyes told her that he was delighted.

"Thank you. Coming from such a beautiful woman, that's a great compliment."

They laughed, pleased with themselves and each other.

Spence was half done his bun by the time she brought up Portia's mother, and the whole subject of psychics helping in investigations.

"I asked Portia to see if her mother could come up with anything about the Stevens baby," Joanne explained. "But she couldn't. At least, not yet. Apparently, she needs something tangible that belonged to the person, in order to clue in on them, or whatever it is she does. The only thing available from the Stevens baby was her footprint. Portia's mother said she'd drop by St. Joe's and have a look at it today." She looked at Spence from under her eyelashes, trying to gauge what he thought of all this.

"I just wondered if you ever used a person like that when you were in the RCMP."

Spence nodded, totally unperturbed by what she was saying. "Yeah, we did on several occasions, particularly in cases like this where there's so little to go on."

"Have you ever heard of this Lydia Bailey?"

Spence shook his head. "No, but that doesn't mean she isn't legitimate."

"Do you think there's the slightest chance she'll come up with anything useful?"

"It's worth a try. Anything's worth a try, and it can't hurt."

"Oh, Spence, I hope it works. Something's got to. The baby's been gone so long now. I get so scared for her, I hardly dare to think about it." Her eyes filled with tears and she tried to blink them back, but Spence noticed.

He reached across the table and took her hand between both of his. "We're doing everything possible, Joanne. Not just the police, but you and me, as well. If it's in the cards to find her, we will, but you've got to accept the fact that some investigations go bad, just like, I guess, some of your patients do. Try not to let it eat at your gut."

She nodded. The size and the warmth of his hands were comforting. But when his fingers trailed up her wrist, she felt something more than comfort.

"All done?"

She was.

"Let's go see what we can find out, then."

"Did you call this woman to say we were coming?"

"Nope. It's way easier to say no on the phone than it is to a real live person at the door."

Joanne climbed on the bike, wondering if all they'd get out of this trip was a long ride on a sunny day, even as she wished fervently, while the bike sped toward Seattle, that she and Spence were doing just that—having a glorious ride with no purpose other than enjoyment.

IN SPITE OF THE DIRECTIONS Spence had gotten from the cops who'd interviewed Natasha, it took some time to find Natasha's sister, Marilyn Rogers. She lived in a duplex in a remote and run-down suburb of Seattle, one that was reached by following a dizzying series of secondary streets.

"There it is." Spence parked the bike and stowed their helmets. Joanne felt nerves tighten in her belly as they approached the house.

"Who are you? What do you want?" The woman who'd opened the door left the security chain in place, so it was impossible to see what she looked like.

Spence told her their names, then explained that they were investigating the abduction of Natasha's newborn daughter.

"I already talked to the police." The chain was still in place. "I gave them everything I knew, which was, like, nothing."

"We're not with the police," Spence said.

"Are you reporters, then? Because I've told you people a thousand times, I don't want to be interviewed." Frustration and anger laced her tone.

"We're not reporters. We have nothing to do with the press," Joanne said quickly, sensing that the woman was about to shut the door on them. "Spence and I were present when your niece was born, Ms. Rogers. I'm a doctor. I delivered her. She was the sweetest little girl." Joanne swallowed hard and then went on. "She had a full head of very dark hair, and these little delicate, long-fingered hands, and the prettiest mouth. Please, won't you talk to us for just a few moments? I know you must be busy. We won't take up much of your time."

There was no response. "Ms. Rogers?" Joanne's voice broke. "I'm...I'm so terribly worried about your little niece. I'd do anything to find her, and I know you would, too. Won't you please just talk to us?"

The appeal worked. Marilyn Rogers slowly undid the safety chain and opened the door.

She was a nondescript woman, short and heavy in the hips, with brown hair caught back in a ponytail. The only characteristic she shared with her sister was her mouth, full and sensual and pouty.

"Come in." She led the way into a tidy but threadbare living room, and they sat, Joanne and Spence side by side on a mustard-colored sofa, Marilyn in a worn blue armchair, fingers nervously interlaced on the lap of her black stretch pants.

"I haven't even seen Tasha for over two years," she said in answer to Spence's question. "She called me once and told me she was expecting and that she wasn't gonna marry the guy. There were these rich folks who were paying her to have the baby so they could adopt it, she said. I told the police about it."

Joanne was profoundly shocked, but a glance at

Spence convinced her that he either already knew, or was expert at hiding his reactions.

"Did the baby's natural father know about these adoption plans, Ms. Rogers?"

Marilyn shrugged. "I dunno. I don't think so. It sounded to me like Tasha hadn't even told him about the baby. She said she needed the money these people were giving her, that she deserved it, losing her figure and feeling sick. She had bad morning sickness."

"Why do you think she was having the baby? Why didn't she just go ahead and have an abortion?" Spence asked next.

Marilyn shook her head. "Who knows. I guess because she could make some money having the baby, instead of spending it having an abortion."

"Do you know for a fact that she was desperate for money?"

Marilyn was losing patience with the questioning. "I told the police all this already. I dunno anything for a fact, like, I only talked to her that one time. But probably she needed money, sure. She wasn't exactly making a fortune as an actress."

"Did she call you that time to borrow money?"

Marilyn's mouth tightened. "No, she did not. We talked about personal stuff, private. Not about money. And anyhow, she knew I was separated, with my own kids to raise. She knew I didn't have any to loan her."

"How did your husband feel about your sister?"

Marilyn glared at Spence, and her face turned magenta. "What's Howard got to do with anything? He wasn't even around anymore when Tasha called me."

"Do you have a phone number or an address where we could reach him? I'd very much like to talk to him, Ms. Rogers."

"No, I do not." It was obvious Marilyn was angry and upset, and Spence changed direction. "Tell me about when you and Natasha were kids. Were there just the two of you?"

"Yeah, just her and me." Marilyn was more relaxed now. "We grew up poor. We were real close in those days, Tasha and I. We lived outside of Blaine."

Joanne remembered driving through the small border town earlier that morning. It was halfway between Vancouver and Seattle.

"Our dad worked in a lumber mill," Marilyn explained. "He was killed when we were just little kids. Tasha always wanted to be an actress. She got the main roles in all the school plays. She was the pretty one, but I got better marks in school." An undertone of resentment crept into Marilyn's voice. "Tasha had a knack for getting what she wanted. She was smart that way." She moved restlessly. "Now, if you don't mind, I gotta go pick up my little girl from preschool."

Spence and Joanne got to their feet.

"Are these your kids?" From the mantel, Joanne lifted a photo of two smiling boys and a little girl. "They're adorable. How old are they?"

"Jason's six, Josh is four and Leanne's three." Marilyn's face creased in a proud smile and her voice changed, grew softer, when she mentioned her children.

"Was Natasha close to her niece and nephews?" Joanne couldn't imagine an aunt not doting on those three.

Marilyn shook her head and the smile faded. "Not really. She's sent stuff at Christmas sometimes. She's pretty busy with her own life. Doesn't have much time for family. Her and my mom are exactly the same in that regard."

The words took a moment to register. "Your mother? But I thought..." Joanne glanced at Spence, and this time she could tell he was as surprised as she. "I somehow had the impression your mother wasn't alive."

"Oh, that's what Tasha said. I read it in one of those magazines. It's her way of getting back at Mom. They never did get along."

"Where does your mother live?" Spence asked.

Clearly, Spence was thinking the same as Joanne. With all the publicity over the baby's abduction, why hadn't the grandmother expressed concern or come forward?

"She's in Florida. She married some old guy who has a trailer down there. They drink quite a bit. I called her to tell her about the baby being stolen from the hospital, but she just said it was Tasha's own fault. No love lost between the two of them."

"What's your mom's name?"

"Carol. Carol Overmyer. Look, I've really got to get going. If you're not there to pick the kids up, they get really upset."

Outside, Joanne walked to the bike, Spence at her side.

He dug the helmets out of the trunk, then looked at Joanne. "So baby Abigail wasn't named after Natasha's dear deceased mother," he said softly. "It sounds as if Ms. Stevens wasn't exactly truthful about a lot of things."

"Sounds to me as if the whole family could use a lot of counseling," she said. "Those poor sweet little kids. And Marilyn, too, raising them as a single parent. It can't be easy for her."

Spence agreed, adding, "I wouldn't have gotten to first base with her if you hadn't been along, Joanne. You're a good interrogator."

She was ridiculously pleased. "Thanks. It comes from years of digging out obscure symptoms from patients who don't want to talk."

"Speaking of talking," Spence said, "I'd very much like to locate Howard Rogers today, but it could take a while, and it's already past one." His eyes searched her face, and there was a trace of hesitancy in his voice. "What would you say to staying in Seattle tonight?"

Her heart gave a little lurch. The air seemed thick with sudden promise. "That's fine with me. I've got nothing to rush back for."

"Good. I'll get us rooms at a downtown hotel and then we can go have some lunch."

He was doing his best to sound casual, but Joanne could tell by the sudden huskiness in his voice that Spence, too, was thinking of the night ahead.

CHAPTER THIRTEEN

THE HOTEL HE CHOSE was not only in the heart of the city, it was also perched right on the waterfront. It had recently been refurbished and it was luxurious. Their rooms were adjoining, two large bedrooms, each with a queen-size bed and a spectacular view of the harbor. The sitting area boasted a lovely old credenza and a sofa covered in elegant florals. There was a fireplace, which looked as if it burned wood, though it was actually gas.

"Do you mind if I order us lunch from room service?" Spence had taken off his jacket, sweater and boots. His close-fitting long-sleeved white tee was tucked into faded jeans that clung to his legs like a soft second skin.

"I have to call Zelaney and find out if they have an address on Rogers. It could take some time."

"Room service is fine." Joanne was standing at the window in Spence's room, admiring the huge cruise ship that seemed to be parked inches away. She'd carefully put her backpack on the bed in the other room.

''There's a menu here. You want to have a look?''

She drew an armchair over and sank into it, still watching the water. It was soothing. Peaceful, relaxed—which she wasn't.

She *was* hungry, though. ''Just order me plenty of food, Spence. I don't care what. Well, not fries, but anything else. I'm starving again. What is it about motorcycles that gives me such an appetite?''

''Fresh air.'' She heard him chuckle, then dial the phone, and she smiled as he ordered soup, sandwiches, fruit salad and lemon pie.

After that, he dialed again and had a long conversation, obviously not with Zelaney, his tone impatient at times. ''Call me as soon as you find out,'' he finally directed, and read the number off the telephone. ''And make it as quick as you can. I'm on the clock here.''

When he was done she said, ''This is a great hotel, Spence. Have you stayed here before?''

''Nope. I came to Seattle a couple of times on police business, and I always thought I'd like to stay here sometime.'' He was prowling around behind her like a huge cat.

''I was wondering if maybe you brought all your ladies to this hotel.'' She was only half joking.

''Listen to me.'' He was beside her before she could move from the window, and his face and voice were intense and serious. ''I'm not that kind of guy, Joanne. I didn't plan to bring you down to Seattle just to get you in a hotel room.''

She drew in a breath and decided, for once in her emotional life, to take a major chance. ''I'm disappointed,'' she said levelly, forcing herself to look straight into his clear eyes. ''I sort of hoped that you *had* planned it.''

He was utterly still for an instant, and then he reached down and tugged her out of the chair. His arms came around her with a ferocity and strength that made her gasp.

''Joanne, Joanne.'' His voice was a groan. ''I want you so much my teeth ache. I've been trying to stop myself from dragging you over to that bed like a damn caveman.'' He buried his fingers in her hair and drew her face to his and kissed her with a hunger that melted the nerves lumped in her stomach, soothed the fear that lived just behind her heart.

''Do you know—'' he interspersed words with kisses ''—what it does to me—'' his thumbs stroked her jawline ''—to feel you pressed against me on that bike—'' his hands slid down, molding her shoulders, and his voice dropped to a sensual growl ''—to feel your legs spread wide on either side of me…''

He was touching her breasts now, cupping them, thumbs slowly circling her nipples through the fabric of her sweater. Her heart bucked and jerked, desire flowing through her like hot liquid fire.

The phone rang.

With a savage curse, he kissed her hard and released her, then stalked over to answer.

An instant later, there was a tap on the door, and when Joanne answered it, a waiter pushed in a loaded food trolley.

Still on the phone, Spence beckoned the man over and signed the check, rolling his eyes at Joanne at the series of interruptions.

The telephone conversation went on and on. Joanne pulled the trolley over to a table beside the window and unloaded it. The smell was intoxicating. Physical desire gradually gave way to feelings of hunger, and she nibbled on a chunk of cantaloupe and then a slice of orange.

Spence was watching her, so she took a slice of watermelon over and fed it to him. He caught her finger in his teeth and sucked at it and then gently bit. She shivered, and he drew her close for a hurried kiss, holding her crushed against him as he listened to whomever was on the other end of the line and murmured assent from time to time.

Joanne leaned against his chest, shutting her eyes and savoring the smell of him, a lemony kind of aftershave, a clean, spicy, arousing male scent that was strictly Spence.

''Thanks, Cameron. Appreciate your help,'' he

said at last, and hung up. He wrapped both arms around her and drew her to his body, groaning with frustration.

"I can't believe this, but we're gonna have to put lovemaking on hold for a couple of hours, darlin'. One of Zelaney's bright young guys located Howard Rogers. He's an auto mechanic working just out of Seattle in a suburb called Renton. Lucky for me, he had an assault charge against him a while back so he was on the system. I have to catch him at work, because there's no home address or phone number on the guy. Cameron called the shop, and Rogers is at work today, but he's off at four." He stepped back a little so he could study her face, read her expression.

"There's more bad news, darlin'. I'm gonna have to leave you here while I go out to see him. I have a feeling he might be more forthcoming man to man than if you were with me."

Joanne was a little disappointed, but she understood Spence's reasoning. Because she was a woman, she had reached Marilyn Rogers more easily than Spence would have; the reverse was undoubtedly true, as well.

"I'll do some shopping while you're gone," she decided. "You do have time to eat before you go, don't you?"

"Try and stop me."

It took less than twenty minutes to devour every

scrap of the food. Then, with one last passionate kiss, Spence headed out the door.

"I'll call you to say when I'll be back," he promised.

"I'll be here, unless of course I meet some handsome sailor on the pier."

"He won't be handsome when I get through with him," Spence growled, winking at her as he closed the door.

Joanne had a long, hot bath and then set off to explore the downtown shops nearest the hotel. She had a wicked, wonderful plan in mind for a gift for Spence.

SPENCE STOPPED at the desk and got exact directions for the fastest route to Renton and the address of the body shop. It was already after three, and there was no time to spare for getting lost.

Traffic was heavy, however, and it was almost four when he pulled the bike up in front of the ramshackle wooden building.

"Howard Rogers?" The huge man he asked gave him a suspicious look, but he jerked a thumb toward the back of the shop. Spence made his way past cars in varying states of disrepair until he reached a rangy man in filthy blue coveralls, who was working on a late-model Corvette.

"Howard Rogers?"

"Who wants to know?" The belligerent tone wasn't encouraging.

"My name's Spence Mathews."

"You're a cop, right?" Rogers shot Spence a resentful glance and went on with what he was doing. "Look, I keep my nose clean. I ain't done nothin' wrong. And I got nothin' to say about anythin'."

"I used to be a cop, yeah, but I'm not one anymore." Spence explained in great detail who he was and why he was there.

"I knew about the kid gettin' snatched. The cops came by right after and asked a zillion questions. Had it in their minds I might have had somethin' to do with it." Rogers shook his head in disgust. "As if I'd do a thing like that. I got kids of my own. What the hell would I want with a baby? And anyway, I was workin' all day that day."

"I know you had nothing to do with it, Mr. Rogers. I only want to talk to you about your wife's sister, get your impressions of her. I spoke to Marilyn this morning. I just want a second opinion.

Rogers spit on the floor. "Marilyn the one who told you where I worked?"

"Nope. She wouldn't say a thing about you. I got a friend in Vancouver to locate you."

"That goddamn trumped-up assault charge," Rogers snarled. "Man has no privacy once the cops get involved in his life." He shot Spence a venomous look. "This car's gotta be finished by quitting time. I need this job. I got kids to support. I got no time to talk right now."

Spence could feel the meeting going south, and he went with a hunch. "Yeah, I know what you mean. It's tough when you're divorced. You don't get to see your kids, but you still have to support them."

"Ain't that the truth." Howard's mouth twisted into a grimace. "You divorced?"

"I was. My wife's dead now." For some reason he couldn't explain to himself, Spence added, "I was driving her and my kid to the airport one day, fighting as usual over visiting rights, and a truck broadsided me. My wife died. My kid was badly hurt."

"Shit, that's bad luck." For the first time Spence had Howard's full attention.

"Yeah. Just like it was bad luck for your baby niece to get snatched from the hospital. If you could tell me anything at all about Marilyn's sister, Mr. Rogers, I'd be really grateful. Look, I know you're busy right now. Could I maybe buy you a beer at quitting time?"

Howard took a long time deciding, but at last he nodded. "Guess so. There's a tavern a few blocks from here. I'll meet you there." He gave Spence directions. "I'll be another hour at least. This sucker's givin' me nothin' but grief."

Spence rode the bike over to the tavern and parked, trying to decide what to do for an hour. There was a drugstore on the corner. He walked over and bought deodorant and a package of disposable razors; the hotel might have them, but no point in taking chances.

He needed one more item, and he set off down the aisles to find it. It made him think about Joanne, waiting for him back at the hotel, and his pulse began to pound.

He wanted to get done with Rogers as fast as he could and return to her. Calling her and telling her what he was doing came to mind, but he decided against it; he'd only been gone a little more than an hour, and she'd said she was going out to do some shopping. He grinned to himself—he should have warned her that there was only so much room in the saddlebags.

He should call Lillian, though, and let her know he wouldn't be home tonight. He stood staring at a display of perfume, wondering what scent Joanne might like. The subtle way she smelled made him want to press his nose against every inch of her, but he couldn't imagine what perfume it might be that drove him nuts.

Nope, he told himself, perfume was too risky—too many choices. Still, he wanted to take her something, some little gift that said how much he valued her company, how much he wanted her in his arms, how much he enjoyed being with her...but what?

Deciding wasn't easy, he admitted after twenty minutes of fruitless wandering up one aisle and down another.

He gave up finally and located the condom section, made a careful choice and added the package to the other items in his basket.

Then a wild and wonderful idea struck him. It would take a bit of courage, but what the heck, he'd never be in this store again, anyway.

He picked out a dozen boxes of condoms and then headed for the section that had wrapping paper. He chose soft pink tissue and a red satin ribbon, grabbed a roll of tape and made his way to the checkout. Luck was with him; no one else was in the lineup, and the woman at the till was mature, with laugh lines that indicated she might have a sense of humor. Her name tag read Louella.

After dumping his purchases on the counter, he paid and then said, "Louella, is there a gift-wrapping service?"

"What you want wrapped, honey?" She didn't look at the condoms, but he could tell by the twinkle in her eye that she'd definitely noticed.

His face was burning, but he ignored it. A man had to do what a man had to do.

"These." He stacked the condom boxes into a

neat pile. "In this." He indicated the tissue. "With this stuff around it."

She threw back her head and laughed, a trilling sound that made Spence laugh, too.

"You're in luck, honey. Only, let's put these handy-dandy little items in a box." She bent and rummaged under the counter, then came up with a large box.

In less than five minutes, she had the box folded in the pink tissue and tied with the huge red satin bow.

"Louella, thank you from the bottom of my heart." Spence slipped ten dollars into her hand.

She glanced at the money and eyed him coquettishly. "She's one lucky lady, honey. She doesn't realize that, you come on back. I'm off at seven."

Feeling hugely relieved, he headed out the door and stowed the package carefully in the trunk of the bike.

It was almost time to meet Rogers. He hurried to the tavern, but before he went in he used the pay phone and dialed his own place.

No one home. No one was ever home these days. Feeling irritated, he found himself wondering if Devon was somewhere with that Palmer kid.

Kid, hell. Palmer was a man.

Spence scowled and waited until the answering machine picked up, then left a terse message saying he'd be back sometime the following day.

Inside the tavern, there were maybe two dozen patrons, most of them men in work clothes, drinking beer, playing pool, leaning on the counter. Spence chose a booth with at least a semblance of privacy and ordered a jug of draft, still thinking about his daughter and Palmer.

He admitted to himself that he hated the very notion of Devon being with Palmer, and he hated himself for minding even more.

He poured a foaming glass of beer from the jug the waiter plunked down on the sticky Arborite.

There was absolutely nothing wrong with Eric Palmer—except that he was disabled. And the idea of Devon being with a man who was permanently confined to a wheelchair made Spence's gut churn and bile rise in his throat.

What kind of life could that be—not for Eric, but for Devon? God knows, she'd been in a wheelchair herself; she understood exactly how it limited everything. And now that she was walking again, Spence wanted normality for her. He wanted her to get an education; he wanted her to fall in love, sometime in the distant future, with some great guy, get married, have kids.

Which brought him exactly to what he'd deliberately avoided each time he thought of Eric Palmer and his daughter. The subject he didn't want to even consider.

What kind of sexual relationship could a woman

have with a guy in a wheelchair? Nothing approaching normal, that was damn sure.

He was relieved to see Howard coming through the tavern door.

"So you found the place okay." Howard slid into the seat across from Spence. He'd taken off his coveralls, but the jeans and checked shirt he wore were anything but clean. He smelled of grease and pungent sweat, and there was a smear of dirt across his forehead.

"Beer?" Spence shoved the spare glass across, and Howard filled it from the jug. "Get your job finished?"

Howard nodded, then swallowed three quarters of the beer in a long, thirsty swig. Spence refilled the glass and motioned to the waiter for another pitcher.

"You not drinkin'?" Howard eyed Spence's glass, which was still almost full.

"Waiting for you." Spence downed half his glass, and Howard nodded approvingly. But then he became more adversarial. "So if you're not a cop," he said in a belligerent tone, "why're you stickin' your nose into this thing with Natasha, anyhow?" He'd obviously thought over everything that Spence had told him. "What's in it for you?"

Back when he was doing investigations, Spence had always found that people responded best if he stuck close to the truth.

"Like I said, I was there when the baby was born. I feel responsible for her. And the doctor who delivered her is a friend. Natasha's suing her now because of a security band that should have been put on but wasn't. So there isn't any one clear answer to your question."

Another half glass of beer disappeared into Howard like water soaked up by a sponge.

"Natasha's suing, huh?" He snorted. "Figures. She was always quick to spot a chance to make a buck, that little…" He didn't finish the sentence, but it wasn't hard to do.

"You've had bad dealings with Natasha?" Spence knew he had to strike exactly the right note to get Howard to open up about his former sister-in-law. "In-laws can cause a lot of trouble for a guy."

"You can say that again." Howard tipped his glass once more. Spence refilled it and drank some beer from his own, trying to stay sober and still make it appear that he was keeping up with Howard.

"You figure Natasha's a troublemaker?"

"A-number-one." Howard's narrow eyes became slits. "She's smart and she's mean. She'd do pretty much anythin' to get somethin' she wants."

"What d'ya figure she wants most?"

"That's easy," Howard sneered. "She wants her mug up on the big screen. She wants to be a friggin' *star.''* Howard's voice dripped venom. "And the scheming little bitch'll do anything to get it.''

"So you figure she's a real ball breaker?''

"A-number-one.'' Howard's glass was half empty again. He held it out, and Spence refilled it. "Have one yourself.''

There was nothing to do but top up his glass and drink some of it. "Sounds like she screwed you over good.''

"You better believe it.'' Howard leaned across the table. His breath was foul, and Spence had to fight not to draw away. "Natasha climbed in bed with me when she was barely fifteen. Marilyn was workin' nights at the convenience store. I shoulda had sense enough to kick her out, but I was drinkin' hard in those days.'' He took three more hefty pulls at his glass. "Anyway, the little bitch blackmailed me. She said if I didn't give her the cash she wanted, she'd tell Marilyn and go to the cops and press charges for statutory rape. I was shit scared, I can tell you.''

"I can see why. What a rotten thing to do.'' Spence nodded sympathetically.

"You better believe it. I sold my gun collection to get the money. I gave her every damn cent she asked for—and would you believe that she told Marilyn, anyhow? Waited awhile and then told my wife that I was the one came on to *her*. It's what broke up my marriage in the end.''

Spence doubted that, but he made the appropriate understanding noises. "What did Natasha use the money for?"

"Acting lessons. Plastic surgery—she had her boobs done." Howard shook his head. "Gives me the willies, phony boobs, don't it you?"

Spence hadn't given it a whole lot of thought, but he assured Howard he felt the same.

"So you want my opinion on this kidnappin' thing?"

Spence nodded encouragingly.

Howard had another long fortifying drink. "She set the whole thing up herself," he announced triumphantly.

"If she did, what do you figure she's getting out of it?"

Howard shot Spence a disbelieving look. "Publicity, man. Get herself noticed, big time. Doesn't take a genius to figure that out. Count the number of times she's been interviewed on the tube. And magazines. I already got three myself where she's written up. I'll bet up in Canuck country there's a helluva pile more. She's dead set on gettin' noticed. That's what it's all about with little old Tasha."

Spence had what he wanted from Howard. For the next fifteen minutes, he let the other man ramble on about missing his children and wanting his wife back. Then, after ordering yet another pitcher, he shook Howard's hand, explaining he'd like to stay and drink, but he had a friend waiting for him back at the hotel—a lady.

After a requisite number of winks and suggestive remarks, Howard settled down to his beer, and Spence made his escape.

As he walked to his bike, it became abundantly clear that he'd had far too much to drink to ride the motorcycle. He couldn't just leave it parked on the street, however; bikes were an easy mark for thieves.

A man passing by told him there was a parking garage several blocks away. It took huge effort, but Spence managed to roll the bike up the hill and down the long block to reach the garage. He parked the heavy machine in a secure stall near the attendant, whom he asked to call him a cab.

The cabbie hadn't gone more than two blocks when Spence remembered the wrapped gift in the trunk of the bike and had to ask that they return to the garage.

He'd also forgotten to call Joanne as he'd promised. The beer had turned his brain to mush.

At the hotel, he hastily paid the cabdriver and waited impatiently for the elevator. He had a sudden sinking feeling that Joanne had probably given up on him and headed for the airport.

He slid his card into the door and stepped inside, every sense tuned.

"Joanne?" The entire suite smelled of something

feminine and sensual and pretty. His heart swelled and he couldn't help but smile. She'd waited.

She came out of the bathroom, and his breath caught in his throat. She was wearing a long, low-cut satin something, midnight blue, ingeniously designed so that even the slightest movement revealed the sinuous curves of the naked body underneath the slippery fabric.

"Hi, Spence. How did it go?"

She was nervous. He could hear the tiny tremor in her tone, and that bit of hesitancy was more arousing to him than utter confidence could ever have been.

"Joanne." He knew he sounded hoarse. "Joanne, I can't think of anything except how gorgeous you look at this moment." He walked toward her, forgetting about the pink-tissue-wrapped box he was clutching in one hand. He put his arms around her, drawing her close for a kiss that began as hello and spiraled out of control so quickly he had to use every ounce of self-discipline to pull back.

"I smell of beer. Sorry about that. And I have to shower." His heart was hammering; his jeans were far too tight. "I'll beat the land record for speed, so just don't go anywhere, will you, my beautiful lady?" He remembered the package and held it out to her.

"For you." And now he wasn't at all sure that

what had seemed brilliant and funny and fitting in that damn drugstore was the sort of thing he should be giving her.

Too late, Mathews.

"Thank you." Her tremulous smile made him want to gather her in his arms again and forget about the shower, but the memory of the pub and the smell of Howard sent him hurrying toward the bathroom and a fast, hot, thorough scrubbing.

He had enough presence of mind to call room service on his way and order a bottle of champagne, adding that the waiter should knock and leave it outside the door. He didn't want any other male, any age, seeing Joanne in that gown.

He shaved faster than he'd have believed possible, and in the shower tried to figure out what he should put on. A thick terry robe hung on a hook on the bathroom door. He toweled dry and donned it.

Joanne was kneeling in the middle of the bed, holding the box he'd given her, still wrapped. She smiled and thrust a shiny purple box at him.

"I thought we'd unwrap these together."

Spence's heart sank, and he tried to hide his apprehension as his fingers fumbled with the bow on his package. He had to fight an urge to reach over and snatch the gaily wrapped pink box of condoms from her before she had a chance to discover what was inside. She'd undoubtedly chosen something for him far more sensitive and fitting. He was a lamebrain idiot.

The purple wrappings fell away moments later and he forced a smile as he opened the small box inside. He stared down at the contents, hardly able to believe what he was seeing.

Condoms.

About the same number he'd chosen for her, but much more varied in color and texture.

He looked up just in time to catch the dumbfounded expression on her face as she opened her box and saw what was inside. Gingerly, she held up one foil-wrapped package between thumb and forefinger, and then burst into uncontrollable giggles.

"I'm not sure I'll be up for this, although I promise you all I've got," Spence said in a rueful tone. "D'you think they'll give us a refund on half if we return them in mint condition?"

Their shared laughter erased every lingering trace of awkwardness. Spence pushed her gently back on the bed and drew her close, letting his hands slide down the slinky gown and learn her shape.

"We'll start slow," he whispered in her ear, using his tongue delicately on that special, secret spot just behind her earlobe, loving the way she shivered under his hands. "We've got all night, and God knows, we've plenty of supplies."

CHAPTER FOURTEEN

JOANNE HAD SPENT all afternoon imagining every detail of making love with Spence, and as the hours passed she'd grown progressively less confident and more nervous, not only over the outrageously expensive, classically simple gown, but also over her brazen gift for him.

She'd never set foot in a condom shop, and she'd had to walk past it half a dozen times to get up the nerve to go in. After that, it hadn't been too difficult; the woman running the place was twenty years older than Joanne, and her matter-of-fact assistance had been invaluable.

Back in the hotel, it had taken every ounce of courage Joanne possessed to put on the bias-satin garment she'd bought at the high-end lingerie shop downstairs in the lobby.

She'd put on panties and taken them off three times before forcing herself to remove them once and for all. She wasn't a virgin, after all, although she certainly felt like it tonight.

The sound of Spence's voice calling her name when he opened the door had sent her into near panic in the bedroom. She'd had to force herself not to tear off the gown and scrabble into her jeans.

And then the acute embarrassment of actually walking out and greeting him made her reasonably sure she was in the first stages of myocardial infarction. Certainly she had tachycardia; her heart was beating inside her chest like the wings of a hummingbird.

The trouble was, she had absolutely no experience at seduction, or even titillation. She'd never done anything remotely as risqué as this in her entire marriage to Henry; she'd never purchased a single negligee for herself, and neither had Henry ever given her one. They wore flannel or cotton pajamas. Their sex life had mirrored their choice of sleepwear—comfortable, quiet, pleasant, restrained.

The look on Spence's face when she finally managed to show herself was worth all the agonizing she'd gone through, however. And his kiss left no doubt that he fully appreciated her efforts, although the sight of the pink-wrapped gift he was holding had made her stomach churn all over again. He'd gone and bought her something terribly romantic; she was convinced of it.

While he was in the shower, she shoved her gift for him in the trash; but then resurrected it, having finally decided she'd give it to him and to heck with it. She was a mature woman. Mature women did

things like this all the time in the few sitcoms she'd
ever watched.

And then the coincidence of their choices left her
openmouthed with amazement, helpless with laughter, which made her forget to be nervous when
Spence joined her on the bed, deliciously damp
from his shower and sexy as hell in a white terry
robe that bared a large portion of his well-shaped
legs.

There was a knock on the door, and he came
back in with a bottle of champagne and two flutes.
He popped the cork, filled her glass and handed it
to her.

"To you, my beautiful lady," he toasted.

She loved the nippy dryness, the soft warmth the
wine created in the depths of her belly.

When they'd had enough wine, Spence took her
glass from her and eased her back on the bed. He
used the last of his champagne to form a pool in
the hollow of her throat, and he sipped from it.

Her body stiffened, and she gasped at the sen-
sations he created in her. Slowly, he began to do
other things, things that made it impossible to think.

She could only feel. She was a doctor; why
hadn't she learned there were nerve centers on her
hands, her neck, her shoulders, that caused involuntary tremors down her spine? How could she
have reached the age she was without being aware
that a man's big and amazingly gentle hands on her

face, tracing her closed eyelids, following the line of her nose, learning the texture of her skin, could make her breathing so erratic?

And all the while, he talked to her, whispered intimate words of admiration, telling her over and over again how beautiful she was, showing her with his arousal that she was irresistible to him.

He was utterly confident, and he made it plain that he enjoyed even the slightest contact every bit as much as she. He murmured extravagant words of praise as he explored over and over again, always with agonizing slowness, her hands, her lips, her ears, her neck, her shoulders, the bend of her elbow, her nape and, at last, when she could hardly stand the anticipation, her breasts.

When she told herself that, logically, this magnificent excess of sensation had to come to an end, that nothing could feel this soul-shattering for long, she learned to her astonishment that it was only beginning. She learned that her body had capacities she'd never imagined, that, indeed, one climax could lead to another, each more intense.

And she learned that she hadn't ever had the slightest inkling of just what making love with a man really meant.

"You awake, darlin'?" he asked sometime later.

"Barely." She'd been dozing, her head resting on his arm.

She was contented, euphoric and so relaxed she felt boneless.

"Howard Rogers has an interesting theory about his sister-in-law I thought you might like to hear."

"Tell me." Joanne's lethargy vanished, and as Spence described Natasha from her brother-in-law's perspective and explained his version of the baby's disappearance, a tumult of conflicting feelings washed over her. In spite of her experience in the ER, she still didn't want to believe a mother could do such a thing, but there was a simple and horrifying rationality to it.

"If he's right," Spence said, "it might be good news from one point of view. If she arranged for her own baby's abduction, Natasha would probably make reasonably certain the child was being cared for. Particularly if she still has hopes of collecting money from the adoptive parents."

Joanne reluctantly agreed. "I've had awful nightmares about some crazed loonie taking that little girl and mistreating her."

"Me, too." Spence's arm tightened around her, and he brushed a comforting kiss across her cheekbone. "I'm not a hundred-percent convinced that Howard's right, but we've both noticed how skillful Natasha is at generating media interest in her situation and at doing interviews. Whether she arranged this or not, the basic problem is still the same—getting that baby girl back from wherever she is.

Natasha's very clever. Tripping her up may be difficult.''

"It's hard to believe any woman would go to those lengths just for publicity.'' Joanne was remembering the terrified expression of the young woman as she lay on the ER floor, pushing her baby from her body.

"You and I both know that people are capable of almost anything. Ambition is a powerful motive.''

"What will you do now?''

"I'll focus on Natasha.'' Spence's voice took on a different note, a hardness that Joanne had never heard before, and she felt his muscles flex. "I'll dig as deep as I can into her life. I'll track down every single friend she's ever had, and every enemy, if I have to. There has to be something that will give her away, and I'll find it. She'll make a mistake somewhere along the line. People almost always do.''

Joanne whistled softly. "I wouldn't want to be a criminal and have you on my trail.''

He laughed, and his body relaxed. "Just try to move to the other bedroom, and see how fast you have me on your trail, lady.''

She rolled over and straddled him. "Two can play at this game, Mr. Tenacity. Now just try to get away from *me*.'' Amazed at her own boldness and smugly delighted with herself, she bent forward and kissed him, then mimicked the path his mouth had traveled on her body.

His moans of pleasure as she made her slow journey down thrilled her. She arrived at her destination and took him gently into her mouth, and he cupped her head in his hands, fingers buried in her hair, and repeated her name again and again.

When he drew her up at last and entered her, he stared deep into her eyes, and as she rocked them both to rhapsody their gaze held steadfast. This time she felt that in some mystical fashion, they became a single soul.

Exhausted, she fell asleep, but she awoke several times to the sound of Spence's soft snore. No matter how deeply he slept or which way she turned, his arms enfolded her, his huge frame moving to accommodate whatever position her body found comfortable. Being cradled this way was a strange and new experience—one she hadn't even known she longed for.

Toward morning she fell into a deep and dreamless sleep. She woke up after a timeless time to the inner knowledge that it was late, that she was in a strange place, that it was gray and raining heavily outside, that the bed beside her was empty.

She sat up, groggy and disoriented, aware that Spence was talking softly on the telephone in the other room. Then she got up and went into the bathroom. She was surprised by the strangeness of the woman who stared back at her from the mirror there. Her hair was wild, her eyes half-lidded, their expression replete. Her lips were swollen, her skin glowing. She grinned at herself. Lovemaking was flattering, and the fact that her body was quite sore in certain strategic places wasn't at all a problem. She stepped into the shower and lathered herself with sweet-smelling soap and shampoo.

By the time she emerged from the bathroom, wrapped in one of the hotel's thick terry robes, Spence had rolled a breakfast trolley over to the window. He'd turned on the fireplace, and the logs snapped and crackled. Welcome warmth spilled from it; Joanne went over and stood with her back to it, soaking in the heat.

"Good morning, pretty lady." He kissed her most thoroughly before he handed her a chilled glass of some exotic and delicious juice.

"Good morning." She held the glass up in a toast, feeling a little shy with him. He knew her now so intimately; it left her feeling vulnerable.

"Come over here and eat. I didn't know what you'd like so I ordered some of everything."

And indeed he had. The trolley was laden with cereal and toast and omelettes and fresh fruit and muffins and an assortment of warm pastries, as well as a delicious-looking piece of fresh pink salmon.

"It's a feast, and I'm starving."

"Me, too." He smiled at her, his beautiful blue

eyes warm and filled with the secrets they'd shared in the night. He, also, was freshly showered. He'd pulled his jeans on, but his chest was bare, and Joanne loved the sight of him, barefoot, half clothed, hair rumpled and still damp. With his broad shoulders and well-developed muscles, he looked like one of the male pinups on the calendar the nurses had hung on the wall of the women's locker room at St. Joe's.

She told him so, then laughed outright when his already ruddy skin deepened in a blush.

He held her chair, and she sat. Then he leaned across and fed her fresh strawberries; served her portions of omelette, bites of salmon; put toast on her side plate; filled her coffee cup.

She was utterly famished, and Spence obviously was, as well. The rain pounded against the window; the fire radiated warmth; she didn't have to hurry to get to work. The combination couldn't have been more perfect.

With fresh coffee and a copy of the day's paper, they moved to the love seat by the fire. Spence studied the sports page and Joanne read arts and entertainment, and they shared snippets of what intrigued them.

"The Mariners are playing at the Kingdome."

"The Seattle Symphony is presenting 'The Best of Opera.'"

"Another football coach just bit the dust. This

new one has to get the team up to speed or his head will roll just like the last one.''

"Dustin Hoffman was in town. They're filming a movie here. I read the book. I can't wait to see what they do with it.''

Spence tossed the paper to the floor and ran his fingers across her forearm. ''Joanne, the weather report says it's going to rain all day.'' He frowned and then blurted, ''Do you have to get back to Vancouver today, or could you wait till tomorrow? Riding a bike in the rain is pretty grim.''

"I don't work until Tuesday. I'd love to stay on.'' The thought of having an entire day with him was intoxicating, and she couldn't help but smile.

"That's great.'' His grin was as exuberant as his tone. ''That's absolutely great. Let's see. What shall we do today?'' His eyes sparkled with mischief. ''There's the game at the Kingdome. I could probably get tickets.''

"Or the symphony. I'm sure there're seats available.''

He snatched up the local activity section of the newspaper and pretended panic. ''Instead of the symphony, why don't we walk in the rain, explore the Pike Place Market, tour the underground passages that were once streets in historic Pioneer Square.'' He gave her a mock pleading look. ''Please, no symphony?''

She pretended to consider, gave an exaggerated

sigh, then said wearily, "Well, all right, then. This once. But you'll have to make it good. I had my heart set on Bach."

Both of them laughed, and then he grabbed her and tickled her, which soon led back to the bedroom and a very long, exquisite delay in going anywhere at all.

EXPLORING SEATTLE was fun, but the rain fell steadily, and by late afternoon Joanne was damp and cold.

"Let's go back to the hotel," she suggested. "I need a hot bath." The memory of that morning's lovemaking made her bold. "The tub's big enough for two," she whispered, and the look he gave her sent heat spiraling into her belly.

In their suite, Spence filled the oversize bathtub and Joanne lit the candles she'd bought at the market. They turned the clock radio beside the bed to an FM music station and slowly undressed each other.

Minutes later, up to her neck in bubbles, cradled in Spence's arms, Joanne sighed with utter contentment and pleasurable weariness.

"Do you know I've never had a bath with a man before," she confessed in a sleepy voice as he slowly and sensuously rubbed soap on her back, her breasts, her belly.

His hands stilled. "Didn't you and your husband play this way?"

"Nope." She shook her head and explained how it had been with Henry. "We had this intellectual connection. We were best friends, but we never did anything like this," she concluded. "I thought what we had was enough."

"He's been gone quite a while. You must have had other relationships. You're a beautiful, sensuous woman."

She had to smile. If that was true, it was news to her. "None that ended up this intimate," she confessed. "I dated. They were men from the hospital. The one I've been seeing most recently is Henry's best friend, Jerry McCormack. Although he's perfectly nice, I haven't any desire to go to bed with him. I don't think he wants to, either."

He laughed. "If he's a red-blooded male, I guarantee you, he wants to."

Joanne grinned to herself. There *had* been several awkward moments with Jerry, but she wasn't about to tell Spence that. Instead, she dared to ask the question she'd wondered about. "How was it with you and your wife, Spence?"

She was curious how their divorce had come about. She couldn't begin to imagine any woman choosing to leave this beautiful, passionate man.

"Sex was always good between us," he said. "But good sex isn't enough to make a marriage work." He was quiet for a long time, his hands soothing on her arms, titillating on her breasts. "I blamed Helen when our marriage began to go sour," he finally confessed. "It took a long time for me to admit that a large portion of the blame belonged with me. I was ambitious in those days. I'd work around the clock on some case or other."

"Did...did Helen—" Knowing how far to go with these questions was hard. "Did Helen work?"

"She was a legal secretary, a very good one. Through a case she was interested in, she got very involved in the women's movement, and more and more unhappy with me and the demands of my job. Devon was just entering her teens. There was lots of friction between her and her mother. Helen accused me of spoiling Dev, and looking back, she was right. I'd come home wanting a quiet evening, and Helen would hit me with everything that had gone wrong that day or that week. She didn't think I did enough around the house or as a parent."

Spence was pensive, his hands still now, looped around her middle. Joanne put her own hands on top of his, holding him to her.

"In retrospect, Helen had a legitimate gripe. I tried, but I let my job take a huge chunk of my life. Helen and I drifted further and further apart. We stopped making love, stopped talking. Then I came home one day, and she told me she'd filed for divorce. She was moving to Calgary to work for a lawyer who represented a newly formed woman's group there, and she was taking Dev with her. It nearly killed me. I could see my daughter whenever I wanted, but I'd have to go to Calgary to do it, or bring her to Vancouver. I knew that was gonna be tough. She was in school. I had a demanding job.''

"Did you and Helen go for counseling?"

"Nope." She felt Spence shake his head. "I knew that if Helen filed for divorce, she didn't want me anymore. My ego was roughed up pretty bad. I'd figured our marriage was just going through a bad patch, that we'd find a way of connecting again." He gave a sad chuckle. "Funny how blind you can be when you want to."

"Did you end up in a legal battle?" Joanne had heard horror stories of the fighting that went on when couples separated.

"Not over material things. I bought out Helen's share of the house and let her take whatever she wanted. The only thing I cared about was Dev. It was hell not having her live in the same city. I flew her to Vancouver as often as I could, and I went to Calgary as often as I could. I tried to get Helen to let her live with me for a year, but she refused point-blank."

He was quiet for a time, and then he sighed and his voice went flat. "The accident happened in November. Helen came through with Dev to go to a friend's wedding. We were fighting over where Devon would spend Christmas.''

Wanting him to relax again, Joanne said, ''Devon's a beautiful young woman.''

She could almost feel his smile. ''I think so, too.''

''And she seems to be doing well with her life. She's getting an education. She has a very nice boyfriend.''

Wrong direction. She felt his body tense all over again.

''He's not her boyfriend.''

Nope, Spence, I'd say he's her lover. Joanne remembered the silhouette in the darkened van, the two young people wrapped in each other's arms. She wasn't about to argue with Spence, but the electricity between Devon and Eric had been hard to mistake.

She decided to change the subject. There was a question she had to ask Spence, one that all this talk about relationships had been flirting with and yet avoiding.

''Spence?''

''I'm still here, sweetheart.'' He was relaxed, but she felt her stomach tighten. The subject was a difficult one, but for her own peace of mind she needed a straight answer.

''You haven't said anything about your, um, your romantic life since your marriage.''

"I wouldn't exactly call it 'romantic.'" The wry humor in his voice was inescapable. "Until the accident, I had sexual relationships with quite a few women—nothing long-term, certainly nothing permanent."

"There hasn't been anyone you wanted to marry?"

"No." The denial was immediate and definite. "I've realized I enjoy sex too much to live without it, but as far as marriage goes, I'll never do it again."

The utter finality in his tone was what hurt her the most.

Leave it at that, Duncan, she warned silently. Before you make a complete fool of yourself, leave it.

But she couldn't. If she'd learned anything from her relationship with Henry, it was the value of bald honesty. She hadn't been honest in her marriage; she was determined not to make that mistake again.

She swallowed hard before she pursued the issue. She *had* to know; she had to hear him say it, loud and clear, so she had no illusions. This was like abrading a wound, she thought distractedly, so that eventually it would heal. Nasty, but necessary. She was surprised at how normal her voice sounded.

"Are you saying that what's between us right now is all there ever will be, Spence?"

He was very still, and she was sorry she was

facing away from him, because she needed to look into his eyes when he answered. He could control the expression on his face, but not in his eyes. She unhooked his hands and turned in the soapy water, kneeling between his outspread legs.

"Yes—"

There was just enough light to see his face. He held her gaze, and she knew he absolutely meant what he was saying.

"—that's exactly what I'm telling you. I should have said something long before now, and I apologize for that."

He put his hands on her shoulders, and that was when she realized she was trembling.

"I've never met a woman like you before, Joanne. You make me feel things I never thought I'd feel again, things I maybe never wanted to feel again. I want you. I love making love with you. I like talking to you. I enjoy being with you. But that doesn't change the facts."

"What facts are those?" To not let him notice how his words were affecting her was almost impossible.

"Just that I'll never marry again. Neither will I live with anyone. Any kind of permanent relationship is out of the question for us." The strained harshness to his voice and the agonized look in his eyes told her that what he was saying was painful.

"I still don't fully understand why." Her voice

was soft but also insistent. She knew she was pushing him in a direction he didn't want to go, yet she
didn't care now. She had to hear it all, know exactly
why he was doing this.

"I promised myself I'd spend my life making up
to Devon for everything I took away from her,
Joanne. She's my first priority, and she always will
be. Because she is, I can't get involved. Anyone
else would have to come second, and I just
wouldn't do that to someone I cared for."

She nodded, marveling at her ability to function
reasonably when what she really felt like doing was
screaming at him. "I understand that *you* feel that
way, Spence. I certainly understand *why* you do."
She tried for a deep breath but couldn't quite bring
it off. "I guess I just don't think Devon wants you
to give up your life for her."

"It's not exactly something I've said to her." He
was getting angry; it showed in his voice. "I'd
never tell her a thing like that. I've never said it to
a damn soul before. The only reason I'm telling you
is so that you understand."

She knew by the way his jaw clenched, the way
his eyes narrowed, that she was now in dangerous
territory, and she didn't give a hoot. She had to
have him hear her truth.

"You don't have to say it to Devon, Spence. She
sees it in your actions. She's already pulling away,
and sooner or later she's going to really resent

you." She'd gone way too far, so she might as well finish it. "She's going to want a life all her own. That's what growing up is all about, isn't it?"

He didn't answer. Instead, he grasped the side of the tub, untangled his legs from hers and climbed out. Water cascaded over her. He looped a towel around his waist and used another to dry his arms and chest with brisk, angry strokes.

"Being a doctor doesn't make you an expert at being a parent, Joanne."

The cold accusation stung, and her hurt and disappointment boiled to the surface. "And being a martyr doesn't get you a medal, Spence."

He turned and left the room.

She sat in the cooling water, trying to stop the waves of painful emotion that rolled through her. At last she got out of the tub and dried herself. Her hands were shaking. Her insides were, as well.

She and Spence needed to talk; they couldn't leave it like this; they'd shared too much to end it with bitter words.

But when she opened the bathroom door, he was fully dressed, pulling on his leather jacket.

"I'm going to get the bike." He'd told her about parking it in the garage. "It'll save us a trip in the morning. See you a little later." His voice was polite and distant, as if she were a stranger.

It was late, long after midnight, and still raining. Riding a motorcycle in the dark on slick streets in a strange city would be dangerous. She wanted him to stay, to talk with her, so they could mend some of the damage. But before she could say any of those things, he was gone.

CHAPTER FIFTEEN

SPENCE SHOULDERED the door of the hotel open and stepped out into the rainy night. He'd have to call a cab sooner or later—he couldn't possibly walk all the way to where he'd left the bike—but at this moment he needed to move, fast and hard.

He strode off down the street, dimly aware how cold and wet it was, but the self-righteous anger that boiled inside him made him impervious to the weather.

What bloody right did she have to accuse him of being a martyr? Where did she get off, telling him how his own daughter felt?

He knew how *he* felt—and it was lousy. Becoming this involved with Joanne had been a mistake, a huge mistake. He'd slipped into it almost accidentally, as a result of the abduction. Ordinarily, he'd never have let himself get involved with someone like her, a doctor, a woman he...

Spence stopped walking. He jammed his hands into his jacket pockets and stood staring sightlessly into the dark window of a closed restaurant.

A woman he...what? Wanted with a physical

ache that wasn't sated in the slightest even after a night and a day of lovemaking?

He started walking again, more slowly now.

A woman who made him laugh, made him think, made him feel like a god damn hero just because he instinctively knew how to please her in bed? A woman who, in spite of being intellectual and arty, seemed willing and able to enjoy the same things he enjoyed?

A woman brave enough to bring sensitive issues out into the open, he admitted reluctantly. A woman who didn't play any games or act coy or pretend that she didn't want a future with him. A woman courageous enough to speak her truths and take the consequences.

Anger slowly faded, giving way to sadness and a kind of yearning. If only things were different, he thought, hunching his shoulders against the rain.

He and Joanne were good together; they were perfectly suited in so many ways.

Get over it, Mathews. She wants what you don't have—time, attention, a future without your load of responsibilities. But you shouldn't have been so hard on her. You had no reason and no right to hurt her the way you just did.

There was a convenience store a long block away, and he hurried toward it. He'd call her and apologize. He had to look up the number of the hotel. An automated voice asked for the room number. He gave it and waited.

The phone rang and rang. No response.

Spence hung up, enraged at the delay, and dialed the front desk. The night clerk checked the number and rang it for him twice. At last, Spence insisted the clerk send someone up to knock on the door, and when that didn't bring any response, he panicked.

God help him, he'd left her in the bathroom. He'd left her upset. What if she'd slipped and was lying helpless and in pain on the tiled floor? What if she'd banged her head and was unconscious…?

He could get the clerk to rouse the night manager.

He could call 9-1-1 and send an emergency team up there.

Instead, he dropped the phone and began to run.

He wasn't certain how far he'd come, but it couldn't be more than ten or twelve blocks. He could get to the hotel faster than any emergency team.

He burst into the lobby and ignored the startled expressions on the faces of the staff at the desk. He pounded the elevator keys, urging the car to hurry down from wherever it was. Then he banged the panel inside the car, trying to make it hurry up to the fifth floor.

He tore down the hallway, card in hand, cursing

when it wouldn't work the first time, or the second. The third time he was careful, forcing himself to do it slowly, exactly right.

He ripped open the door and hurtled inside.

''Joanne? Joanne? Hey, Joanne?''

He raced into the bathroom, then did a quick tour of the adjoining bedrooms. It took only moments to determine that she was gone.

He sat down on the bed. Told himself his heart was hammering from the long run, the fear he'd felt. That he needed to calm down, think this thing through logically and sensibly.

She'd be either at the bus depot or the airport. He could probably locate her by making a few calls. He might even be able to catch up to her if he rushed.

He reached for the phone, but then set it down slowly without dialing. This way was by far the best; it had ended things clean—no messy strings to tie up, no tearful scenes to suffer through, he told himself.

His brain repeated those words like a mantra, and he wanted to believe them. They were all true, weren't they?

So why did he feel as if he'd been smashed by a semi?

After a long time he decided that the logical thing to do was go to bed, get some rest. That way he could get an early start the following morning.

He went through the motions, but it didn't work. He was still wide-awake an hour-and-a-half later. He finally got up and went into the other bedroom, when he slipped between sheets that didn't smell of their lovemaking and her perfume.

He tossed and turned and eventually lay on his back, staring at the ceiling until the clock finally said it was morning.

Riding a motorcycle demanded total attention. Twice on the long drive home Spence came heart-stoppingly close to losing control of the powerful machine. He hadn't slept, and he blamed his care-lessness on that, but the truth was that he was think-ing about Joanne.

He had unfinished business with her, he finally concluded. He'd promised her he'd do his best to get the baby back, and a promise was a promise.

He'd call Bud as soon as he got back to Van-couver and ask for a leave of absence so he could devote all his time and energy to the Stevens case.

And, of course, that decision had nothing what-soever to do with avoiding seeing Joanne at St Joe's.

SPENCE DIDN'T have to call Bud. As he wheeled his bike down the street late that afternoon, he saw that Ansell's little green sports car was parked in front of his house.

And so was the blue van that belonged to Eric Palmer.

Spence's heart sank, and then he felt irritated. He was weary. The last thing he wanted to do at the moment was be social to Devon's friend, but it appeared there was no way to avoid it. He parked the bike in the garage and opened the kitchen door, plastering on a smile he knew was stiff and unnatural.

"Hi, Dad. Good trip?" Devon was making a salad at the counter. Eric was sitting sidewise in his wheelchair, close to her, stretching so that he could wash lettuce under the tap.

"Not bad, Dev." He couldn't stop his voice from changing as he added, "Hello, Eric." He knew he sounded guarded and a lot less than cordial. Well, it was the best he could do, he told himself resentfully. It was asking too much today to manufacture a welcome for Eric that he didn't genuinely feel. Couldn't honestly feel.

Never would feel, he amended angrily, wishing the young man in the wheelchair were anywhere except in his family's kitchen.

"Hello, Mr. Mathews." Eric was polite, but there was reserve in his tone and in the glance he shot Spence. He was no fool; he clearly knew Devon's father wasn't exactly overjoyed to see him.

Call me 'Spence.' It was so obviously the right time to invite the boy to do so. Spence knew that.

He also knew he wasn't about to extend the invitation.

Instead, he turned his attention back to Devon. "Where's your gram?"

"She and Bud went for a walk. They should be back in a while."

Devon was sending him a beseeching look with her eyes, a look that Spence had never been able to resist. It was on Eric's behalf; she was asking him to be nice, to try harder. This time, it didn't work on him.

"We made pizza." She leaned over the back of Eric's chair and looped her arms around his neck. With her chin, she indicated several aluminum-foil-wrapped trays sitting on the table. "And we're having spinach salad and garlic bread. We're a great team when it comes to cooking, mostly because Eric knows how to do stuff. You haven't eaten already, have you, Dad?"

He hadn't, but he wasn't hungry. "I grabbed a burger not long ago." he lied. "I'll skip the pizza. I'm gonna have a shower."

"There's frozen chocolate ice-cream cake for dessert. Eric brought it." The warm smile she exchanged with the younger man would have melted ice cream through asbestos, and Spence's gut roiled at the sight of it.

The ice-cream dessert had always been Dev's favorite, a treat that Spence bought on special occasions just for his daughter. He knew it was irrational and childish to resent Eric for finding out what Devon liked and providing it. But knowing it didn't stop Spence from resenting Eric like hell.

Standing under the hot water in the shower didn't help a single thing. His brain just jumped from one uncomfortable scenario to the next. He had vivid images of Joanne, smiling and windburned as she climbed off the back of his bike, naked as she stepped into the bathtub, flushed and intense and unbelievably sensual lying beneath him.

When he forced those images out of his mind, all he could see was Devon, smiling at Eric, touching his shoulder, her exotic eyes brimming over with…

Spence turned the taps off so hard the noise reverberated—a thing he'd told the women they must never do. He toweled himself dry with enough savage energy to take paint off concrete.

He wanted nothing more than to toss some clothes on and sneak out without saying another word to anyone, but he had to talk to Bud; he planned to throw himself into the Stevens investigation and stay so bloody busy he wouldn't have time to think.

Ansell and his mother had returned from their walk. As Spence pulled on jeans and an old rugby shirt, he could hear Bud's raspy, hearty voice in the kitchen, followed by Eric's voice, then repeated bursts of feminine laughter. Even that pleasant sound irritated Spence.

Nobody was *that* funny.

It took enormous effort to paste a pleasant expression on his face and walk into the kitchen. Everyone was grouped around the old Arborite table, munching on huge slices of cheesy pizza. It sounded as if they were all talking at once.

"Spencer." Lillian beamed with pleasure at the sight of him. "Grab a plate. These young chefs have really outdone themselves. They even made the crust from scratch. The only time I tried that, it tasted like dried wallpaper paste."

The pizza did smell good, but Spence wasn't about to join in. He repeated his story about having already eaten and added that he was going out again; he had something important to check on. Before anyone could ask questions, he added, "Bud, if you could spare me for a week or two, I'd like to pursue this abduction investigation with Zelaney."

Bud, friend that he was, immediately and enthusiastically agreed that Spence should do exactly that.

"I've got a couple of applications from guys who say they're experienced and are lookin' for work. I'll give them a shot at your spot till you get back."

"Thanks, Bud." Spence waved at the others and hurried out the door, wondering where the hell he could go on a Monday evening to while away four or five hours. His car was in the double garage; he hardly ever drove it, preferring to take the bike whenever possible. He'd had enough of the bike today, though.

As he turned the key in the ignition and then backed out of the driveway, he thought about Devon and her persistent demands that he teach her to drive. It was past time he gave in. He knew—he'd always known—that it was his own fear for her safety that made him reluctant. Because of her damaged hip, Devon's reaction time with her right leg was much slower than he considered safe. But maybe he was being unnecessarily cautious; he'd tell her that he'd take her out for lessons really soon.

That decision made him feel marginally better.

Almost as if it had a mind of its own, his car ended up at the Vancouver City Police downtown station, where Zelaney and his team were centered.

Spence knew from experience that on a case as urgent as the abduction, there would be investigators working around the clock. Zelaney had given him access to any files he wanted to read. Spence found a relatively quiet corner and methodically began to study every single item in the bulky folder.

When he next looked up, eyes blurry and muscles aching from hours of concentration, he was amazed to find that it was 2:15 in the morning. He felt enormously relieved to realize that just maybe he was exhausted enough at last to go home and sleep...as long as he managed not to think about Joanne.

CHAPTER SIXTEEN

HE'D SHOWN HER a whole new world, and then he'd ruthlessly shoved her out of it and closed the door. He'd been cold and insulting. He hadn't even bothered to call her since she'd come home. He wasn't the kind of man any self-respecting woman in her right mind would trust with her heart.

So why couldn't she get Spencer Mathews out of her mind?

Joanne drove through the early-morning traffic on her way to work, eyes scratchy, body heavy with weariness. It was Thursday, her third day of work since that endless bus ride home from Seattle. And last night, like the other nights since she'd come back, she'd probably had a maximum of four hours' sleep. She could go to sleep at bedtime; she just couldn't stay asleep.

She wheeled into the employees' parking lot, assuring herself she wouldn't detour past the spot where she knew Spence's motorcycle was usually parked. But just as she had each of the other mornings this interminable week, she couldn't stop herself from checking.

The bike wasn't there. It hadn't been there all week.

Well, he worked shifts, she reminded herself. He was probably on nights or afternoons.

And what difference did it make whether he was at St. Joe's or not, whether she saw him or didn't? Whatever had been between them was over; he'd made that patently clear.

Angry with herself, she hurried up the stairs and into the ER, hung up her jacket in her locker, pulled a fresh lab coat on over her chinos and shirt, and prayed for a shift so busy she'd have no time to think about Spence or her own wretched state of mind.

"Joanne, good morning." Portia's face was freshly scrubbed, but her bloodshot eyes clearly indicated that she'd been up far too long. "I'm just heading off to catch some sleep. Last night was crazy. We had eight high school girls brought in one after the other—AMS, ALOC."

Altered mental state, altered level of consciousness, Joanne interpreted.

"There was a beach party and somebody laced the lemonade with LSD. We did a toxic screen and the drug showed up in every single one of them."

Joanne shook her head. "I thought LSD was out of fashion now. We haven't seen any for a while. Are they all okay?"

Portia nodded. "Six were released. Two are still

here. And there're some pretty irate parents raising hell right now down at the police station.''

''I should hope so.''

''Mom came in and I showed her the baby's footprint.''

With everything that had gone on during the past few days, Joanne had almost forgotten about Portia's mother and the footprint.

''The good news is the baby's alive. She saw her in a pink plastic bathtub. The little girl was lying on a table in what she thought was a house trailer. She thought the child was sleeping.''

''Did she see anybody with the baby?''

''A woman with lots of red hair.''

''No address or anything?'' Joanne knew that was too much to hope for, as she wasn't surprised when Portia shook her head. ''That's the bad news. Mom tried, but this place seemed to be pretty isolated—no street numbers or anything. There were huge mountains around, and water not far away.''

That description could fit the entire province of British Columbia, Joanne mused cynically.

''Not much help, huh? I'm sorry about that.''

''At least she saw the baby alive.'' Joanne did her best not to show how utterly despondent she felt.

''Dr. Duncan?'' One of the interns stuck his head in the door, forehead creased in a worried frown. ''I've got a twenty-nine-year-old football player in cubicle three with what looks like hypertrophic cardiomyopathy. Could you come and have a look? His coach brought him in. The guy's parents are giving me a real hard time. They say I don't know what I'm talking about.''

Joanne's heart sank. Of all the problems she encountered in the ER, hereditary forms of heart disease were the most upsetting for her to deal with; they brought back the sense of frustration and helplessness that had surrounded Henry's death. And when they presented in young athletes like this one, the impotence she felt was overwhelming. Certain forms caused an enlargement of the heart muscle, resulting in a blockage of the flow of blood out of the heart. The young person didn't suspect a problem until it showed up under extreme stress. In all too many cases, death was the outcome.

''I'll be right there, Kaleb.''

The workday had begun. With a final word of thanks to Portia, Joanne hurried out into the ER, and just as she'd hoped earlier, one crisis came hard on the heels of the next for hours at a time, leaving no space in her mind to think about Spence or even the missing baby.

SPENCE WAS NOW reasonably certain that Natasha knew where the baby was and who had taken it, but he had to convince Zelaney that his suspicions were valid.

"We interviewed this Rogers guy. He didn't tell us anything like what he told you," Zelaney protested when Spence voiced his reasons for suspecting Natasha.

"Howard doesn't like cops. He doesn't reveal much when he's sober, either."

"So you've got the drunken ravings of a guy who admits he boinked a fifteen-year-old kid—*his own sister-in-law,* for crissake. That's statutory rape." Zelaney was highly skeptical. "We've had a tap on Stevens's phone since she got out of the hospital. We did round-the-clock surveillance on her until last week. *Nada.* She's as clean as soap." Zelaney shook his head. "Y'ask me, somethin' should have shown up by now if she's involved. The phone tap's still in place, but I had to pull the surveillance. That double murder on the west side two days ago means I'm short of manpower."

"If you can spare just one guy to give me a break for a couple of hours at night, I'll work the surveillance on her."

Zelaney assigned Const. Harlan Ross to spell Spence in the stakeout on the apartment, but another three days of observing Stevens, following her each time she went out, yielded nothing.

Spence's weariness and frustration grew in direct proportion to each long, futile hour that dragged past watching Stevens.

At ten on a Saturday morning, Spence met with Zelaney at a coffee shop.

"I dunno how long I can keep Ross on the job. I'm getting flak from upstairs on it," Zelaney said.

Spence knew the system; he'd already guessed that he'd be working alone before long.

"You still convinced she's involved?"

Zelaney obviously wasn't. Spence nodded, although he'd had his own doubts during the tedious days and nights he'd spent watching. "Sooner or later she'll slip, but the question is how long it'll take. My guess is she has to be in contact eventually with whoever has the baby. Nothing yet on the phone tap?"

Zelaney hesitated. "One call came in from a woman at eight this morning. Could be nothing. She didn't identify herself. Natasha obviously knew who it was. Called her 'Agnes.' Anyways, Agnes asked how Natasha was doing and then said the kids were getting her down. She had cabin fever and needed a break real bad. Natasha promised to call her back."

"Did you get a trace on the call?"

"Yeah. It was from a pay phone at a gas station out in Abbotsford, and nobody there noticed this Agnes making the call. The guy running the station was busy with the morning rush. Said he vaguely remembered a redheaded woman with a car full of kids pulled over by the rest rooms. Maybe just a friend of Natasha's?''

''Maybe.'' Spence was thoughtful. ''Maybe not. An hour ago I tailed her to that convenience store on Main. She bought milk and bread and then made a call from the pay phone. Now, why call from a pay phone when she's got a working telephone at her place? It drove me nuts not knowing what she said and to whom. I wonder if it was to this Agnes,'' Spence mused. ''Any chance you could tap that one, as well?''

''The phone at the convenience store?'' Zelaney rolled his eyes, but finally, very reluctantly, nodded. ''Okay. I still think you're barking up the wrong tree, but I'll put the boys from Special Section on it.''

''This is one smart, tough young lady,'' Spence emphasized. ''She had the balls to blackmail her brother-in-law. She's bright enough to suspect we might have her calls monitored. She might even have noticed your guys were watching the apartment. She's not gonna do anything stupid at this stage. I'm still puzzled by how the abductor knew the baby wasn't banded in the hospital. You absolutely sure Stevens doesn't have a cell phone tucked away somewhere? Any aspiring actress would have a cell.''

''No cell registered in her name. We checked.'' Zelaney looked a trifle embarrassed. ''We just found out she might have had one at the hospital when the baby was born, though. Apparently the adoptive parents gave her one to use while she was pregnant, then asked for it back after the abduction. The adoptive father says Stevens was racking up a sizable bill with it.''

"Maybe he suspects Natasha isn't exactly trustworthy. Is there any way to check on whether or not a call was made from that cell right after the baby was born?''

"None. The cell's digital. There's no way to trace digital calls.''

TWO HOURS LATER, Spence was slumped in his car drinking coffee from a thermos, when Natasha's battered little vehicle pulled out of the parking garage with her at the wheel. Keeping a reasonable distance behind, Spence followed her to a mobile phone mart. The store was crowded, so he took a chance and went inside. He stayed just long enough to confirm that Natasha was purchasing a cell phone.

Once she'd left the store, he approached the clerk who'd served her. "Do your mobiles need charging, or can they be used immediately?''

"Usually they have to be charged for twelve hours. But if you need one right away, we keep a couple of floor models powered up. I just sold one to a lady, but there's another around here some-where. Just let me—''

''Another time, thanks.''

A feeling of urgency swept over Spence. He was certain Natasha would be using the cell to contact her partner. Somehow they had to monitor that call.

As soon as he was outside the store, Spence was on the phone to Zelaney, explaining what he'd learned from the clerk. ''We've got to get a record of the calls she makes from that mobile phone, and we've got to set up the tap right away,'' Spence urged. ''It's too much of a coincidence. That call comes this morning from this Agnes. Stevens calls back from the pay phone. Now she runs out and gets a cell that's already charged. Something's go-ing down.''

Zelaney sighed heavily. ''I just sent Special Sec-tion over to the convenience store. They're gonna think I've gone audio happy. Okay, Spence, I'll get them going on this, as well, but we'll have to have access to the damn thing to place a mike in the mouthpiece. How the hell we gonna manage that?''

Spence thought it over. ''Have one of your guys call her immediately and say he's from the store. Tell her the phone she just bought is defective. Dream up some technical jargon that sounds logi-cal. Replace that one with one that's wired. Get the manager of the store to cooperate, in case she phones him back and checks. Deliver the new one to her right away. She's probably already making calls on the one she has.''

They could already have missed the call that was crucial. Spence's gut was churning with frustration.

''Might work.'' Zelaney sounded anything but enthusiastic. ''I'll get on it.''

Spence did his best to curb his impatience. ''I'm heading back to her apartment now.''

Enthusiastic or not, Zelaney was true to his word. Within a half-hour, Spence watched a truck marked with the store's logo drive up. Spence recognized the plainclothes policeman who made his way up to Natasha's apartment with the new cell phone.

Ten minutes later, Natasha hurried out of the building and walked quickly up the street to a small park.

Spence followed on foot and, with a growing sense of excitement, noted that she looked around carefully before settling on a deserted park bench. It was starting to rain, but that didn't seem to bother her. From her bag, she pulled out the cell and dialed, then had a long conversation.

Spence was too far away to see the expression on her face or hear what was said. He stood in the deep shadow of a group of pine trees, praying that Special Section had done their work well and the conversation was being recorded; he had a gut feeling that this was the break in the case everyone had been waiting for.

Natasha was back in the apartment by the time Spence's portable rang. The tension in Zelaney's voice told Spence his hunch had been right.

"I'm getting a warrant based on a call Stevens made a few minutes ago. Soon as it's signed, we're on our way to pick her up. I'll fill you in when we get there."

"You know where the baby is?" Every muscle in Spence's body was aching with tension.

"Not certain, but we've got a probable location in Abbotsford."

"Pretty good bet the baby's there?"

"We should know in a few minutes. The boys are on their way. They'll notify me immediately."

Spence's heart hammered. It wasn't arresting Natasha he cared about. It was recovering the baby, safe and sound.

Let it be that way, he pleaded silently as he waited anxiously for Zelaney. *Safe and sound.*

He'd phone Joanne when they found the baby, Spence promised himself. That would fulfill the promise he'd made to her. It would at least be an honorable ending to their relationship.

But the baby wasn't in Abbotsford. At the address was a run-down trailer crouched on a half-acre of land by the river, and the dreary little place was deserted.

Someone had been there recently, Zelaney was told; the smelly old trailer was warm, and food was in the fridge. The police settled in to wait, in the hope that whoever lived there would return.

The trailer and all the utilities were registered to a George Pitt, whom police were trying to locate. Nothing in the trailer indicated that anyone named Agnes had lived there.

But children had been around, Zelaney related to Spence. Toys, soiled diapers—some of them newborn size—baby formula and baby clothing littered the trailer, and two cribs were crammed into one small room.

Zelaney cursed when the news came, and Spence's heart constricted. They both knew this was the dangerous time. This was when whoever had the baby could panic and do something irreversible.

Natasha, at first the picture of injured innocence but minutes later, when confronted with the phone call, alternately cursing like a stevedore and spitting like an angry cat, was picked up and taken to police headquarters for questioning.

Spence went along. He wanted to listen to the recording of the call that Natasha had made from the park.

On the tape, she was obviously furious, although she tried to hide it. Her voice had a nasty bite; her words were clipped.

''...Where the hell have you been? I've been trying to get you for the past half-hour,'' Natasha began.

Just as he'd feared, she'd attempted to make the call before they got the recording device in place. Spence sent up a silent thank-you to providence for intervening.

"I was outside hanging up clothes on the line." Agnes sounded belligerent.

"I thought we had an agreement," Natasha went on. "And I thought I told you *never, never* to call me. The cops have my apartment phone bugged. For all I know the whole place is wired. You've put the whole damn plan at risk by breaking our agreement. You do see that, don't you?"

The other woman's voice was high and edgy, and she, also, was clearly angry. "Yeah, well, this is going on too long, ya hear me? I'm stuck out here in the middle of bloody nowhere with nobody to talk to. The kids are drivin' me crazy, that baby of yours cries all the time. It's gettin' on my nerves bad."

"It won't be for much longer, Agnes. I promise." Natasha's tone changed drastically. "We agreed on a month. That's not that much longer." Now Natasha was as compassionate and soothing as a professional housemother.

She was really not a bad actress, Spence thought.

Agnes swore. "Screw a month. That's another, what?—another ten days? I can't go that long."

"Then just another day or so, okay? That murder case got me bumped off the front pages, but it'll probably cool down soon. We have to time this right so we get the max in publicity, you know that."

Agnes's voice grew spiteful. "How much more do you want? You got yourself plastered all over the papers already, on TV, in magazines—and what am I getting out of it? *I'm* the one taking the risks here, not you." She drew in a breath and then the real issue became clear. "And where the hell is my money, Natasha? You got paid for some of those stories. You said you'd send money. I gotta buy stuff. I got needs."

Spence's blood ran cold. Agnes sounded like an addict. Addicts didn't make good foster mothers. He grew even more apprehensive as the conversation progressed.

Natasha made promises, obviously trying to soothe and calm the other woman.

"...The cops are smart. They're gonna find me sooner or later," Agnes whined at one point. "I'm gonna just drop your kid off somewhere."

In spite of her acting ability, Natasha clearly was growing agitated. "Stick to the damn plan," she urged. "At least do the phone thing. Call the cops and tell them where you're leaving the baby. They can't trace the call unless you stay on the line. They have no way of telling who you are."

Spence shook his head. Natasha's motherly instincts weren't impressive.

The next part of the tape was chilling.

"...I'm not sticking my neck out any farther than it already is," Agnes said. "I'm dumping her, and you better get that money to me or I'll—"

"You'll what?" Natasha's voice changed, becoming hard and mocking. "You can't very well blow the whistle on me without getting yourself in deep shit, now can you, Agnes?"

The other woman spewed out obscenities, and then hung up.

Spence was horrified.

Where would Agnes leave the baby?

It was late afternoon, Vancouver's skies were gray, rain was falling in earnest now and the evening and night would be chilly. How long could a tiny baby survive if left outside? Would Agnes make the phone call Natasha had mentioned, or would she simply abandon the child without thought for her survival?

She'd make sure the little girl was found in time, Spence tried to assure himself. No matter how desperate she was, Agnes wouldn't want a murder charge on her hands.

Please, let her stay rational enough to figure that out.

Tension grew almost unbearable as one hour passed, then another.

Spence realized he had to call Joanne. She had a right to know what was happening, he told himself as he dialed her home number. Besides, she was a doctor; they'd need one on hand, wouldn't they? He sent up a fervent prayer that the baby would still require a doctor's attention when she was found.

But a part of Spence also realized that contacting Joanne had little to do with what was right, or necessary, or expedient. They'd been in this thing together from the beginning.

He needed Joanne at his side when it ended.

CHAPTER SEVENTEEN

JOANNE REREAD the directions on the box and without much hope dumped the spice mix into the noodles she'd just reconstituted. She was hungry, but the gluey concoction didn't look at all like the colored picture on the box.

She was on the verge of scraping it into the garbage and calling for a pizza, when the phone rang.

"Joanne, it's me."

"Hello, Spence." At the sound of his voice, every shred of hunger disappeared, replaced by a confused mixture of emotions. Longing and desire and exasperation and—she couldn't begin to deny it—overwhelming love.

"Joanne, I'm calling about the baby."

Quickly, before she could say a single word, he told her what had happened during the past hours. Her insides contracted anew as every concern but the baby's welfare was shoved aside.

"Where are you?" She noticed, as if listening to a stranger, that she'd restored to her brisk, no-nonsense ER voice. When he told her, she said, "I'll be there right away."

She remembered to turn off the stove burner. She remembered to grab a raincoat and her medical bag. Years of training in Emerg did come in handy, she thought wildly as she raced for her car.

The atmosphere at police headquarters reminded Joanne of those tense moments before the arrival of ambulances in the ER, with staff gowned, adrenaline pumping, all systems prepared and ready. The difference here was that the wait was interminable.

Spence had been watching for her. When she hurried through the door, he was there. For an instant their eyes locked and the world contracted until there were only the two of them. She came within an inch of throwing herself into his arms, but something distant and forbidding in his expression stopped her in time.

He was wearing his familiar uniform, jeans and a black sweatshirt with the sleeves shoved up to his elbows. He looked older—weary, tense, somber. The lines on his forehead and around his eyes were more pronounced; the hollows of his cheekbones, deeply carved and dramatic. And Joanne could tell that, purposefully or not, he'd removed himself from her orbit.

''Come this way.'' His quiet voice, superficially calm, broke the spell, and she trailed him to a large, smoke-filled room where Zelaney and three other men were all talking on telephones, quietly but intensely.

Zelaney nodded to her, hung up, then beckoned Spence over. Joanne followed, and Zelaney indicated an empty chair, but she didn't sit down. She couldn't.

"We've located George Pitt. He's in a Surrey nursing home." The municipality of Surrey was a forty-minute drive from downtown Vancouver. "Agnes is his daughter," Zelaney went on. "Her full name's Agnes Mary Wells. She's got a rap sheet from way back for possession and soliciting. She did six months five years ago. Nothing much since then."

Spence swore under his breath. "Any current address, other than the trailer?"

Zelaney shook his head. "Pitt insists she's straightened out recently. He told her she could have the trailer because she's got two little kids and their genetic donor's in maximum security in Matsqui doing two to five for armed B-and-E."

In prison for two to five years for breaking and entering. Fortunately, Joanne was familiar with police jargon.

"How old are her kids?" Spence asked next.

"Three and four."

"No need for baby formula or newborn diapers, then."

"No doubt she has the Stevens kid." Zelaney tilted the chair back and rubbed his forehead with his fingers. "The big question is, where will she dump her?"

"Nothing useful from Mother Natasha?"

Zelaney shrugged. "I've got a couple of female detectives in with her. She's playing hard-ass. Her lawyer's on his way over."

Spence nodded and then turned to Joanne, courteous as always, as dispassionate as if she were a stranger. "You want some coffee? A sandwich? There's a machine. It's not exactly gourmet..."

Joanne swallowed hard and declined. He led the way over to an unused desk in a corner, held a chair for her. She sat down. He went behind the desk and shuffled through a stack of paper.

"Still raining out there?" He spoke without looking at her.

Spence, I love you. Don't you know that?

"It's pouring." Her hands clenched, and she had to force herself not to imagine a baby too small to even roll over by herself, lying somewhere with cold rain pelting down on her unprotected face and tiny body.

"She'll likely leave her where there's cover. She's got kids of her own." Spence said it as if reading Joanne's mind.

Why couldn't he read her mind about other things?

"Of course she will." *Except that she's scared*

*of being seen, so she won't go where there're peo-
ple, will she.*

There was no need to voice it. Spence knew.

Silence fell, and they waited.

A UNIFORMED COP rushed to the door when the call
came in to the front desk. "The manager of the
burger place at the foot of Davie says a street person just walked in with a small baby. Claims he
found it in Stanley Park. He gave the baby to the
manager and then just left."

Everyone in the room leaped up.

The officer answered the unspoken concern on
all their minds.

"The guy says the baby's crying."

A cheer went up, and Joanne breathed, "Oh,
thank You, God." Relief swiftly gave way to professional considerations. "We'll need an ambulance
down there."

"Zelaney's already put a call in for one," Spence
told her. "C'mon, let's go."

Spence grabbed her by the hand and tugged her
with him as he rushed outside. She retrieved her
medical bag from the trunk of her vehicle.

A uniformed young woman waited for them in a
white police car. Spence opened the rear door for
Joanne and then absently put his hand flat on the
top of her head as she climbed in, as if she were a
suspect he was ushering into the car. It illustrated

for her exactly how distraught he was beneath his facade of utter calm, and for a moment she felt an overwhelming sense of tenderness for him. He hid his innermost feelings so well.

It was her first time in a squad car, although she'd ridden in ambulances during her medical training. Some detached part of her marveled at how muted the siren was with the windows shut, and how murderous she felt toward other drivers who were slow to get out of their way.

With a screech of tires, the driver stopped beside the fast-food outlet, and then Joanne and Spence were out and racing for the entrance. An ambulance pulled up right behind them, and the attendants followed them inside.

The restaurant was busy; almost every table was occupied. And as word spread that a baby had been found, more people tried to come in for a look.

Zelaney quickly put two officers at the door, with instructions that no one except police and ambulance personnel were to be allowed inside. A television news van pulled up outside, then another.

Joanne would remember only later how quiet it became in the place, despite the number of people. Over the murmur of voices rose the best sound in all the world, the sound that brought tears to her eyes and a lump to her throat.

It was the indignant, demanding, hungry cry of a very small baby. One of the female employees was holding her, and when Joanne identified herself as a doctor, the woman handed her over.

The baby was wrapped in a scratchy and scruffy gray cape that smelled of woodsmoke and dank wool. Joanne rolled the cape back. Inside its folds, the baby was well protected. She was wearing a fuzzy blue one-piece zippered snowsuit with a hood and, when that was undone, a knitted red toque and pink terry pajamas. The outer layers of her clothing were damp, but the pajamas felt dry. Joanne noted that everything was clean.

"Is there somewhere private and warm we could examine her?" It seemed that no immediate attention was required, so Joanne cradled the small, squirming body against her, hoping against hope that first impressions were accurate and that the small girl was unharmed.

The manager hurried Joanne and the ambulance crew along a narrow corridor to a small office. Spence and the female police officer came along. They stood well back as Joanne and the medics laid the baby on a desk and swiftly removed her clothing, a procedure that brought screams of outrage from the tiny female, but delighted those who were annoying her.

A quick but thorough check showed she was nourished and healthy, with no apparent bruising or signs of abuse. Her temp was normal, although her extremities were chilly. Her heart and lungs were clear and her diaper was wet, which showed she wasn't dehydrated. Her eyes and ears appeared free of infection. Blood pressure and pulse were within the normal range. Joanne reported her findings aloud, and the police officer wrote them down in her notebook.

"You're the most beautiful little girl in the world," Joanne crooned as she replaced the minute undershirt and snapped the pajamas into place. The baby's wails were increasingly desperate, and she sucked hungrily on her fist between bouts of screaming. The attendants wrapped a blanket around her, and Joanne held her. She felt reluctant to let her go, even for a moment.

"She seems absolutely fine, but she's pretty hungry. She likely hasn't eaten in a while. That's what's making her feel cold." Joanne made a quick decision. "It'll take us a while to get to St. Joe's and the nursery, and there's no emergency now," she added. "I saw a drugstore just down the street. Could someone buy a disposable feeding bottle and a can of infant formula? And a diaper. She's badly in need of a change. Let's make her as comfortable as possible right away. She's had a stressful day."

"She's had a stressful life," Spence remarked under his breath, and Joanne nodded agreement. Their eyes met briefly, and then Joanne turned her attention to the baby again.

Within moments, a policeman was back with the

items Joanne had requested. She changed diapers as
the manager warmed the milk. The baby's choking,
greedy gulps when the bottle was presented brought
smiles to everyone's faces.

The manager was the one who asked, "What'll
happen to her now?"

"She'll be put in the care of Social Services and
placed in a foster home," Joanne explained. "But
first we'll keep her under observation at St. Joe's
for a couple of days, just to make certain we
haven't missed anything."

Getting out of the restaurant was a challenge.
News vans and reporters and curious onlookers
were blocking the street. Zelaney's men held the
crowd off, as Joanne and the emergency attendants
climbed into the back of the ambulance. The baby
sucked contentedly at her bottle.

Members of the press surged forward. They
thrust microphones at Joanne, and barraged her ex-
citedly with questions.

Joanne caught one last glimpse of Spence just
before the ambulance sped away. He raised his
hand to her in the familiar little salute she knew so
well.

But this time he seemed to be saying goodbye.

SPENCE WATCHED the ambulance, lights flashing
and siren blaring, disappear up Davie Street.

"We've located the guy who found the baby,"

Zelaney said. "We're bringing him in to the station to see what he can tell us. He's an addict, well-known to the cops who patrol the park. His street name is Sir Galahad because of that cape he wears. It's the one he wrapped the baby in. He's harmless as long as he hasn't used any bad dope. And I've got a team watching the trailer. We were counting on Agnes going back there, but now that the media have gotten the scoop on the baby, she might get antsy."

Spence rode with Zelaney back to headquarters.

"I owe you a drink, Spence. We wouldn't have put two and two together as quick as you did on this case," Zelaney admitted. "I'll be free in an hour or so. How about I take you out for some dinner."

Spence thought the invitation over for a moment, then decided against it. "Another time, Gordon. Right now I should get home. I haven't spent much time with the family the past while."

"Tell me about it. Marcie says the only reason we've lasted twenty-five years is that we don't spend enough time together to get in fights." Zelaney reached out a hand and shook Spence's, and his voice when he spoke was gruff and sincere. "Thanks for all your effort and your expertise, buddy. I wish you'd come work for us. The VCP are a cut above the RCMP. You'd like it here."

They both grinned. The rivalry between the two forces was old and good-natured.

Spence drove home slowly, wondering why he didn't feel more elated about the successful ending to the case. He *was* relieved and delighted about the baby's safe recovery. Of course he was. But he couldn't summon up the usual euphoria that he'd felt at other, similar, times when a case wrapped up.

Joanne's image kept flashing into his mind, and all he could think of was the radiance of her face, the tremor in her lovely voice, the tears in her soft green eyes as she pronounced the baby healthy.

He smacked a hand on the steering wheel in frustration. Why did this one particular woman have to burrow under his skin and stubbornly refuse him peace?

Their time together and their reasons for getting to know each other were things of the past now. The passion, the closeness they'd shared, had resulted from their common concern for the Stevens baby, he assured himself.

It wasn't unheard of for two people united in a common cause to get into a sexual relationship. It didn't mean they were—what was the buzzword these days?—*soul mates.*

When he got home, Lillian's car wasn't in the driveway, but a soft light shone through the closed blinds in Devon's room. Spence suddenly felt guilty. He'd hardly seen his daughter the past few days. He certainly hadn't talked to her apart from a quick greeting in passing.

Maybe she'd like a pizza. He'd go pick one up. He'd get a video, as well. They hadn't spent an evening like that for months. He'd tell her that he was planning to teach her to drive. In fact, he decided on the spur of the moment, he'd get her a car of her own once she learned.

Thinking to surprise her with that news, he went quietly into the house and down the hall to her room.

"Dev?" He knocked and then opened the door.

Devon lay on her bed enfolded in Eric's arms, naked except for her underwear.

CHAPTER EIGHTEEN

THE SHOCKING IMAGE branded itself on Spence's brain, seared there as if branded.

Devon's long legs entwined with Eric's. His jeans in a heap on the floor.

Eric quickly flipped a comforter over her. They both stared up at Spence. Their young faces reflected shock, but Spence could also see the remnants of passion in swollen lips, dazed eyes.

There was an endless, stunned moment when Spence felt paralyzed, unable to move or react in any way. And then pure outrage replaced inertia.

"You." Spence's voice was guttural. He jerked his thumb at Eric, barely able to control the murderous impulse that urged him to go over and lift the young man bodily out of his daughter's bed, hurt him with his fists, literally toss him out the front door.

"Leave this house, Palmer," he ordered. "Get out of here, right now. And don't ever show your face around here again."

Devon raised herself on an elbow and glared at Spence. Her voice was trembling; her expression, mutinous. "Be careful what you say, Dad. Because if Eric goes, so do I."

"Don't you dare threaten me, young lady," Spence thundered. He was far beyond reason. His hands were shaking, and so was his voice. "Get dressed, both of you. Devon, I'll talk to you later." He fumbled for the door.

"Mr. Mathews, wait."

Spence paused, but he didn't turn around.

"I think you should know that I've asked Devon to marry me. She wants to wait awhile." Eric managed to sound both dignified and in control, despite the circumstances.

"I'm relieved to hear that she has at least that much sense left." Spence felt as though he were choking on bile.

"We've decided to live together, Dad." Devon threw the news at him like a weapon, and it wounded him to his soul.

"We'll see about that," he finally stated, then left the room. He had the absurd, childish urge to slam the door hard behind him, but instead he shut it softly and then stood stock-still, breathing as if he'd run a fast mile.

He was sitting in the study, still breathing hard and staring blindly at the television, when Devon came in with Eric close behind her.

"We'd like to talk to you, sir." Eric rolled his chair over so that he was facing Spence.

Spence shut the television off and waited, glaring at Eric, not trusting himself to say a word.

"I apologize" Eric began, "for being in Devon's bedroom tonight. It was thoughtless, and I'm sorry for putting her and you in an embarrassing situation." He met Spence's scathing gaze without flinching. "I realize you don't like me, Mr. Mathews, but under the circumstances there are some things about me you should know." Eric's voice hardened, and against his will, Spence felt a trace of respect for the younger man.

"First and foremost, I love Devon with all my heart, and I plan to make sure she's supported in anything and everything she chooses to do. I intend to take wonderful care of her. For a while, finances will be tight, but my prospects after I graduate university are good. I already have an offer of a job, and my father has agreed to help us out in the meantime. I'll pay him back, every cent, when I graduate next June. Until then..."

Spence stiffened. He instinctively knew this next part was something he absolutely didn't want to hear.

"...until then, we've rented an apartment together," Eric went on, "and we're moving in this weekend. We'd both be pleased if you'd come and see the place."

A torrent of objections raced through Spence's head.

Devon was too young, too inexperienced, too fragile…

"She doesn't even know how to drive." The moment the words were out, Spence wondered what the hell had possessed him to say them. Of all the things wrong about this, driving wasn't at the top of the list.

Devon answered. "I'm learning, Dad. Eric's teaching me. I got my learner's license last week." There was no accusation against him in her voice, Spence noted wearily. She just sounded proud and happy.

"I'd rather you and I were on speaking terms, Mr. Mathews, because otherwise this'll be hard on Dev."

Eric had a relentless streak, and he was tough, Spence acknowledged. Again, he felt a trace of admiration for the younger man. But resentment quickly overpowered it.

Spence felt he'd been backed into a corner and given an ultimatum, and it made his hackles rise.

"I think my daughter knows I don't deliberately do things to hurt her," Spence snapped.

God, I hope she knows that. One glance at Devon, though, told him otherwise. Her eyes were shiny with unshed tears, and her lips were trembling. There was such frustration, such resigned anger on her face, Spence couldn't bear it.

And then he seemed to hear Joanne uttering

words that had offended him, words he'd rejected. *"Sooner or later, Devon's going to really resent you."*

If he went on the way he was, he'd lose his daughter. Was he willing to pay that price for the sake of his pride?

Giving in took every shred of self-control and maturity, but he did it.

"Sounds as if your minds are made up," he managed to say, almost choking on the words. "Where's this apartment you've rented?"

They told him. It wasn't an area of town he wanted Devon living in, but again he held his tongue. "Do you two have any furniture?"

His abrupt change in attitude had visibly surprised the young people.

"Some, not much." Devon was being cautious. She obviously expected Spence to revert to his former stance at any moment. "Eric's folks gave us a sofa and a couple of chairs. The apartment has a fridge and a stove."

"You're welcome to take the furniture from your bedroom, and there's some other stuff around here you can have, as well. I've been planning to replace this rug," Spence improvised, "and you can have that antique writing table from the front hall." She could remove everything in the whole bloody house, for all he cared. With her gone, the place would be empty anyway. "And, of course, I'll go on supporting you financially, Dev. More than anything I want you to finish your education.''

Eric's hands bunched into fists at that and his voice was strained and stubborn. ''That won't be necessary, sir. I've arranged my finances so that I can support Devon.''

Devon's chin came up. ''Knock it off, both of you. I'm not a kid. I'm not some helpless little twit who needs big strong men to look after her. I can pay some of my tuition myself. I've got a part-time job at the library, and I can always use the insurance money from the accident.''

The situation called for diplomacy. Spence wanted that insurance money kept in trust for her, invested so she always had an income to fall back on if she needed it.

He drew in a breath and forced himself to appeal directly to Eric. ''You said your father's helping you out financially. It would please me a lot if you'd let me help Dev in the same way, just until you're both finished your education.''

Spence could see Eric struggling with pride on one hand and practicality on the other.

''Please, Eric.'' Love was all that made humility possible for Spence.

''We'll talk it over, sir.''

'''Spence.' Call me 'Spence.''' Saying it wasn't easy, but there was no backing up, and although the situation was almost killing him, he might as well go ahead with as much generosity as he could muster.

"Thank you, Dad." Clearly, Devon had been waiting for this sign. Her face crumpled, and she threw her arms around Spence's neck and buried her face on his shoulder.

The embrace would have been more comforting to Spence if he hadn't smelled Eric's aftershave on her skin.

"Well, what's happening here?" Lillian's cheerful voice interrupted the awkward scene, and Spence was pathetically grateful.

"You guys are celebrating the baby's safe return without me, right?" she continued. "I just heard about it on the car radio." She gave Spence a proud smile. "Congratulations, dear. It must feel wonderful to know you helped bring her back safely."

For a few moments, personal issues were put aside as Devon and Eric asked questions and Spence recounted the story of the baby's recovery.

And then Devon told her grandmother the news about the apartment and her plans to move in with Eric on the weekend.

Spence watched his mother's reaction, expecting surprise and shock and, he hoped, disapproval. But Lillian merely seemed pleased, and once again he felt a strong sense of betrayal.

At last Eric left, and Devon went to her room to pack.

Lillian made tea and brought a cup in to Spence. "You probably would rather have a stiff shot of whiskey, after all that's been going on," she remarked, smiling as she sat down on the sofa beside him. "Goodness knows, you ought to be celebrating tonight, with the baby safe. And where's Joanne? I would have thought the two of you'd be drinking champagne together."

Spence didn't respond. Instead, he turned and looked straight into his mother's eyes. "You knew Devon and Eric were planning this, didn't you, Mom." His voice was accusing, and he didn't care. He'd counted on Lillian's support, and she'd let him down.

"Not exactly. Not that they were planning to move in together this soon," Lillian said in a maddeningly calm tone. "But I did know they were in love. It was plain as anything to see, if only you'd chosen to." She gave Spence a long, considering look. "He's a fine boy, Spencer."

"I'm sure he is." Spence didn't plan to say anything more, but the words tumbled out, anyway. "I know he is, God damn it. He's also permanently confined to a wheelchair. What kind of future can Devon have with a man like that?"

"The kind of future she wants, obviously. If anyone understands exactly what it means to be in a chair, it's Devon. Remember that she used one herself for long enough."

Spence's voice rose. "How could I ever forget? Which is exactly why I want something different for her. I want—" Spence struggled with the thoughts. "I just want her to have a normal life. Is that so much to ask?"

"Oh, Spencer." Lillian sounded weary and sad. "Parents always want that for their children." She put her hand on his arm and gave it a gentle squeeze. "The trick is letting them decide what's normal, and being glad for them when they figure it out."

"They were in Devon's bedroom when I came home tonight," Spence burst out. "I walked in on them."

"Oh, dear." Lillian shook her head, but she still wasn't unduly surprised. "That's such a nasty shock, isn't it, finding out your child is sexually active? I still remember clearly the day I came home and discovered you and Nancy Hargraves naked on the sofa."

Spence had entirely forgotten that little incident, and he didn't appreciate Lillian's recollection of it at just this moment. Neither could he point out to his own mother that what had gone on between him and Nancy Hargraves was precisely what he'd prefer for his daughter; healthy, uncomplicated sex.

"She's gonna want kids someday" was all he could think of to say.

"And she and Eric can have them, if that's what

they want," Lillian stated with certainty. "I've been doing some research on sexuality and spinal cord injury. There've been so many advances since I stopped nursing. I'll give you the material I photocopied, if you like."

Spence understood then that Lillian had searched out answers not for herself, but for him.

"I guess I should read it." He sounded ungracious and didn't give a fiddler's damn.

"Good." Lillian sipped at her tea, then sighed. "Spencer, there's something else we need to discuss."

For one awful moment, he thought she was going to ask him about Joanne again. He didn't want to even start explaining why he wasn't seeing her any longer. It was like using a wire brush on a deep wound. He tensed and waited.

"Spencer, I'm moving out, too."

Her announcement took him totally by surprise.

"You're moving out? Why the hell are *you* moving out?" He felt his entire family was suddenly abandoning him.

"Privacy, Spencer." Lillian's tone was dry, as if he ought to have known without asking. "I've always had my own place—you're aware of that. I want it again. Being here with you and Devon was always temporary, just until she became independent, and that certainly seems to have happened."

"When are you moving?" He felt as if he'd been

belly-punched and then immediately smacked on the head.

"Actually, I put a deposit today on a ground-level town house over on first avenue, near Oak Street. It's small, but it's just a couple of blocks from the ocean. I can move in right away."

There wasn't much to say.

At least *she* would be living in a good neighborhood. "I'm really sorry you're leaving, Mom. I guess I never thought it through enough—you needing your own place."

Lillian stared down at her teacup. "I've been seeing a lot of Bud again, Spencer, and he's given me an ultimatum. He said he was giving you one, too."

"He hasn't yet. What about?"

"Yours concerns Vector. He has a buyer and he needs to know what you're planning for your future." She waited a moment and added with a wry grin, "Mine was a bit more personal. It was like that old saying about bowel movements and pots."

Shit or get off the pot. In spite of how he was feeling, Spence had to smile.

Lillian pondered for a moment, then shrugged and shook her head. "I'm not sure exactly what I'll do about it. But I do know I want my own space, no matter what happens between us."

"Bud's a great guy, but I don't have to tell you that. You already know."

"I do." Lillian took his hand in hers, and held it for several moments in silence.

"Sometimes I worry that I've passed on some obscure genetic malfunction to you, Spencer— something that prevents either of us from trusting anyone with our hearts."

"What do you mean by that?" He gave her a quizzical look, trying to figure out whether she was joking.

"Simply that both of us seem to run away from intimacy, even when the right person comes along."

"I wouldn't say that." He was angry with her all of a sudden. "I was married for seventeen years. That's not exactly running from intimacy. And you've always maintained that one shot at marriage was enough for you."

"Maybe it's time we both reconsidered."

He'd had absolutely enough for one day.

"Maybe it's time we rustled up some food, Mom."

He just knew she was going to bring up Joanne next, and he wasn't certain how much longer he could hold on to his fragile composure if she did. He leaped to his feet. "I'm gonna call the pizza delivery place. You want your usual?"

Lillian gave him an exasperated glance, but then she shrugged and smiled at him resignedly. "Yes, please. I'll go whip up a salad. I could die of scurvy unless I have something green pretty soon. With you not here, Devon and I've been living pretty much on Chinese takeout and tinned soup. Lots of monosodium.''

Spence made the phone call, wondering if he'd be able to choke down even a bite of the pizza when it arrived. The sick way his gut felt tonight, he might never be hungry again.

Maybe living here alone wouldn't be that bad, he tried to console himself. At least he wouldn't have to pretend he wanted pizza when he didn't. He wouldn't have to get home for dinner on time. He'd no longer have to concern himself with whether Devon had a ride to wherever she was going. There'd be no one to object when he turned on the sports channel, or to complain when he left the toilet seat up, or borrow his sweatshirts and return them smelling of perfume.

He'd probably adjust to living alone pretty fast.

CHAPTER NINETEEN

JOANNE DRAGGED her suitcase into the hall and locked the door to her apartment. Her tickets were in the jacket of her stylish new silk pants suit, and the taxi was waiting downstairs to take her to the dock. The *Sea Princess* would depart this afternoon for Alaska—for a seven-day cruise along the Inside Passage—and she'd be on it.

She'd always thought going on a cruise alone would be the loneliest thing a person could do, but she'd been wrong. Nothing could be worse than the acute aloneness she'd felt this past while, right here in her own home.

For the first few days after the recovery of the baby, she'd foolishly believed Spence would either call or come to see her at work. When he didn't, she realized once and for all that it was over—and that was when she'd become angry, with him for being a fool but mostly with herself.

She, too, was a fool, sitting around waiting for him like a lovesick teenager, she'd decided.

Then she'd noticed the advertisement on television for the cruise. She'd called immediately and booked an outside cabin.

By some miracle, she was able to trade a block of shifts with one of the other ER physicians, and Portia had come along as adviser on a massive shopping spree to make sure Joanne had exactly the right wardrobe.

To hell with Spencer Mathews. She was going to enjoy herself on this trip or die trying, she thought grimly.

And when she got back, she'd let Philip McCormack know she was available.

Portia's assurances that love would win out in the end were both naive and ridiculous.

BY THE TIME BUD was able to arrange the work schedule so Spence was back on regular shifts at St. Joe's, both Lillian and Devon had moved out. Spence helped both of them get settled, stubbornly refusing their separate invitations to stay for dinner.

Zelaney had kept him informed on what was happening with the abduction case. Natasha Stevens had fired her lawyer and made several impassioned speeches to the press protesting her innocence, but late on the night the baby was recovered, the police located and arrested Agnes Wells. She was buying drugs from a downtown supplier whom the police had under surveillance.

Zelaney told Spence that at first Wells was antagonistic and denied any knowledge of the abduction. But when police made it clear to her they had a record of the phone call between her and Stevens, and that aside from the drug charge she was facing charges of kidnapping, abandoning a child, endangering a child's life and criminal negligence, Agnes crumbled.

The skinny little red-haired woman told Zelaney how she'd met Natasha in the waiting room of a doctor's office; Natasha was there for a pregnancy test. They'd become friends, and after watching a television documentary about abducted babies, Natasha had researched the whole thing and come up with the plan to have Agnes abduct hers.

They'd make a fortune, Natasha had claimed; she'd sell her tragic tale to the tabloids and the publicity would turn her into an instant celebrity. This would result in stints on talk shows and, eventually, acting jobs. They'd split the tabloid money equally. Then, when the press lost interest in the story, Agnes would make an anonymous call to the police and leave the baby where it'd be found immediately. That would generate interest all over again.

They hadn't known anything about the security bands at the hospital, Agnes claimed. When her last baby was born, no such precautions existed; it was pure dumb luck that Natasha's baby hadn't been banded, or Agnes would have been caught right away. As for having Agnes pose as a photographer, they'd gotten the idea from another abduction that had happened in a town in British Columbia five years earlier.

Wells's children were now in the care of Social Services, and she was being held until the case came to trial.

The first day back on shift, Spence found an excuse to visit the ER just before noon.

Joanne had a right to know how the investigation had played out, he assured himself. He pondered what he'd say when he saw her. He'd keep it casual, he resolved. He'd ask how the baby was doing; he'd read in the paper that she was in a foster home and that the people who'd wanted to adopt her were being checked out as possible parents. He'd tell Joanne he wanted to be friends, if that was possible. *Was* it possible?

After a sleepless night of deliberation, he decided to omit that part. He couldn't be around her without wanting to hold her, make love to her. Being "friends" wasn't going to do it. Yet what other option was there? He had to see her; it was like an obsession.

But Joanne wasn't at work, and when Spence buttonholed one of the ER nurses, she told him Dr. Duncan had taken holidays. No, she didn't know when the doctor would be back. And no, neither did she know where the doctor had gone.

Spence tried to convince himself that was probably for the best. But he couldn't explain why he rode the bike miles out of his way just to drive past her apartment building each night to check whether there were lights on.

There weren't, and he couldn't explain the desolation that swept over him each time he looked up at those dark, empty windows.

Truth was, he was in a black mood these days. After the thrill of assisting with the abduction, he found that working as just a security guard at St. Joe's was boring and depressing. Each shift seemed endless, and he realized that Bud was right. He needed a job that challenged him more than this one did.

Being at home wasn't much better than being at work. After a few desperate and interminable evenings spent watching the sports channel, eating TV dinners and trying not to think about Joanne and what she might be doing, Spence began to search for reasons not to go home.

He played handball at the YMCA with anyone who wanted a game, which was great because it left him exhausted—but a man couldn't make a new career out of handball. Besides, he'd developed a nasty temper, cursing when he lost points because his mind wandered, which made it tough to get partners.

Consistently, there were messages on his answering machine from both Lillian and Devon, asking him to come for dinner. Consistently, he ignored them. He could only be polite for a limited amount of time these days, and he was afraid it wouldn't extend through an entire evening.

One night he rode the motorcycle to Squamish and back, taking the twisting curves a lot faster than was absolutely safe, trying to force his mind to ignore the empty space on the seat behind him. He made the trip only once; he might be a little depressed, but he didn't want to end up a statistic.

He found out which movie theaters had early showings and sat through several double features, unable to remember afterward what the plots had even been about, so he quit going.

When he found himself actually considering having a beer after work with Murray Kellerman, Spence realized things had gone way too far.

That was the evening he called Bud, relieved beyond measure when his old friend suggested they have dinner together at Bud's favorite Italian restaurant.

Walking into the familiar old building at six that evening brought back a flood of memories for Spence. It was the place Bud had brought him all during his growing-up years, either to celebrate some triumph or to bust him on his bullshit.

As usual, no matter how early Spence was, Bud was there before him. A bottle of Chianti and a platter of antipasto already sat on the table, and Bud was just finishing a spirited conversation about seafood with the proprietor, who greeted Spence with the familiar strong handshake and the eye-stinging pat on the cheek he'd always bestowed.

A long, serious discussion about the specials on the menu followed. At last, decisions about dinner were completed, and Bud and Spence were left alone.

"I see they caught that woman who took the baby," Bud commented, and for a while they talked about the abduction.

"How's it going at work, Spence?" The waiter came by with hot bread and refilled their wineglasses, and Spence waited until he was gone to respond.

"I need to talk to you about that." He took a deep breath and then said what had become clear to him. "I don't think I can go on much longer being a security guard, Bud."

"Well, hallelujah. I like hearin' you say that, son. I hope this means you're ready to get in on the administrative end of the business and let me retire."

Spence had given that a lot of thought in the past few days, and he'd made up his mind. "If that's still an option, I want to give it a try."

"It sure as hell is," Bud crowed, holding up his wineglass in a toast. "I've been waitin' a long time to have you take over Vector, Spence."

Bud's positive reaction touched Spence deeply.

"Now, if your mother would just—" Bud stopped and abruptly changed the subject. "By the way, how's Joanne? I liked her a lot, Spence. Seemed to me she was pretty fond of you. You feel the same about her?"

Bud never pried into his romantic life. Spence gave him a long, curious look. The waiter came by with their first course, a hearty bean soup, and when he'd left, Spence said, "Mom send you on a fishing trip, Bud?"

Bud rubbed a hand across his jaw and had the grace to appear embarrassed.

"Damn it all, son, she asked me to ask you, and I'm putty in that woman's hands. She figures you and Joanne are a good match, and that you're gonna blow it."

His mother was right. He'd already blown it.

"Just tell her I'm not seeing Joanne anymore." Spence drank half his wine in one gulp. "I'm sure Mom already knows that. What she probably wants to know is why."

Bud didn't say anything. They both spooned up soup for a while, and when the silence grew unbearable, Spence added, "Joanne's a beautiful woman, but I'm not in any position to get involved with her, Bud. And it's not fair to let her think otherwise. I've got too much baggage. She deserves better."

Bud looked him straight in the eye. "There's no man I know better than you, son. You're the best, and don't you ever think different." His tone held utter conviction, and Spence had to fight to keep the mist in his eyes from turning to tears and rolling down his face.

"You in love with Joanne?"

Bud's directness made it hard to lie, and Spence realized he was too emotionally exhausted even to try. He'd been lying to himself for days now— weeks. To tell the truth at last was a relief.

"Yeah, I guess I am." His chest hurt with the admission. "But I'm a bad candidate for any kind of relationship. I screwed up my marriage. There were signs along the way, and I ignored them all. Then I had the accident. I know technically maybe it wasn't all my fault, but some of it was. Regardless of fault, it ended Helen's life, and it changed Devon's forever. I can't help but feel responsible for that."

Bud clicked his tongue. "You've gotta let it go, Spence." He sounded exasperated. "Bad things happen, and they can be an anvil around our necks, weighing us down for the rest of our lives, if we let them."

Spence gave Bud a tortured look. "Easy for you to say. What if I got into this thing with Joanne and it turned out I couldn't be a good husband to her, either? What if it's just not in me? Matter of fact, I don't think it is.''

Bud was shaking his head. ''You've got things ass backward where men and women are concerned, Spence, which is something I know a lot about. If you love this woman and you let her get away, you're making a big mistake, one you'll live to regret.'' He bent his head over his soup, but he wasn't eating any more than Spence was. ''Didn't you ever wonder what happened between your mother and me all those years ago?''

Spence frowned, not sure where the conversation was going. ''Sure I wondered. I asked Mom about it once. I asked you, too, if you remember. Both of you gave me some sort of run around.''

''Didn't want to hurt you, son.'' Bud sighed deeply and pushed his bowl away. ''See, it involved you.''

''Me?'' Spence frowned. ''How so?''

''From the beginning, Lillian wanted us to get married. And I might have if it hadn't been for you. A little boy with big blue eyes, hungry for a daddy—you scared the tar out of me. And Lillian wanted more kids, too. She was clear about that and honest with me from the beginning.''

The waiter retrieved the soup bowls and put down huge plates of pasta with seafood sauce. When the ceremony with the grated cheese and the pepper and refilling the wineglasses was finished and the waiter left, Bud took up the story again.

"I was crazy in love with Lillian back then, same as I am now. But in those days, I had it in my head I didn't want to get married, and I sure as blazes didn't want to father any kids or raise any who thought of me as their daddy."

Spence couldn't control the overwhelming hurt and confusion that Bud's words elicited. *He'd* been the reason his mother and Bud had never married?

Bud guessed how Spence was feeling. "Now, don't for one minute start takin' on guilt about that," he warned, absently forking up some pasta and chewing it before he continued. "Came from the way I grew up. Had nothin' to do with you. No point in going into details except to say there were eleven of us and no money. The man who fathered us was about as bad as they come. I got scars on my back from beatings he gave me because I tried to stop him from hitting my mother. I was convinced I couldn't be anybody's husband, and sure as hell wouldn't be a success as a father. What did I know about any of it but what I'd learned first-hand? And no way on God's green earth was I gonna take a chance that I'd be the same as him."

Bud grew silent again, and Spence waited, every muscle tense. He had the feeling that what Bud was saying was massively important to him, but he wasn't yet sure how.

"Then your mom got pregnant."

Shock rippled through Spence. He'd never guessed, never even suspected.

"And instead of standing by her, I ran." The lines in Bud's face were suddenly deep, the sadness in his eyes old and haunting. "I was gone four months. Took me that long to realize I couldn't live without Lillian." His voice softened. "Or you, either, Spence. It finally penetrated my thick skull that I might just be able to do an okay job of being your daddy. So I came back. And I found out she'd had a miscarriage that nearly killed her."

Memories stirred in Spence, of hay and an attic bedroom. "The summer I was seven. I stayed with my grandparents because Mom was sick."

Bud nodded. "She nearly died. And she wanted nothing more to do with me after that."

Spence thought back on that time, and he couldn't help but recognize how much easier his own growing-up years would have been with Bud as his stepfather.

"I tried to change her mind every way I knew, but she was too hurt. I kept after her and kept after her, and damn if she didn't go and get married to Lamotta—I thought at the time to spite me. Worst moment of my life, when she got married."

"Mine, too." Spence had hated Willis Lamotta from the beginning. Until now he'd never understood why his mother had married the man. Now he could see that she'd been running from Bud and the pain of his desertion.

"So you know the rest of the story," Bud said in a somber tone. "I got married, too, after a while. Wasn't fair to Marlene, and it didn't last. I take full blame for that, also." Bud's normally jovial face was downcast. "Neither your mother nor I have had what you'd call real happy lives, and that's because of me, Spence. Because I made the same mistake you're making—thinking that the past determines the future."

"But you've always been the man I considered my father." Spence's voice was thick, and he had to clear his throat.

"Thanks, son. Goes both ways." Bud's eyes were wet, and he swiped at them with his sauce-stained napkin and tried for a grin that didn't come off. "Life's funny, huh, Spence?"

They made a show of eating their dinner, but neither had much appetite.

The waiter finally took away their plates, and Bud, acting on long habit, ordered coffee and spumoni ice cream for both of them.

"Tomorrow morning you come by the office. I'll get hold of my lawyer and the accountant. We'll hammer out the details of our new partnership," Bud declared.

"Thanks, Bud. For everything." The words didn't begin to cover the gratitude Spence felt, or

the love and admiration that welled up in his heart
for this man who was brave and generous enough
to bare his soul and his wounds in an effort to keep
Spence from missing an opportunity for happiness.

THE INVITATION was on his machine when Spence
got home that night. Devon's voice was tentative.

"Dad, it's Eric's birthday on Saturday. I'm making dinner and his parents are coming. I really wish
you'd come, too." There was sad resignation in her
voice when she added, "I know you won't, but I
really miss you, Dad."

Spence dialed Joanne's number first, but no one
answered. His heart sank as he listened to her voice
on the machine. Closing his eyes so he could picture her face, he tried to think of something to say
to her voice mail, and couldn't. What he needed to
tell her was too complex and important to put on
an answering machine. He hung up finally without
saying anything at all.

Next he called Devon and accepted her invitation
to Eric's birthday party.

CHAPTER TWENTY

DEVON AND ERIC'S apartment was small, and it seemed to be overflowing with bodies when Spence arrived on Thursday evening.

A short plump woman in a tight black dress answered the doorbell and gave him a wide, welcoming smile. "You must be Devon's father. Come on in. I'm Mary Palmer. That's my husband, Edward, over there, and my sons, Rob and David. Eric and Devon are in the kitchen with the door shut. They won't let me in to help. I'll take those if you like—"

Spence handed over the bottles of wine and the clumsily wrapped gift he was holding, just in time to shake hands with Eric's father, a tall burly man with graying fair hair and the shoulders of a line-backer. Spence could easily see what Eric would look like in middle age; he was exactly like his father. Eric's two brothers were more like their mother, short and dark.

Spence had just been introduced to them, when the kitchen door burst open and Devon hurried to greet him, her limp barely discernible tonight.

"Dad I'm so glad you came." Her blue eyes were radiant. "You've met everyone? I asked Grandma and Bud, but they were going to their yoga graduation, can you believe it?" Devon giggled. "It's probably good they couldn't make it. We'd have had to feed people in the hallway."

She was wearing a scarlet dress that he hadn't seen before. It clung to her slender waist and flared around her hips. Spence thought he'd never seen her as beautiful.

"How lovely you are, Dev. That's a pretty dress."

Her smile deepened and her smile grew soft. "Eric got it for me."

Eric came out of the kitchen just then and wheeled over to them, offering his hand and a wide smile. "Glad you could make it, sir—Spence."

"Happy birthday, Eric." Spence gave Eric's hand a firm shake, and he managed a smile that was almost natural.

"Thanks, I'm having a great day. Devon's made certain everything's perfect." He smiled up at her, and the look they exchanged was intimate and filled with affection.

"How about a drink, Spence? We have wine and beer, or scotch if you prefer." Eric was doing a good job of being host.

"A beer sounds great."

Eric brought it promptly in a chilled mug.

"You a football fan?" Edward Palmer drew Spence into the discussion the men were having over wide receivers.

Soon Devon asked everyone to squeeze in around the table. Spence couldn't help but be aware of the warm affection among the Palmers. They joked and teased and laughed as the simple meal progressed, and clearly Devon was already very much a part of the family. Everyone complimented her on the lasagna, and she gave credit to Mary for teaching her how to make it.

Dessert was a rather lopsided chocolate birthday cake covered with candles. Eric declared it perfect, and Devon's pride in her accomplishment was touching for Spence to see.

Eric opened his gifts, an array of thoughtful but inexpensive items—sweatshirts, aftershave, socks.

Spence grew tense when it came time for Eric to open the gift he'd bought him. He'd put a lot of thought and energy into finding it, and he hoped Eric would understand what the gift was intended to convey.

The wrappings fell away to reveal a beautiful wooden chess set, similar to the one Spence's grandfather had left him. Everyone exclaimed, and Eric was obviously delighted.

"Thank you so much, Spence. I'll treasure this, and I'll make good use of it."

"You're very welcome." Spence cleared his

throat, and his voice was gruff. This next part was the tricky bit, because it put control for whatever friendship might be between them squarely with Eric. "I thought maybe we could have a game together sometime."

Eric gave an enthusiastic nod, his smile wide and eager. "How does next Monday night sound?"

It was agreed. For the rest of the evening, Spence joined in the conversation, but part of him was observing, watching the interplay between Devon and Eric, noticing the small, step-saving things Eric did for her: making trips to the kitchen to refill water pitchers, carrying dishes, insisting when the meal was over that he and his brothers would clean up.

There was nothing overt about his concern for her; it was subtle, and Spence doubted that even Devon was consciously aware of it. Everything was done naturally and without fanfare, but it was evident Eric was determined to do anything he could to prevent Devon from getting overtired.

Seeing the beautiful and vivacious young woman his daughter had become, Spence felt as if the shackles he'd imposed upon himself since the accident were falling away. Devon was visibly happy, palpably in love, obviously adored and cherished.

What more could a father want for his child? Aside from preferring that eventually his stubborn daughter would marry Eric instead of just living with him, Spence couldn't think of anything.

Watching them together, Spence suspected that might happen before long.

By ten-thirty the party had ended. It was a warm, dry May evening, and Spence had ridden his motorcycle. The moon was full; the city, quiet.

He was already halfway home when he gave in to the urge to detour past Joanne's building.

A soft light shone in her window. Spence drove past slowly, heart hammering. He knew it was too late to ring her buzzer, but at the end of the street, he changed his mind. Making a looping turn, he came back.

He had to tell Joanne tonight, now, that he loved her. He'd delayed far too long already. He wanted to marry her; he wanted to spend his life with her; and every hour wasted was one less they'd have together.

He pulled the bike up to the curb and sat there a moment, rehearsing what he'd say, worrying over what her response would be. He'd been an idiot. Maybe he'd lost her forever—

A black Lincoln Continental drew up in front of the apartment building, directly under a street lamp. A tall, regal-looking man in a tuxedo climbed out and went around to open the passenger door, and Spence froze when Joanne emerged from the vehicle.

He'd never seen her in evening dress. She seemed to shimmer under the street lamp, feet in high black sandals, hips and waist wrapped in midnight blue, arms and shoulders enfolded in something black and fuzzy. Her shining silver-blond hair was a glimmering halo around her lovely face.

He heard her say something, but he couldn't catch the words. They laughed together, Joanne's head tilted up to look at her partner. The man took her hand in his, and they began to stroll toward the lobby.

Spence's body went icy cold, then a killing rage came over him—a jealousy so profound that it was all he could do not to act on it. He understood in that instant how men could murder for love. He watched, breath coming short, and slowly his rage gave way to a numbing recognition.

He didn't own a tuxedo. He didn't drive a Lincoln. Wherever they'd been tonight wasn't somewhere Spence would likely go. This was the world Joanne deserved; this man was the type she belonged with.

Spence reached blindly for the key in the bike's ignition.

You're gonna give up, just like that? I never figured you for a coward. I thought you said you loved the lady.

It could have been Bud's voice, or maybe it was his own. Spence drew a ragged breath and climbed off the bike.

He had to sprint to catch them before they got

through the outer door and inside the building. Joanne was already reaching for her key in the dainty little satchel she carried.

"Joanne. Joanne, wait up." His commanding voice boomed out. He sounded exactly like Murray Kellerman, and Spence was elated, because it stopped them in their tracks. The man slid an arm protectively around Joanne's shoulders as, surprised, they turned in unison toward Spence.

HER INSIDES began to tremble at the sight of him. What was he doing here, now, at the very moment she'd made up her mind to take the necessary next step with Philip McCormack?

She'd invited him up for coffee. Afterward, she wouldn't resist when he put his arms around her. He was a perfectly sweet man; it wasn't his fault that she felt nothing when he kissed her. He probably wouldn't even know. Women were lucky that way. A bodily response wasn't essential to the procedure.

The hospital fund-raising dinner they'd attended had been the usual combination of too much wine, too many courses and too many dull speeches.

She didn't care. She hadn't even been bored, because somewhere in the past few weeks, Joanne had perfected the ability to split off—to smile and respond to what was happening around her while in her mind she was somewhere else.

That somewhere was the back of a sleek black two-wheeled machine with wings of chrome, swooping, dipping, soaring along a road high above the ocean.

"What are you doing here, Spence?" Her voice trembled along with the rest of her. She'd longed for this man, been furious with him, wept with frustration because of him. She'd spent a ridiculous amount of money to be a prisoner on a cruise ship for seven endless days and nights, just because of him. And now she absolutely wasn't about to let him see the devastating effect he had on her.

"Do you know this person, Joanne?" Philip sounded aggressive.

"Yes, I know him." Deliberately, she moved closer to Philip, fiendishly pleased when his arm tightened around her and Spence's expression indicated that he'd noticed.

"I need to talk to you, Joanne. I need a second chance." Spence's voice was as tense as Philip's arm.

"This isn't the time or place." Now Philip's voice was authoritative. He reached for the key in Joanne's hand.

She resisted. This was her party.

Philip bristled. Spence hesitated.

Joanne waited.

Spence's blue eyes were intent on her face, his voice husky, each word distinct. "I've been such a bloody fool, Joanne. Please forgive me.'' There was agony in his tone. "I love you. I don't think I can live the rest of my life without you.'' He drew a deep breath, then said in ringing tones, "Will you marry me?''

She let him suffer, but only for one long moment. "Yes,'' she said. "Yes, yes, I will. Yes.''

And she walked away from Philip, into the waiting circle of Spence's arms.

EPILOGUE

Spencer, Joanne, say hello to your new son. He's got fine lungs, this wee boy.''

Dr. Morgan Jacobsen's chocolate-brown eyes were jubilant over the top of her mask. She held the squalling newborn up for his mother and father to admire before she handed him to the neonatalogist, who whisked the baby off to a separate area of the delivery room to thoroughly check him over.

Morgan turned back to Joanne. ''Rest while you can, mother. Your second little angel will likely be here within minutes.'' She patted Joanne's thigh.

''You're a superstar, Doctor. You're waltzing through this delivery as if you'd done it a dozen times before.''

Joanne didn't feel as though she was waltzing. The labor hurt worse than anything she'd ever experienced, ever imagined, and the pain utterly enraged her. How could she have assisted so many times at delivery and never fully appreciated how terrible it felt?

''He's perfect. He's beautiful. Joanne, I love you, darlin'. I love you so much.''

Spence's words pushed away her anger for a moment, but then she remembered that she was only half done. She scowled up at him, needing to tell him that this was it; these babies were the only ones she'd ever agree to have; she'd never get pregnant again; labor hurt way too much and delivery was agony. But at that moment the next contraction hit full force.

"Here we go, Joanne," Morgan said. "Push, sweetheart. There we go. Baby's crowning. What a mop of dark hair. See it in the mirror?"

Joanne didn't give a hoot about the stupid mirror. An eruption was going on inside her. She was splitting in pieces. She was—

"Stop now. Don't push. Pant, pant. That's perfect." Morgan's calm voice seemed to come from a long distance away. Joanne panted frantically, cursed silently.

"Next contraction, we're gonna have us a baby," Morgan promised.

Us? What us? *She* was the one in agony here. Where did Jacobsen get off with this *us* crap?

"Hang in there, beautiful lady. You're almost done." Spence wiped Joanne's forehead with a cool cloth and it felt heavenly, but then the pain came again, monstrous and blinding. She pushed with all her strength, all her will, all her reserves, all her anger…and felt the second baby slide like a sea creature out of her body.

And like a miracle the pain was gone. Awe and joy replaced Joanne's bad temper.

"It's a girl. It's a gorgeous wee girl. You've got a boy and a girl, Mr. and Mrs. Mathews. Congratulations."

Joanne began to laugh and weep at the same time, as Morgan held up her daughter. The infant was red, wrinkled, blood-smeared and indescribably beautiful. A nurse carried her away to join her brother and to be checked head to toe.

"I won the bet. You owe me ten bucks," Morgan called gleefully to the anesthesiologist, as she delivered the afterbirth. "I told you we wouldn't need you horning in on this production. I told you this lady could deliver twins vaginally."

Because of Joanne's age and because the birth was a multiple, Morgan had lined up the troops in case a C-section became necessary. Joanne, though, had insisted on a vaginal delivery, and Morgan had fully supported her decision.

"Both perfect specimens. Nine on the Apgar. Lungs like opera singers." The beaming neonatalogist held the babies, one tucked under each arm. He handed them over to Joanne and Spence.

They wore knitted toques, one pink, the other blue. Joanne was holding her squirming son. One small foot had already escaped from the flannel blanket that swaddled him. She counted the small toes and then fingered the blue security band firmly attached to a minuscule ankle. A torrent of memories assailed her.

Almost three years had passed since the abduction, but for Joanne the memory of that fateful morning in the ER was suddenly as fresh as yesterday. She heard Natasha's cries of pain, and she remembered how that other little girl had squirmed that morning, wet and wailing in her arms.

She looked up at Spence. His eyes lingered on the security band, and when they met hers she could tell that he, too, was remembering.

"Such great things came of a bad beginning," he murmured now, as he had so often since their marriage.

The baby girl born that long-ago morning was now Christine Marie, the adored adopted daughter of Dirk and Betsy Halstead. Natasha Stevens and Agnes Wells were each serving time for their roles in the abduction.

"We're done here, Joanne. Let's get you and these squirts up to your room so you can get some rest."

Joanne was both exhausted and exhilarated. She couldn't wait to show the babies off to Lillian and Bud, Dev and Eric. And she knew that at this very moment the hospital grapevine was undoubtedly spreading the word throughout the ER that Doc Duncan had popped her twins. The next few hours were likely to be anything but restful as her friends and colleagues made visits to her room.

"Devon and Eric want to practice on our two so they're experts when their own baby arrives," she told Morgan.

The past three years had been eventful. Devon and Eric were married just six months after Spence and her; and three days after that wedding, Lillian and Bud surprised everyone when they flew off to Hawaii and got married quietly on the beach in Honolulu.

Joanne and Devon had become pregnant within two months of each other. Joanne had eavesdropped on hilarious conversations between Spence and Eric as they played chess each Monday and conferred earnestly on the most effective remedies for morning sickness and heartburn.

"Devon's doing just great. It's Eric I'm worried about." Morgan giggled. "He came close to passing out when we did ultrasound. I'm gonna have to have smelling salts ready for him in the delivery room."

Joanne snuggled under the heated flannel blanket the nurse had wrapped around her. She was being wheeled along familiar corridors to the maternity ward, her babies close behind her, all of them under Spence's watchful eye.

He saw her looking up at him and winked, catching her hand and holding on, fingers laced through hers.

"We'll have to trade in the motorcycle for a utility van." He should have looked regretful, but he was smiling as though he'd just won the lottery.

"Do that and I swear I'll buy us season tickets to the symphony," she threatened.

"You fight dirty, Mrs. Mathews. Okay, we'll keep the bike."

"Absolutely." She thought of sunshine, of winding roads beside the ocean, of French fries and wild lovemaking in green hidden glades on trails too narrow for anything but a motorcycle.

It might be a while before they rode again, but the day would come. The trails and the bike would be there when she and Spence were ready. They had time; they had a lifetime of days to live to the fullest.

The stretcher stopped for a moment as the aides checked in at the nursing station, and Spence bent over and pressed a lingering kiss on Joanne's lips. He whispered ruefully close to her ear, "I'm glad we've got a son and a daughter, darlin', because I could never put you through that again. So much pain—it was awful."

She was drowsy, and staying awake was getting harder and harder. "It wasn't that bad," she murmured. "I was thinking…maybe a little brother or sister for them…would be nice. In a year or so. I always…wanted a big family, Spence…''

With a smile on her lips and his hand holding hers, she slipped into sleep, and dreamed of tomorrows rich with possibility and promise.

HARLEQUIN *Super* ROMANCE®

A LITTLE SECRET

*One day you're single, no kids—
the next, you're a father of a child
you never knew you had.*

HIS DADDY'S EYES by *Debra Salonen*

(Superromance #934)

The little boy's eyes were a deep shade of blue, the same
shade as the pair that stared back at Lawrence Bishop from
the mirror every morning. Could the child really be his? To
find out, Lawrence has to confront the child's aunt—and what
he learns will change his life forever.

On sale August 2000

Available wherever Harlequin books are sold.

HARLEQUIN®
*M*akes any time special ™

Visit us at www.eHarlequin.com

HSRALS

If you enjoyed what you just read,
then we've got an offer you can't resist!

Take 2 bestselling
love stories FREE!

Plus get a FREE surprise gift!

Clip this page and mail it to Harlequin Reader Service®

IN U.S.A.	IN CANADA
3010 Walden Ave.	P.O. Box 609
P.O. Box 1867	Fort Erie, Ontario
Buffalo, N.Y. 14240-1867	L2A 5X3

YES! Please send me 2 free Harlequin Superromance® novels and my free surprise gift. Then send me 6 brand-new novels every month, which I will receive before they're available in stores. In the U.S.A., bill me at the bargain price of $3.80 plus 25¢ delivery per book and applicable sales tax, if any*. In Canada, bill me at the bargain price of $4.21 plus 25¢ delivery per book and applicable taxes**. That's the complete price, and a saving of at least 10% off the cover prices—what a great deal! I understand that accepting the 2 free books and gift places me under no obligation ever to buy any books. I can always return a shipment and cancel at any time. Even if I never buy another book from Harlequin, the 2 free books and gift are mine to keep forever. So why not take us up on our invitation. You'll be glad you did!

135 HEN C22S
336 HEN C22T

Name	(PLEASE PRINT)	
Address	Apt.#	
City	State/Prov.	Zip/Postal Code

  * Terms and prices subject to change without notice. Sales tax applicable in N.Y.
 ** Canadian residents will be charged applicable provincial taxes and GST.
    All orders subject to approval. Offer limited to one per household.
    ® is a registered trademark of Harlequin Enterprises Limited.

SUP00   ©1998 Harlequin Enterprises Limited

In her acclaimed series *Love Letters*, award-winning author LISA JACKSON sweeps you away with three dramatic tales of the men and women who learn the ABC's of love.

Love Letters by

LISA JACKSON

Family Affairs...

The manipulative patriarch of the McKee family has mysteriously died, but he left behind letters to his children to set right some of his misdeeds—particularly where they concern matters of the heart....

Don't miss **LOVE LETTERS**
On sale August 2000 at your favorite retail outlet.

Silhouette®
Where love comes alive™

Visit Silhouette at www.eHarlequin.com

PSBR3LL

HARLEQUIN
SUPERROMANCE®

You are now entering

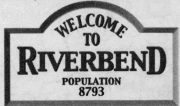

WELCOME TO RIVERBEND

POPULATION
8793

Riverbend...the kind of place where everyone knows
your name—and your business. Riverbend...home of
the River Rats—a group of small-town sons and
daughters who've been friends since high school.

The Rats are all grown up now. Living their lives and
learning that some days are good and some days
aren't—and that you can get through anything
as long as you have your friends.

Starting in July 2000, Harlequin Superromance brings
you Riverbend—six books about the River Rats and
the Midwest town they live in.

BIRTHRIGHT by Judith Arnold (July 2000)
THAT SUMMER THING by Pamela Bauer (August 2000)
HOMECOMING by Laura Abbot (September 2000)
LAST-MINUTE MARRIAGE by Marisa Carroll (October 2000)
A CHRISTMAS LEGACY by Kathryn Shay (November 2000)

Available wherever Harlequin books are sold.

HARLEQUIN®
Makes any time special ™

Visit us at www.eHarlequin.com   HSRIVER

Romance is just one click away!

love scopes

➤ Find out all about your guy in the Men of the Zodiac area.

➤ Get your daily horoscope.

➤ Take a look at our Passionscopes, Lovescopes, Birthday Scopes and more!

join Heart-to-Heart,
our interactive community

➤ Talk with Harlequin authors!

➤ Meet other readers and chat with other members.

➤ Join the discussion forums and post messages on our message boards.

romantic ideas

➤ Get scrumptious meal ideas in the Romantic Recipes area!

➤ Check out the Daily Love Dose to get romantic ideas and suggestions.

Visit us online at

www.eHarlequin.com

on Women.com Networks

HEUT2

#930 THAT SUMMER THING • Pamela Bauer
Riverbend

Charlie Callahan is the original good-time Charlie. At least, that's what everyone thinks, especially Beth Pennington. After all, she was once briefly—disastrously—married to him. And now she's sharing an inheritance with Charlie! Isn't it ironic?

Riverbend, Indiana: Home of the River Rats—small-town sons and daughters who've been friends since high school. These are their stories.

#931 P.S. LOVE YOU MADLY • Bethany Campbell

Darcy's mother and Sloan's father are in love. But Darcy's sister is aghast and Sloan's aunt is appalled. And that leaves the two of them trying to make everyone see sense. No problem, right? But then their parents break up just when *they're* falling in love.... Compared to what these two go through, Romeo and Juliet had it easy.

Guaranteed to be one of the funniest romances you'll read this year!

#932 CATHRYN • Shannon Waverly
Circle of Friends

Cathryn McGrath of Harmony, Massachusetts, is the ideal wife and mother—her children are happy, her house is beautiful, her marriage is perfect. Except it's not.... Her husband is having an affair with another woman! Then Cathryn's marriage irrevocably ends, and she resumes her friendship with Tucker Lang—former bad boy of Harmony, who shows her that there's life after betrayal, love after divorce.

#933 HITCHED! • Ruth Jean Dale
The Taggarts of Texas

Rand Taggart may have been swindled out of a fortune by his old college roommate, but he can inherit a *second* fortune—provided he's happily married by his thirtieth birthday. In order to save her sister's name, Maxi Rafferty is going to help him out—and complicate her life and Rand's with this seemingly straightforward marriage of convenience!

#934 HIS DADDY'S EYES • Debra Salonen
A Little Secret

There's one thing in Judge Lawrence Bishop's past that could come back to haunt him. Two years ago he spent a weekend in the arms of a sexy stranger. Then Lawrence learns the woman is dead—but her fifteen-month-old son is living with her sister, Sara Carsten. Lawrence does the math and pays Sara a visit. What he tells her—and what he sees with his own eyes—rocks both their worlds.

#935 DEEP IN THE HEART OF TEXAS • Linda Warren

Heiress Miranda Maddox has been kidnapped and held prisoner. Jacob Culver, a fugitive and the man known as "the hermit," rescues her, and against his own inclinations, agrees to guide her back to her home. In the process, Miranda discovers that someone in her family ordered her kidnapping—and she learns to trust Jake. She also learns that sometimes trust leads to love....

SOUTH CAROLINA LIBRARY

L.C.C. SOUTH CAMPUS LIBRARY

Some of the postures contained in this publication should only be attempted under the supervision of an experienced yoga practitioner. If in doubt, please contact your doctor or local yoga center.

Copyright © Jessie Chapman 2002. This book is copyright.
Apart from any fair dealing for the purposes of private study, research,
criticism or review, as permitted under the Copyright Act, no part may
be reproduced by any process without written permission.
Inquiries should be addressed to the publishers.

Published by:
Ulysses Press
P.O. Box 3440
Berkeley CA 94703
www.ulyssespress.com

Library of Congress Control Number 2002101120
ISBN 1-56975-314-8

First published by HarperCollins Publishers, Sydney, Australia, in 1999.
This edition published by arrangement with HarperCollins Publishers Pty Ltd.

Printed in Canada by Transcontinental Printing

1 3 5 7 9 10 8 6 4 2

Cover: Rachel Hull in *Eka Pada Rajakapotasana*
Cover photograph by Jessie Chapman
All internal photographs by Dhyan

Yoga models: Aloka, Jessie Chapman, Ronit Robbaz Franco,
Rachel Hull, Mathew James, Louisa Sear, and Peter Watkins

RA
781.7
·C467
2002

DEC 2 1 2004

JESSIE CHAPMAN

photographs by
DHYAN

Postures, sequences and meditations

Ulysses Press

YOGA

IN FOCUS

Contents

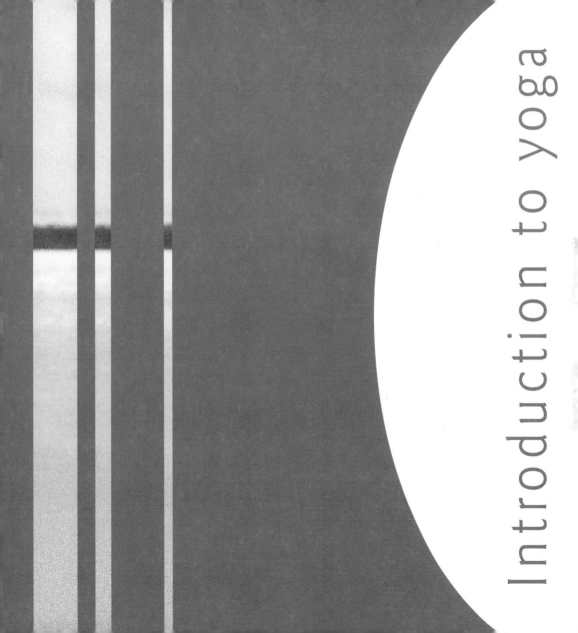

Introduction to yoga

What is yoga?

The word yoga symbolizes the union of oneself with all that is.

Through the practice of yoga we experience increased self-awareness and feelings of centeredness, clarity and balance in our everyday lives. We are more able to make important choices necessary in realizing our potential. Yoga is an internal practice that is unique to each individual. Whether you first come to it through the postures, the philosophy or through meditation, you will be enriched with personal insights and revelations.

Yoga aims to balance all the aspects of the self: physical, emotional, mental and spiritual and to bring out the best in each individual. It offers us a way to live a healthy and harmonious life. The mental and physical disciplines taught in yoga are tools for overcoming the limitations we place on ourselves, such as unhealthy lifestyle habits and mental or physical imbalances.

Yoga is a spiritual practice. It teaches us to journey within, to get to know ourselves and, ultimately, to live in harmony with our soul and the "universal soul" or "god."

Yoga through the ages

Yoga has been practiced and passed on for thousands of years. Originating in India, the first references to yoga, its philosophy and its many postures were discovered in some of the oldest written manuscripts ever found.

In ancient India scriptures were written in Sanskrit, a sacred language spoken and understood only by the educated and privileged few. For hundreds of years yoga remained inaccessible to the masses because of this language barrier. However, as interest in yoga grew, its philosophy became more refined and more widely understood.

A lot of what is known of yoga today is due to the collected works and translations of Patanjali—an Indian sage and yogi from around 300 BC. Patanjali wrote what are known as the *yoga sutras*. These *sutras* are short teachings offering wisdom and insights into yoga philosophy. They were easily grasped and passed down by word of mouth by those yoga students who could not read or write.

With the dedicated study and practice of yoga teachers and practitioners throughout India, yoga soon spread to other parts of the world. Today there are many styles of yoga available, each with its own emphasis. However, the teachings and the essence of yoga remain the same throughout time.

The eightfold path

In the *yoga sutras* Patanjali set down the eightfold path to the strengthening and evolution of the body, mind and soul. This eightfold path is made up of mental and physical disciplines.

Patanjali referred to each discipline as a "limb." Each limb develops with practice and is connected to the seven other limbs. The eightfold path is not a step-by-step manual to enlightenment—different aspects of the path may unfold at different stages in our lives.

The eightfold path helped illuminate the philosophy behind yoga, making yoga more accessible to the spiritual seeker.

The eight limbs of yoga

1.) YAMA

These are five universal ethics that act as a guide for us to live in harmony with one another in a shared and peaceful world.

Ahimsa—non-violence, physical or otherwise

Satya—truthfulness to oneself and to others

Asteya—non-stealing

Brahmacharya—chastity. This does not necessarily refer to celibacy, rather to the containing and harnessing of one's sexual energy for other purposes.

Aparigraha—non-hoarding or avoiding over-consumption

2.) NIYAMA

These are five personal disciplines that relate to the body and mind. As you practice yoga, you will naturally begin to tune into these disciplines.

Saucha—purity and cleanliness. This can refer to the body, mind and environment.

Santosa—contentment. With contentment comes happiness in the moment, rather than looking to the past or future.

Tapas—devotion and dedication. This could refer to a teacher, spiritual path, or any topic of interest. *Tapas* encourages inspiration and personal growth.

Svadhyana—study, observation and awareness of the self

Isvara Pranidhana—devotion to "god" or the "universal one"

3. ASANA

These are the physical postures that aim to develop a healthy body and mind. Yoga *asanas* stretch and strengthen the body and release unwanted toxins. As the body grows stronger, so does your mind and willpower, preparing you for sitting quietly in meditation.

4. PRANAYAMA

These are the techniques for correct breathing. Through increasing our intake of *prana*, or life force, and learning to breathe fully, our energy levels increase and our life is enriched.

5.) PRATYAHARA

This is the withdrawal from the search for constant stimulation and satisfaction in the world, turning the focus inward to experience happiness from within.

6.) DHARANA

This is the practice of concentration that leads to calming the mind. Entering into a quiet, meditative space becomes more effortless and more desirable.

7.) DHYANA

Dhyana is meditation. Through this practice we experience the mind emptying itself of thoughts and desires and the whole being benefits from this "time out."

8.) SAMADHI

This is the experience known as "enlightenment," where you live completely in the moment, in union with all around you. It is the ultimate goal of yoga practice.

Asana

Asana means posture. It is the third limb on the eightfold path with the aim of developing a healthy body and mind to live a full and balanced life. The body is stretched and loosened, strengthened and cleansed.

The *asanas* were designed to help individuals maintain a healthy body and to prepare it for breathing exercises and sitting quietly in meditation. After a session of postures, the body is more flexible and the mind is clear and quiet. Slipping into a meditative space comes more naturally.

Yoga *asana* classes are popular all around the world. Many people choose yoga over other forms of physical exercise because of the calming and clarifying effect it also has on the mind. Not only do the postures help tone and cleanse all the systems of the body, but your sense of mental and emotional well-being greatly improves. You begin to feel your quality of life improving on all levels.

This book is a guide to inspire the beginner to yoga practice. It presents a broad range of classic yoga postures developed by experienced yoga teachers that are safe and effective for beginners. The more advanced postures, which have no practical instructions, are purely inspirational and are not meant to be practiced from this book.

As a general guide, start with standing postures to warm up and strengthen the body. Continue with sitting and twisting postures to stretch the body more deeply. Then use a backbend, counterbalanced with a forward stretch. Wind down the practice with an inverted posture and some quiet sitting and breathing. Always end the session with a version of *Savasana*, or another relaxation posture.

Getting to know the postures

Your energy levels vary from one day to the next and so may your enthusiasm for particular postures! Some days you might feel tired and emotional; other days on top of the world with abundant energy to spare.

Your body may go through many changes as you encourage it to open and strengthen in places you may never have been in touch with before. You will soon discover the areas of your body that are strong or weak, soft or tight. Do not strain or force your body into a posture. Let your body be in the pose and soften with the breath; your muscles will slowly become more supple.

Get to know the postures. With regular practice, the body becomes stronger and more flexible and the joints loosen. You may start out by trying only a couple of postures a day, building up your practice over time. As your awareness of the postures grows, so will your body's natural ability to perform them.

This is yoga, the body and mind working in unison.

Yoga through the day

Traditionally, yoga is practiced before or at sunrise when the atmosphere is still and the mind is peaceful. However, yoga can be practiced at any time of the day. Experiment with your yoga and get to know your body and how it changes throughout the day.

Yoga practiced in the morning gives you lots of energy to enjoy all the day has to offer. Your body may be quite stiff after sleeping all night, so warming up slowly is important. The greeting the day sequence (page 138) warms up the body quickly and is a good way to begin any practice.

Practicing yoga in the afternoon is a different experience altogether. Your body is already warmed up and you may find you have a lot less resistance to a posture you found difficult in the morning. Choose postures that will help you achieve a specific effect. Relaxation postures can help you wind down at the end of a day and calm a busy mind, or more dynamic postures can help restore much needed vitality and energy.

Evening yoga is a beautiful way to complete the day. Simply sitting quietly and concentrating on deep, full breathing is a perfect way to prepare the mind and body for a restful sleep.

Sacred space

It is best to practice yoga in a clean, quiet, dry environment free from the distractions of telephones, people and loud noises. However, if you have to make a choice between practicing with your children at home or not practicing at all, then of course, go ahead and practice. The kids might even get inspired to join in!

To create a sacred space for yoga if you are not part of a class you just need a little imagination. Try setting up a spare room as an inner sanctuary. Alternatively, just lighting a candle on your bedroom floor is enough to create a peaceful atmosphere. You can practice in a completely empty space, symbolic of an empty, open mind, or you can make the space special with flowers, peaceful pictures and essential oils or incense.

Varying your practice environment can also be exciting. Practicing out in the fresh air is a good way to connect with nature. Find a beautiful setting that is tranquil and clean. An early morning stretch on the beach followed by a quick dip is great, as is a peaceful spot among birds in a garden.

Clothing and equipment

The beauty of yoga is that the only equipment you need is the ground you stand on—and it's free! However, as the ground is sometimes cold or uneven, it is preferable to use a rug or mat on a flat surface. Thin rubber yoga mats are helpful so you don't slip around, and they are a neat package if you are traveling and want to be sure you have your yoga "space" wherever you go.

Yoga is usually best practiced barefoot and it is preferable to wear natural fibers that allow the skin to breathe. So wear loose, comfortable clothes that don't constrict your circulation. The body cools down in relaxation and you want to be sure you don't feel cold while you are lying down. Have a long-sleeved top, a blanket and maybe some socks handy to put on when you begin relaxation. An eye bag is also good for relaxation because it not only blocks out the light but its weight calms the nerves and muscles around the eyelids for deeper relaxation.

The other props you may need can be adapted from household items. Blocks are helpful for the standing postures. If you can't reach the floor you can place a hand on a block, or a pile of books. Straps, or a piece of strong fabric, are helpful in forward bends if you can't reach your toes. A bolster or cushion to lie over and open up the chest is good. Blankets are also useful for many sitting postures.

Commonsense rules

If you're physically or mentally exhausted, do some soft, passive poses that relax the body and rejuvenate the mind rather than tiring yourself out even more by practicing dynamic standing postures.

Avoid practicing stimulating postures late at night as you may find yourself so energized you can't sleep properly.

Don't practice yoga on a full stomach. Leave time after eating and drinking before practicing. An empty stomach makes for a lighter practice.

Precautions

Yoga postures have numerous benefits for the body and mind, but care should be taken when practicing them. Remember that nobody knows your body better than you do, so become aware of what does and doesn't feel right. Don't push or strain yourself into a posture. If you are experiencing pain, slowly release out of the posture as you exhale.

If you know or suspect you have a medical problem, be sure to seek medical advice before practicing yoga. Tell your yoga teacher about any physical problems you may be experiencing, no matter how small they may seem. An experienced teacher will be able to guide you into postures that suit your individual needs.

If you are pregnant and have never done yoga before, do not attempt any postures without first consulting your teacher. Many postures may be dangerous for the baby, but your teacher can give you safe variations. See the pregnancy sequence on page 152.

Most women experience lower energy levels when menstruating. Stick to very passive postures that keep the body cool and don't tire you out. Do not do any inverted postures. The menstruation sequence on page 146 offers relief from menstrual pain and is beneficial throughout the menstrual period.

Breathing

The importance of breathing

Learning to breathe correctly is the best health insurance you can invest in. With the world running at a faster pace than ever before, stress and anxiety are becoming the main cause of modern-day illnesses. Stress causes the chest to tighten and the breath to shorten. The systems of the body soon begin to run inefficiently.

When you breathe slowly and correctly, the muscles relax. The heart and lungs expand and the circulation of oxygenated blood throughout the body increases. When you are feeling inspired (which literally means "to breathe in") and full of life, you can be sure that your body is receiving plenty of oxygen, particularly to the brain.

The philosophy of yoga holds that the air we breathe is full of *prana*, or life force. *Prana* is the energy that links the body with the soul, and unites our body and mind with our higher self. This *prana* gives us vitality to live a healthy and energy-filled life. Living life to our fullest potential goes hand in hand with correct breathing.

Breathing and meditation

The breath can be a focal point for meditation. When you are in a posture, observe the inhalation and exhalation of your breath. Whenever you find your thoughts wandering, return your awareness and concentration to your breath.

The mind empties of thoughts and relaxes.

After a meditative yoga practice, you will feel completely refreshed. Usually you will find any problems you were carrying before you started your practice have become more manageable. With a clear mind comes a new perspective on life.

The breath as a tool

Learn to use your breath as a tool. Developing slow, deep, rhythmic breathing allows you to move in and out of postures with ease and awareness.

When you are in a posture, use your breath to release and open tight muscles. Take your awareness to the muscles in the body that are tight or in spasm. Once you have isolated the area, take your breath there. Concentrate on letting go and softening with the exhalation. Feel the tightness melting away.

Deep, full breathing

Breathing correctly makes all the difference to our mental and emotional states. Natural breathing is slow, deep and full and indicates a relaxed state of mind. Short, tight breathing indicates a stressed and anxious body and mind.

Correct breathing is unforced, and the lungs receive maximum air. Pure, oxygenated blood circulates through the body, keeping it healthy and free of disease.

Learning to breathe correctly may require some commitment and focus but, with practice, it will become second nature. Since air is our "food" for life, the better we breathe, the richer our life will be.

To breathe fully, first breathe in through the nose and direct the air into your abdomen. Feel your stomach expand. Then draw the air up into the lungs. The rib cage slowly expands sideways as air fills the lungs. When breathing out (through the nose), first relax your chest slightly, then your abdomen. This expels all the air from the lungs. Keep the inhalation and exhalation smooth and of equal depths.

Practice breathing correctly whenever you remember, throughout the day. With practice, natural healthy breathing will occur without you needing to focus on it consciously.

Breathing well affects your whole life. If your breathing is full and relaxed, so your life will be. Your body will function more effectively and be less prone to stress and disease. Your mind will be clearer and more focused. Your energy levels will increase, as will your inspiration and vitality.

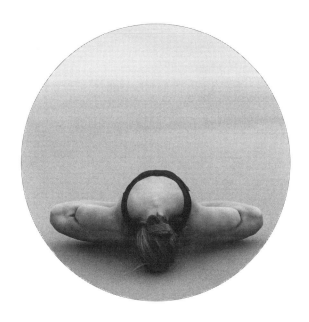

Sitting with the breath

The ancient Indian yogis believed that each individual is born with a certain number of breaths to live. They taught that the way we breathe is of vital importance to our quality and quantity of life. To slow down the breath is, in this sense, extending our lifetime. Sitting and observing the breath and increasing its length takes focus and practice. The amount of energy you have will increase dramatically, as will your vitality and enjoyment in life.

Sit in a comfortable position with your spine straight. A straight back balances the spine and allows oxygenated blood to flow easily through your body. Let your shoulders relax: down and back to open your chest, heart and lungs. Rest the backs of the hands on your knees. Relax your facial muscles as well as your head, neck and shoulders. Keeping still while you are sitting requires discipline and practice. Use the wall for support if you need to but make sure you keep your spine erect. To draw your attention inward and away from external distractions, close your eyes and focus on the inhalation and exhalation.

Postures in practice

Standing postures produce many physical benefits. They strengthen the body and increase flexibility. The postures flex and strengthen muscles and tendons in the legs, help to develop a supple back, and tone the spinal cord and the whole nervous system. They massage and cleanse the internal organs, and improve breathing too.

As you practice these postures, you will begin to stand, walk and sit with more awareness. You will feel as though you have grown inches taller.

Remember to check with a medical practitioner first if you suffer from any medical problems. Don't try standing postures if you suffer from high blood pressure, heart problems or nervous disorders, or if you are in the first three months of pregnancy or in the first three days of menstruation. Take extra care if you have knee or back problems.

You can avoid potential problems by becoming more aware of your body and its response to certain movements. If a posture causes pain, slowly release out of it with your breath.

Tadasana

TADA—MOUNTAIN

Positioning: Stand with your feet together with the heels and toes touching. Bring your awareness to the soles of your feet and distribute your body weight evenly between the right and left side, back and front. Lift your calves, kneecaps and thighs up toward your hips, activating the muscles in your legs. Activate and tuck your buttocks under. Draw your abdomen in slightly. Feel your spine extending up out of your hips, and relax your shoulders down and back to open up your chest, heart and lungs. Activate your arms and extend out through your hands and fingers.

Breathing: Inhale and exhale using deep, slow breaths to expand your chest fully.

Focus: Keep the point of balance between the body and mind being relaxed as well as activated, and focus your eyes softly and directly ahead at eye level.

Hold: For ten breaths or as long as it is comfortable.

Benefits: As the vertebrae separate, the spine elongates and the spinal muscles are strengthened. This is an especially beneficial *asana* for anyone with bad posture as it aligns the skeleton correctly.

The whole body is filled with energy and awareness. Mind and body unite to align and center the body's weight. Standing straight and tall, the whole body is revitalized.

Vrksasana

VRKSA—TREE

Positioning: Stand in *Tadasana*. Bend your right leg and place the foot into your left thigh so it feels locked in. Move your right knee back to open up your hip. Keep your left leg muscles activated and lifting. Center your body weight so you don't slant over onto your standing leg. Have your hands in prayer position in front of your heart. Drop your shoulders and roll them back. Open your chest and relax your facial muscles.

Breathing: Breathing should be deep and full, lifting and opening your rib cage up and out to the sides as you inhale.

Focus: Have your eyes gaze at a point directly in front of you, and breathe softly and evenly through your nose.

Hold: For ten breaths. Exhale to release your right leg down and repeat the posture on the other side.

Variation: Place one hand on a wall for support to maintain your balance.

Benefits: This posture teaches balance and strengthens and stretches the leg and feet muscles. It also soothes the mind and nervous system and develops concentration.

It is a great feeling to find your balance and maintain it. Once you find your balance, enter into a quiet, empty mind space free of thoughts.

Trikonasana

TRIKONA—TRIANGLE

Positioning: From *Tadasana* place your feet about four feet apart. Turn your left foot in 15 degrees and your right foot out to a 90-degree angle. Spread your toes and the base of your feet and activate your leg muscles, lifting them upward. Extend your arms out at shoulder height. Inhale and stretch and lengthen the right arm and side of your torso over to the right, then exhale as you place your hand onto your right foot, or wherever it reaches along your leg. Extend your left arm up and tuck your chin in as you turn your head to face your left hand. Extend your arms away from each other, forming one straight line.

Breathing: Use your breath as a tool to extend and turn your left hip backwards. Inhale and exhale fully, feeling your whole body come alive.

Focus: Let your eyes focus beyond your left fingertips, slowing down your breath. Keep your body aligned and balanced.

Hold: For five breaths. Inhale to come up and out of the posture. Repeat on the other side.

Variations: Practice the posture with your back up against a wall, moving your left hip, back and shoulders toward the wall for maximum opening. If your neck becomes sore, turn your head to look down at your right foot.

Benefits: This posture stimulates and massages the nervous system, internal organs, digestive system and muscles of the spine. It also relieves tightness in the lower back and tones the lateral muscles of the torso.

The body learns coordination as it extends sideways to form a triangular shape. The whole body opens out and the muscles of the legs and torso are toned.

Parsvakonasana

PARSVA—SIDEWAYS; KONA—ANGLE

Positioning: From *Tadasana* place your feet about four feet apart. Turn your right foot out 90 degrees and your left foot in 15 degrees. Inhale and lift out from your waist, extending your arms away from each other. Exhale as you bend your right knee into a right angle, and place your right hand on the floor on the outside of your right foot. Inhale and extend your left arm over your head, keeping your buttocks activated and your leg muscles strong. Tuck in your chin and look back toward your left hand. Extend the whole left side of your body into one straight line and stretch out from your toes through your fingertips.

Breathing: Inhale and exhale deep, full breaths.

Focus: Keep your eye gaze beyond your left fingertips. Focus on the left side of your torso turning and opening upwards, keeping both arms activated and slowing down your breathing.

Hold: For five breaths. Inhale out of the *asana* and repeat on the other side.

Variations: Place your right hand on a block if you can't reach the floor. Turn to look down at the right foot if your neck becomes sore.

Benefits: This posture stimulates the nervous system and internal organs, tones and cleanses the spinal muscles, and strengthens the legs and the muscles around the knee joint.

Precaution: Be careful if you have weak knee joints.

At first, there seems a lot for the body to coordinate in this posture. But with practice, your muscles will build up cellular memory to "remember" how it's done.

Virabhadrasana I

VIRA—WARRIOR FROM INDIAN MYTHOLOGY

Positioning: From *Tadasana* place your feet about four feet apart. Turn your right foot out 90 degrees and your left foot in 45 degrees. Inhale and lift out of your waist, extending your arms upward. Turn your hips and body to the right so you are now facing the same direction as your right foot. Exhale and bend your right knee into a right angle, keeping both legs activated. Rotate your left hip forward so it is parallel to your right hip. Bring your palms together above your head and focus on your spine extending out of your hips. Look up to your hands. Feel your chest expanding with deep, full breaths. Relax your shoulders.

Breathing: Take deep, full breaths, expanding your chest fully.

Focus: Keep your eyes focused on your hands or directly ahead, and slow down your breathing.

Hold: For five breaths. Inhale to release up and out of the posture. Repeat on the other side.

Variations: If your neck becomes tired, look forward. Have your hands on your hips to avoid lower back strain or tired arms.

Benefits: This posture lengthens and tones the spinal muscles and nervous system, and strengthens the legs and the muscles around the knee joint.

In this **dynamic** posture the chest is **puffed outwards,** symbolizing a **warrior** ready for action. The legs are the firm **foundation** for the extension of the upper body.

Virabhadrasana II

VIRA—WARRIOR FROM INDIAN MYTHOLOGY

Positioning: From *Tadasana* place the feet about four feet apart. Turn your right foot out 90 degrees and your left foot in 15 degrees. Align the heel of your right foot with the inner arch of your left foot. As you inhale, extend your arms out to the side and lengthen out from your waist. Exhale and bend your right knee to a right angle, opening your right hip. Keep your left leg straight, with the outside of your foot touching the ground, and your buttocks activated. Lean your torso back slightly toward your left leg, so your spine sits straight up and down. Keep your arms stretching away from each other at shoulder height. Turn your head to face your right hand and relax your neck and shoulders.

Breathing: Inhale and exhale softly through your nose.

Focus: Keep your eye gaze beyond the right hand. Focus on opening your chest and hips, and on breathing slowly.

Hold: For five breaths. Inhale as you come out of the *asana* and repeat on the other side.

Variation: Perform the posture next to a wall, pressing your legs, buttocks, back and shoulders against the wall.

Benefits: This posture tones the spinal muscles and nervous system and strengthens the legs and the muscles around the knee joint.

Precaution: This is a strenuous posture, so take it easy. If your knee joints are weak, be particularly careful and stop if you feel sore.

This is another posture inspired by the mythological warrior. The body and mind are open, activated, focused and prepared for action.

Virabhadrasana III

VIRA—WARRIOR FROM INDIAN MYTHOLOGY

Positioning: From *Tadasana* move into *Virabhadrasana I* (page 36). Exhale and extend your torso over your right leg while lifting your back leg off the ground. Extend your arms out straight, and your left leg straight out to the height of your hips. Keep your back flat and your hips parallel; the standing leg needs to be activated and firm to maintain steady balance. Extend out through your arms and fingertips and relax your facial muscles. Your arms, torso and raised leg should form one straight line.

Breathing: Breathe softly and evenly through your nose.

Focus: Keep a soft eye gaze beyond the fingertips, slowing down your breath and keeping your body balanced and in correct alignment.

Hold: For five breaths. Inhale back to *Virabhadrasana I* to release from the pose. Repeat on the other side.

Variation: Rest your hands on a bench for balance and support.

Benefits: This posture strengthens and tones the legs, arms and trunk muscles, develops willpower, and teaches the mind and body to work in unison to coordinate and balance.

In this third warrior *asana* the body forms a straight line and learns balance and coordination. The posture helps develop inner strength and focus.

Ardha Chandrasana

ARDHA—HALF: CHANDRA—MOON

Positioning: From *Tadasana* move into *Trikonasana* (page 32). Exhale and bend your right knee as you bring your right hand to the floor in front of your foot. Straighten your right leg as you raise your left so the two legs form a right angle. Activate your buttocks, extend out of your left foot and feel the whole front of your body opening. Rotate your left hip around and back and activate the muscles of the leg you are standing on to maintain your balance. When you have your balance, raise your left arm straight up. Tuck in your chin and turn your head to look up to your hand. Feel your chest opening out.

Breathing: Breathe softly and evenly through your nose.

Focus: Keep your eye gaze beyond the left hand, opening up your left hip. Focus on finding and maintaining balance and breathing slowly.

Hold: For five breaths. To come out of the posture, inhale as you move back into *Trikonasana*, then back to *Tadasana*. Repeat the posture on the other side.

Variations: Place your right hand on a brick. Use a wall to support your back and legs and maintain balance.

Benefits: This posture strengthens the legs and buttocks and teaches focus, balance, and coordination of body and mind.

Coordinating your body into this posture requires mental and physical focus. With practice it can be accomplished gracefully.

Parsvottanasana

PARSVA—SIDEWAYS; UTTAN—EXTENSION

Positioning: Place your feet about four feet apart. Fold your arms behind your back with the thumbs into the crease of your elbows. Inhale and lift up out of your waist. Exhale and rotate your right foot out 90 degrees and your left foot in 60 degrees. Turn your hips and body to face the direction of your right foot. Inhale and drop your head back slightly, moving into a small back arch and opening up your chest. Exhale and extend forward to lie your torso over your right leg. If you can rest your chin on your shin, keep your leg muscles activated and rotate your right hip back and left hip forward so they are in line with each other.

Breathing: Take deep, full, even breaths, extending down a little more with each exhalation.

Focus: Keep your eye gaze toward your foot, concentrating on keeping your hips even, lengthening your spine and activating your leg muscles.

Hold: For five breaths. Release up with the inhalation. Rotate your feet and repeat on the opposite side.

Variation: Bring the palms of your hands together in a prayer position behind your back for a more intense shoulder stretch. For stability, place your hands on the floor on either side of your leg.

Benefits: This posture stretches the back muscles, massages the spinal nerves, stretches and opens the leg muscles and stimulates the intestines for good digestion.

In this *asana* the legs create a wide, triangular, stable foundation. From this the torso is free to extend and lengthen.

Padottanasana

PADA—FOOT/LEG: UTTAN—EXTENSION

Positioning: From *Tadasana* place your feet about five feet apart. Put your hands on your hips. Inhale and extend up and out of your waist. Exhale and extend forward and halfway down so your back is flat. Slowly exhale all the way down, drawing in your torso fully toward your legs. Place the palms of your hands on the floor between your feet with your elbows bent, and hang your head down, resting the crown of your head on the floor if possible. Activate the muscles of your legs for support and stability, move your body weight forward onto the front of your feet and feel your back relax and the vertebrae separating. Lift your shoulders.

Breathing: Breathe slowly and evenly through your nose, releasing your torso forward and down with the exhalation.

Focus: Keep your eye gaze on the tip of your nose, lifting your shoulders back toward your ears, softening your back and keeping your body weight moving forward.

Hold: For five to ten breaths. Inhale to come up, bringing your hands onto your hips.

Variations: Rest your hands on a block if you cannot reach the floor. Extend your torso only halfway if you find this posture difficult.

Benefits: This posture releases tight hamstring muscles, tones the legs and buttocks and calms the mind as the head rests forward.

The legs are the support while the head, torso and arms release forward and down. Feel the opening in the leg muscles. The stretch feels great!

Uttanasana

UTTAN—EXTENSION

Positioning: Stand with your feet apart at hip width. Inhale and extend your arms up over your head, placing your thumbs into the crease of your elbows. Exhale and slowly release forward into the resting pose, activate your leg muscles and lock your knees. Move your body weight forward slightly onto the balls of your feet, and feel your vertebrae separating as the weight of your head, neck and shoulders draws your torso down and in toward your legs.

Breathing: Slow down your breathing and relax.

Focus: Keep your eye gaze down past the tip of your nose, or, for deep relaxation, close your eyes. Feel your spine elongating.

Hold: For ten breaths or as long as you like. Release your arms and inhale as you come up.

Variations: Bend your knees if your back feels sore. Rest the crown of your head on a cushioned chair if hanging forward is uncomfortable.

Benefits: This posture relaxes the mind, improves blood circulation and digestion, softens tight spinal muscles and reduces fat around the abdomen.

Whenever you are feeling **tired** or **stressed**, let your body and mind **rest** in this posture. Hanging forward **quiets** the mind and **cools** the body.

Garudasana

GARUDA—EAGLE

Positioning: Stand with the feet together in *Tadasana*. Place your hands on your hips. Bend your knees and cross your right leg over the left. If possible, tuck your right foot round and lock it behind your left ankle. Find your balance. Next, raise your bent arms to shoulder height, cross your left arm over the top of your right arm and, if possible, bring the palms together. Keep your elbows bent at a 90-degree angle and in line with your shoulders. Extend your forearms away from your head, and lift out of your waist for a spinal extension. Relax your head, neck and shoulders.

Breathing: Breathe evenly through your nose.

Focus: Find a point in front of you at eye level, and maintain your balance and stillness of mind.

Hold: For ten full breaths or as long as it is comfortable. Release and repeat the posture on the opposite side.

Variation: If it is too difficult to find your balance in this posture, practice with the hands on the hips.

Benefits: This posture strengthens and tones the muscles and nerves of the legs, loosens the joints in the legs, relieves sciatica in the legs, stretches the shoulders and teaches balance and focus.

This posture teaches balance and coordination. Once you find yourself still in the posture, your mind relaxes and the breath becomes your main point of focus.

Utkatasana

UTKATA—POWERFUL

Positioning: From *Tadasana* inhale, raise your arms above your head and place the palms of your hands together. Exhale and bend your knees, keeping your heels down toward the ground. Lock your elbows, extend your spine out of your hips, lift your rib cage and breathe fully up into your chest. The torso naturally leans forward; however, try to keep your back straight and moving into an upright position. Tuck your buttocks under.

Breathing: Breathe softly through your nose.

Focus: Keep a soft eye gaze up to the hands, sitting a little lower. Keep your arms activated, flex your ankles and slow down your breathing.

Hold: For five breaths. Slowly release into a standing position as you exhale.

Benefits: This posture strengthens the back, legs, arms and torso and develops supple ankles.

This **dynamic** posture **activates** the whole body. The lower body "sits" firmly in midair. The upper body **lifts** and **extends**.

Parighasana

PARIGHA—GATE

Positioning: Kneel on the ground with your hands on your hips. Exhale and extend your right leg out to the right, keeping the foot in line with your hip. Place your right hand on your leg down toward the foot. Inhale and raise your left arm up and extend out from your waist. Exhale and extend your left arm over your head with the palm facing down. Tuck in your chin and look back toward your left hand. Feel the deep stretch in the muscles of the side of your torso and raised arm, keeping your left hip above your left knee.

Breathing: Breathe fully and use the exhalation to release further down your leg, releasing into the side stretch.

Focus: Keep your eye gaze beyond your left hand, releasing the muscles on the sides of your torso. Focus on releasing out of your hip.

Hold: For five breaths. Inhale to come up and change sides.

Benefits: This posture stretches and tones the abdomen, chest, arms and lateral torso muscles. It also stretches and softens the back muscles, massages the internal organs and tones the spinal nerves.

This **intense** side stretch **massages** and **cleanses** your **internal** organs and brings back **life** to the side of the **torso** as it **stretches** and **opens**.

Sitting postures calm the mind and soothe the nervous system.

There are many varieties of sitting postures. Some forward-bending postures lengthen, stretch and tone the legs. Others are more focused on elongating the spine and opening up the chest and shoulders.

Because the body is resting on the floor, the sitting postures require less energy and are less strenuous than the standing postures. However, they are very effective in stretching and releasing deep into the body.

Sit on a blanket or yoga mat to cushion the body from the ground.

Stay in each posture and experience its full benefits by concentrating on your breathing while you relax and let go into the pose. Releasing muscles as you exhale is an effective, gentle and safe way to increase your flexibility.

Using a belt in some of the postures helps to extend forward and keep the hips and torso in correct alignment.

Sitting postures

Sukhasana I

SUKHA—HAPPY

Positioning: Sit on the floor with your legs crossed. Place the back of your hands onto your knees, relax your shoulders down and roll them back to open up your chest. Focus on your spine lifting and elongating and breathe fully, expanding your chest. Keep checking to make sure your back is straight.

Breathing: This comfortable *asana* is ideal for sitting and focusing on taking deep, full, even breaths in and out through your nose.

Focus: Keep your eye gaze at a point in front or have your eyes softly closed. Focus also on keeping your back lifting, with your spine straight, as well as on opening your chest by rolling back your shoulders.

Hold: For as long as it is comfortable, then cross your legs the opposite way and repeat the posture.

Variations: Sit your buttocks on some blankets. Sit up against a wall if your back muscles are weak.

Benefits: This posture is a comfortable position to sit and practice meditation. It strengthens the spinal muscles, gently opens up the hips and stimulates blood flow to the pelvic region.

This easy cross-legged posture strengthens and straightens the back and gently opens the hips. Enjoy the calm as you sit in this centered position.

Sukhasana II

SUKHA—HAPPY

Positioning: Interlock your fingers and turn the palms outward. Raise your arms up over your head as you lift out of your waist and activate the muscle of your arms. Keep your head, neck and shoulders relaxed.

Breathing: Breathe fully and evenly as you lift and expand your chest.

Focus: Keep your eye gaze at eye level and at a point ahead. Lengthen out of your waist and keep your back straight.

Hold: For five breaths. Then interlock your fingers the opposite way and perform the posture on the other side.

Benefits: This posture separates the vertebrae, stimulates blood circulation through the spine and stretches the muscles of the sides of the torso. It gently opens the hips and stimulates blood flow to the pelvic region.

This simple upward lift brings life to the whole upper body. The extension stretches deep into the shoulder and arm muscles, releasing tightness and stress.

Dandasana

DANDA—STICK

Positioning: Sit with your legs stretched out and your back upright. Open up your chest by rolling your shoulders back. Feel your body correctly aligned and your weight even on your right and left buttocks. Lock your legs and arms and activate the muscles.

Breathing: Breathe fully, keeping your breath slow and even. Feel your rib cage expanding and contracting as you inhale and exhale.

Focus: Keep your eye gaze down toward your feet, and your chest and spine lifting upward. Focus also on rolling your shoulders down and back and relaxing your facial muscles.

Hold: For ten full breaths.

Benefits: This posture opens the chest, lungs and heart, teaches the spine correct posture and strengthens the muscles of the legs. The stillness of the posture quietens the mind.

The back is **erect** and the legs and arms are activated and **straight** in this posture. Become **aware** that the **whole** body is **activated.**

Baddha Konasana I

BADDHA—BOUND: KONA—ANGLE

Positioning: Sit with the soles of your feet together. Let your knees relax down toward the floor and the muscles around your hips soften. Interlock your fingers around your toes and lift out of your lower back. Roll your shoulders down and back, and lift and open your chest.

Breathing: Take deep, full, rhythmic breaths. Send the awareness of the exhalation to your hips, softening and letting go in the hips.

Focus: Keep your back straight and let go in your hips.

Hold: For ten breaths or as long as it is comfortable.

Benefits: This posture soothes the sacral nerves, strengthens the back muscles, releases tension in the hips and stimulates circulation to the pelvic region and reproductive organs.

This posture increases circulation to the pelvic organs. It soothes menstrual pain and helps maintain healthy reproductive organs.

Baddha Konasana II

BADDHA—BOUND: KONA—ANGLE

Positioning: Lifting from the front of your body, stretch your torso up and bend forward and down toward the ground. Aim for your abdomen to rest along the floor, then your chest, then your chin. To open your hips further, place your elbows on your knees, working them to the floor.

Breathing: Get in touch with your breath. With a deep exhalation, relax and let go in your hips.

Focus: Feel your hips softening and opening, relax your head downward and calm your mind.

Hold: For five to ten breaths.

Variation: Rest your head on a bolster or a pile of pillows.

Benefits: These are the same as for *Baddha Konasana I*, only a little more intense. Resting your head forward and down relaxes the mind.

This forward-extending posture opens **deep** into the hips, **releasing** stiffness and **stimulating** blood flow to the pelvic organs.

Janu Sirsasana

JANU—KNEE; SIRSA—HEAD

Positioning: Sit with your legs stretched in front of your body. Bend your right leg and place the heel of the foot into your groin. Open up the sole of your foot to face upward and feel your right hip opening. To come forward, inhale and lift out from your waist, lengthening from the front of your body. Either hold onto your feet or a belt looped around the feet and, with the exhalation, extend over your outstretched leg. Rotate your abdomen to the left so your torso is lying straight along your outstretched leg. Rest your abdomen, chest and head comfortably onto your leg.

Breathing: Breathe slowly, releasing your torso forward and down a little more each time you exhale.

Focus: Turn your eye gaze toward your foot. Focus on relaxing your back muscles and abdomen.

Hold: For five breaths. Inhale out of the posture and change sides.

Variations: Place a blanket under the knee of your outstretched leg to relieve tight leg muscles. Stay with your back upright and hold onto a belt looped around your feet if extending forward is painful. Place a bolster on your knees and rest the forehead onto it if lying forward is difficult.

Benefits: This posture stimulates blood flow to the internal organs. It tones the abdominal and leg muscles and loosens the hips.

Precautions: Do not practice this posture if you have chronic arthritis, sciatica or a slipped disc.

Your head lies forward in this position, calming the mind and cooling the whole body. Empty your mind of thoughts by focusing on the soft sound of your breath.

Triang Mukhaikapada Pascimottanasana

TRI—ANGLE; MUKHA—FACE; PADA—FOOT;
PASCIMOTTASANA—POSTERIOR EXTENSION

Positioning: Start with both legs stretched out in *Dandasana*. Bend your right leg back. Place a pile of blankets under your left buttock if you need support. Keep your knees pressing together. Roll your right calf muscle out. Have the sole of your right foot facing upward and the heel touching the hip. Once you are comfortable, extend up out of your waist while inhaling. Extend your arms and torso forward as you exhale. Hold onto your feet as you lie your head down onto your leg.

Breathing: Breathe deeply and slowly, lifting your chest forward with the inhalation and releasing down with the exhalation.

Focus: Send your eye gaze toward your foot, relaxing your head and neck, elongating your spine and quietening your mind.

Hold: For five breaths. Inhale out of the *asana* and repeat on the other side.

Variations: Place a blanket under the knee of the extended leg. Stay with your back upright, holding onto a belt looped around your feet if extending forward is painful. Alternatively, rest the forehead down on a bolster.

Benefits: This position stimulates blood flow to the internal organs and nervous system as well as toning the abdominal and leg muscles.

Precaution: Be careful if you have weak knees.

Keeping the body weight evenly distributed between both hips is a challenge in this posture. Take your awareness inward as you concentrate.

Virasana I

VIRA—A HERO

Positioning: Sit your buttocks on your heels. Slide your heels out to the side so that your buttocks release onto the ground and sit between your heels on the floor. At this point, decide whether you will need to sit on some blankets to relieve pain in your legs, knees and ankles. Draw your knees in toward each other. Stretch the sides of your torso up. Roll back your shoulders and open your chest. Rest the backs of your hands on your knees.

Breathing: Breathe evenly in and out through your nose.

Focus: Use a soft eye gaze at a point ahead, keeping your back straight and the bones of your buttocks down.

Hold: For as long as it is comfortable.

Variations: Kneel with your legs on a pile of blankets to relieve tight ankles and feet. Sit your buttocks on a pile of blankets to release strain in your legs.

Benefits: This posture activates the digestive system and is good for relieving indigestion if practiced after a heavy meal. It strengthens pelvic muscles, knee and ankle joints, stimulates blood flow to the pelvic organs and is a good posture for meditation if the body is comfortable staying in it.

Practice this posture to **open** up **tight** knees and ankles. Once you can sit in it **comfortably** it becomes a **soothing,** **resting** pose for any time of day.

Virasana II

VIRA—A HERO

Positioning: Sit in *Virasana I*. Inhale and raise the arms above the head. Exhale, bend and extend the torso and arms forward and down. Rest the forehead on the floor. Keep the buttocks back to the heels.

Breathing: Maintain natural breathing, softening into the pose with the exhalation.

Focus: Keep the focus on the breathing. Close your eyes and sink your forehead to the floor.

Hold: For five breaths. Exhale when you release up.

Benefits: This posture tones the muscles of the pelvis and stimulates blood flow to the pelvic organs, which helps to maintain healthy functioning of the reproductive organs. It also helps relieve sciatica.

This forward-extension posture stretches deep into the ankle and knee joints, opening and releasing tightness. The spine extends and gently stretches.

Parvatasana

PARVA–MOUNTAIN

Positioning: Sit in a comfortable cross-legged position. Inhale and raise your arms, placing the palms together above your head. Bend your elbows slightly. Relax your shoulders down and open your chest.

Breathing: Inhale and exhale in slow, even breaths.

Focus: Keep a soft eye gaze at a point in front or have your eyes softly closed, keeping your arm muscles activated and lifting and focusing inward on a quiet space empty of thoughts.

Hold: For five to ten breaths. Exhale to release your arms down and repeat the posture with your legs crossed the other way.

Benefits: This posture strengthens the arms, lengthens the spine and softens the hip muscles. It develops willpower and quietens the mind.

With the hands raised in prayer position, this is a beautiful posture that invokes a quiet and meditative space.

Navasana

NAU—BOAT

Positioning: Find your balance on the front of your sitting bones. Raise your legs halfway in toward your chest and extend your arms out parallel to them. Move around until you feel you are centered. Lift your lower back in and up so it doesn't collapse.

Breathing: Inhale to raise your body. Breathe slowly and evenly while you are in the posture. Exhale to release your body.

Focus: Extend your eye gaze beyond the feet, pulling your back in and up and activating your stomach, leg and arm muscles.

Hold: For five to ten full breaths.

Variation: For a more intense pose, raise and straighten your legs and lock your knees. The arms stay parallel to the floor. Your torso and legs will form a "V" shape.

Benefits: This posture stimulates digestion and strengthens the abdominal muscles as well as the back, legs and arms.

This posture teaches alignment, balance, centering, and focus. With practice, you will appreciate the feeling of lightness that comes with Navasana.

Twists are powerful postures that help maintain a clean and healthy body. Twists soften tight back muscles, release toxins and improve the circulation of blood and oxygen through the spine. The internal organs are massaged and the intestines are stimulated to promote good digestion and bowel function. If you spend a lot of time sitting at a desk, a regular spinal twist will help relieve a tired, sore back.

These postures should be practiced carefully. Use exhalations to soften and release deeper into a twist. Twist to both sides of the torso for equal lengths of time and rest after twisting.

When releasing from a spinal twist you may feel a rush of energy. Often the twist affects the body so powerfully that the release of toxins and blocked energy is immediate.

If you suffer from any spinal problems, seek medical advice before attempting the twisting *asanas*. Do not attempt the twisting postures if you are pregnant.

Twisting postures

Bharadvajasana

BHARADVAJA—AN INDIAN SAGE

Positioning: Sit on your buttocks with your legs bent sideways to sit beside your left hip. Place your right foot underneath your left foot. Inhale up out of your waist and twist your torso and head to the right. Place your left hand beside your right knee and your right hand on the ground behind your right hip. Inhale and raise your right arm and wrap it around your back to hold onto your left elbow. Rotate your right shoulder and elbow back, and turn your head to look over your left shoulder.

Breathing: Breathe slowly and evenly. Bring your awareness to the point where the spine is twisting and release deeper into the twist with your breath.

Focus: Keep your eye gaze beyond your left shoulder, and lift and open your chest.

Hold: For five breaths or as long as it is comfortable. Practice the posture on both sides.

Benefits: This posture tones the spinal muscles and nervous system and relieves tight shoulders or a stiff back.

This simple, effective posture relieves backache. The twisting action softens tight muscles, releasing tension and stimulating blood flow through the spine.

Maricyasana Twist

MARICI—AN INDIAN SAGE

Positioning: Sit on the ground with your legs stretched out. Bend your right leg and place the foot close up to the groin, so your thigh touches your abdomen. Inhale and turn to place your right hand on the ground behind your right hip. Lock your left arm in front of your right knee, pressing your knee into your arm. Inhale and lift out of your hips, thinning your waist. Exhale and turn to look back over your right shoulder. Keep your left leg straight and the muscles activated.

Breathing: Use the breath as a tool to lift and turn into the twist. As you inhale, lift your spine. As you exhale, turn and twist your spine and spinal muscles.

Focus: Keep your eye gaze beyond your right shoulder, and your bent knee upright.

Hold: For five breaths. Release your arms and repeat on the other side.

Benefits: This posture stretches and tones the spinal cord, relieves backache, rejuvenates the brain and gives the internal organs a cleansing massage.

This twisting posture gives an internal massage to the body's systems. It cleanses sluggish internal organs and releases toxins.

Spinal Roll

Positioning: Lie flat on the ground with your legs straight. Extend your arms out to the side with the palms facing down. Inhale and bend your knees into your chest. Exhale and turn your head to face down beyond your left hand. Exhale and release the bent legs down to the right onto the ground. Place your knees in close to your right armpit. Keep both shoulders flat on the floor.

Breathing: Breathe deeply.

Focus: Keep your eye gaze beyond your left hand. Focus on softening the back and keeping your shoulders on the ground.

Hold: For five breaths. Inhale, raise your legs back to the center and change sides.

Benefits: This posture tones the spinal cord, stretches back muscles and releases tension in the upper back.

The muscles supporting the spine can easily become tired and inflexible. This simple twist keeps your back soft, supple and healthy.

Backward-bending postures

Urdhva Mukha Svanasana

URDHVA—UPWARD: MUKHA—FACE: SVANA—DOG

Positioning: Lie on your stomach with your legs straight and your elbows bent to place your hands beside your shoulders. Rest your forehead on the floor. Inhale and raise your head, shoulders and chest off the ground. Squeeze your buttocks and extend out of your lower back. Straighten your arms and roll your shoulders back and down. Open your chest. Drop your head back and start to work into the backbend with your breath. Lift out of your lower back. Look up to your third eye (the point between your eyebrows).

Breathing: As you exhale, gently release deeper into the backbend. Breathe deeply and slowly.

Focus: Send your eye gaze up to your third eye, stretching the front of your body and focusing inward.

Hold: For five breaths.

Benefits: This posture keeps the back supple and healthy, regenerates the muscles of the torso and relieves back pain, helping slipped discs. It also massages the abdominal organs and stimulates and tones the sexual organs.

This backward-bending *asana* relieves backache and develops a supple spine. The chest opens out, encouraging deep, full breathing.

Salabhasana

SALABHA—LOCUST

Positioning: Lie on your stomach with your legs straight and your arms resting alongside your body. Place the backs of your hands on the floor. Rest your forehead on the floor. Inhale fully and raise your head, chest, arms and legs off the floor. Breathe normally as you hold the position and raise a little higher. Squeeze your buttocks and keep your legs together and straight as you lift.

Breathing: Inhale to raise up; exhale to release down. Breathe normally as you hold the position.

Focus: Keep your legs together and open your chest.

Hold: For five breaths.

Variations: Try raising just your head, chest and arms off the floor or just your legs, with your arms, chest and head resting. Alternatively, raise one arm only, then change sides, or raise one leg only and then change sides.

Benefits: This posture strengthens the chest and heart, massages and cleanses the kidneys, liver, intestines and other abdominal organs and stimulates the intestines for healthy bowel function. It aids in eliminating diseases of the stomach, strengthens the spine and tones the nerves of the spine and limbs.

Precautions: Do not practice this posture if you have a weak heart or a hernia.

The body lifts to form a small arch. All the muscles at the back of the body lift and strengthen, helping develop a strong, healthy back.

Mini Backbend

Positioning: Lie on your back. Bend your legs. Place your feet up to your buttocks, hip width apart. Extend your arms alongside your body with the palms facing down. Exhale and slowly roll up off the floor. Get in touch with each vertebra as you roll up. First lift your buttocks, then your lower back, middle back and chest. Keep your shoulders down. Squeeze your buttocks and lift your hips up high.

Breathing: Exhale to come into and out of the full posture. Breathe normally as you hold the pose.

Focus: Send your eye gaze down to your navel, opening your chest, lifting your hips and keeping your knees in toward each other.

Hold: For five breaths.

Benefits: This posture massages the abdominal muscles and organs and stimulates blood flow through the spine. It keeps the spine supple, elastic and revitalized, the pelvic organs healthy, and tones the legs and buttocks.

This backward bend helps the spine and the whole body to regenerate rather than degenerate, keeping it stretched, supple and full of life.

Inverted postures stimulate the flow of pure oxygenated blood to the whole body. Blockages in the organs, muscles and nerves are cleared and the body works more effectively. The oxygen supply increases and the body receives more "life force."

Stress and anxiety are reduced as the increased circulation flushes out toxins and purifies the glands, improving the functioning of the body. Accumulated wastes in the legs are removed and replenished with fresh, energizing blood. The breathing slows down and deepens, and the intake of oxygen increases with the outflow of carbon dioxide.

The inverted postures are great stimulants for the brain. Being upside down, more pure oxygenated blood is directed to the brain. Consequently, the mind is invigorated and refreshed.

It is not advisable to practice inverted postures if you have high blood pressure or a weak heart. Do not practice *Salamba Sarvangasana* if you are menstruating or pregnant.

Inverted postures

Adho Mukha Svanasana

ADHO–DOWNWARD; MUKHA–FACE; SVANA–DOG

Positioning: Kneel on the ground. Place your hands on the ground in front of your knees and spread your fingers wide apart. Step your right foot back, then your left foot. Straighten your legs, with your feet hip width apart. Inhale and raise your buttocks and hips. Lower the crown of your head toward the floor. Relax your neck and lift your shoulders back and toward your ears. Release your chest through your shoulders, and work your heels to the ground.

Breathing: Breathe deeply in the posture.

Focus: Keep your eyes focused between your feet on the floor, opening your shoulders, and lifting your hips and buttocks. Focus also on locking your knees, opening the backs of your legs and keeping the palm and heel of your hands pressed to the floor with your fingers spread evenly apart.

Hold: For five to ten breaths. Exhale to release out of the posture.

Variations: Place your head on a bolster for a resting pose and keep your knees bent if your legs are tight.

Benefits: This posture strengthens the arms, tones the sciatic nerve and stretches the ankles and backs of the legs.

Precaution: It is not advisable to practice this posture if you have high blood pressure.

Each limb is stretched out in this posture. The inverted position calms the mind and nervous system and cleanses and massages the internal organs.

Inverted Legs I, II and III

Positioning: Lie flat on your back with your legs up against the wall. Press the buttocks firmly into the wall. Press your lower back to the floor. Gently activate your leg muscles. Rest the back of your hands on the floor and tuck in your chin.

Breathing: Breathe through your nose softly and slowly. This will calm your whole body.

Focus: Close your eyes (or cover your eyes with an eye pad for deep relaxation) and feel the blood flowing down through your legs.

Hold: For five minutes or as long as it feels good. To release out of the posture, bring your knees to your chest and roll to the side.

Benefits: This posture relieves tired feet and legs and refreshes the mind.

Variations: In Inverted Legs II, spread your legs apart. This stimulates blood flow to the hips, pelvis and reproductive organs, and stretches the inner leg muscles. For Inverted Legs III, bend your knees and place the soles of your feet together. The hips open and blood flows to the reproductive organs.

Fatigue and sluggishness are washed away by pure, oxygenated blood and replaced with vitality and alertness.

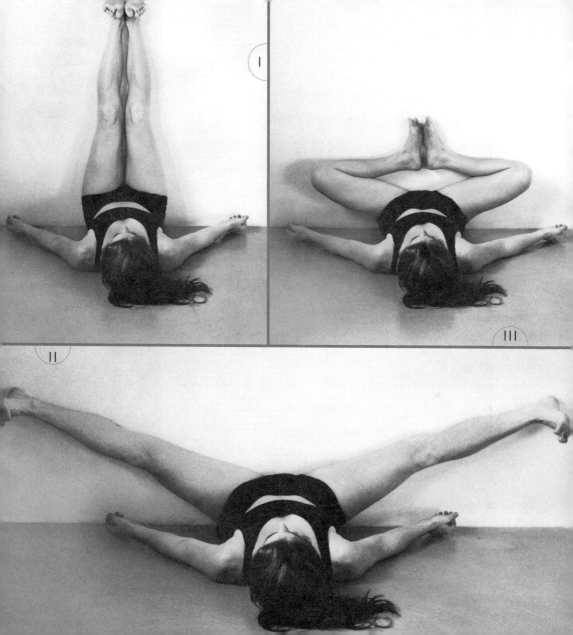

Salamba Sarvangasana

SALAMBA—SUPPORTED; SARVANGASANA—BODY BALANCE

Positioning: Make a neat pile of two or three blankets and lie with your back and shoulders on it. Rest your head onto the floor. Bend your knees and bring your feet into your buttocks. Raise your legs off the floor and place the palms of your hands into your upper back for lift and support. Bring your legs into a vertical position, forming a straight line with your legs and torso. The elbows should sit at shoulder width apart, and the elbows, upper arms and shoulders together support the body. Tuck in your chin and keep your legs lifting.

Breathing: Use normal breathing.

Focus: Keep your eye gaze on your navel. Concentrate on the sound of your breathing, relaxing your head and neck and keeping your body steady and straight.

Hold: For a few breaths. If pressure develops in the head or eyes, come out of the pose immediately. Exhale to release down, remove the blankets and rest with your body flat on the floor. Do not turn your head or neck in this posture.

Salamba Sarvangasana continued over the page

This shoulder stand is known as the "mother *asana*" for its powerful healing and calming effects on the systems of the entire body.

Benefits: This posture relieves mental and physical fatigue and improves the functioning of the circulatory, digestive, nervous, glandular and reproductive systems. It supplies the brain with plenty of oxygenated blood, stimulates the thyroid gland and tones the muscles of the arms, legs and spine. It also stimulates the elimination of fats around the waist, massages the abdominal and reproductive organs and promotes healthy bowel function.

Precautions: It is not advisable to practice this posture if you have a weak heart, high blood pressure or if you are pregnant or menstruating. Ask for assistance from a qualified yoga teacher before attempting this posture for the first time on your own.

Relaxation postures are a restful "retreat" for the body, mind and soul. They will leave you feeling completely rejuvenated.

All body systems rest. The nerves relax completely, and muscles release stored tension.

The sound of the breath is the main focal point. The mind learns to empty itself of busy thoughts and develop concentration.

By practicing conscious relaxation, the mind and body ultimately perform better in everyday life. Our interaction with the world improves, along with our feelings of inner peace.

For sufferers of anxiety and stress who find being relaxed, still and quiet truly difficult, the following relaxation *asanas* will help give the body and mind the rest they need so much.

Practice the relaxation postures in a warm and quiet environment away from any distractions. The use of an eye pad to cover your eyes deepens relaxation, relieving tired eye muscles.

Savasana I

SAVA—LIFELESS BODY

Positioning: Lie flat on your back with your arms slightly away from your body and your palms facing upward. Have your legs separated a little and let the feet fall toward the floor. Tuck in your chin slightly. Adjust your body so that it feels centered and comfortable and close your eyes. Bring your awareness to any part of your body that is tense and relax that area. Resolve not to move your body throughout the practice. Feel your body sinking through the floor, deeper and deeper into relaxation, but do not allow yourself to fall asleep.

Breathing: Slow and rhythmic.

Focus: Observe your breath. Whenever you find yourself thinking, return your awareness to your breath. Relax the muscles of your whole body, from the muscles of your scalp, your face, and down to your toes.

Hold: For ten minutes at the end of every yoga practice, or for a few minutes between postures, especially after dynamic postures. To release from the pose, roll to the right, then slowly come up to a sitting position.

Variations: Cover your eyes with an eye bag to relax your eye muscles and relieve headache. You can also use a small pillow to rest your head on or to place under your knees if lying flat is uncomfortable for your back.

Benefits: This posture relaxes the entire body, rests the nervous system and quietens the mind. It develops concentration and awareness and aids in relieving insomnia if practiced before sleeping.

The body is completely still; there is no movement apart from the breathing.

The mind is awake to the delicious experience of deep relaxation.

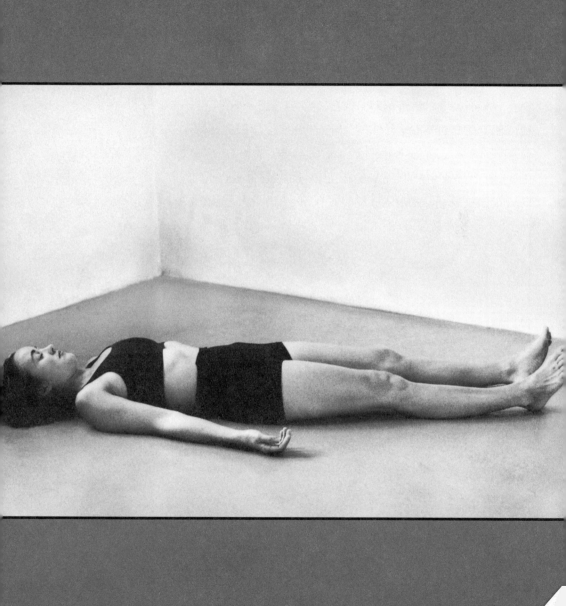

Savasana II

SAVA–LIFELESS BODY

Positioning: Use a bolster or place two or three blankets into a neat pile and fold one blanket in half for a head rest. Sit on the floor with your buttocks touching the edge of the bolster. Stretch your legs out and lower your body down over the bolster, opening your chest. Rest your head on the folded blanket and tuck in your chin. The buttocks stay on the floor and the chest opens. With your body now completely relaxed, listen to your breath. Feel your chest rising as you inhale and sinking as you exhale.

Breathing: Take deep, slow, full breaths through your nose.

Focus: The eyes are closed. Focus on your third eye (the point between your eyebrows). This point of focus develops awareness and intuition. Listen to the sound of your breath and relax every muscle in your body.

Hold: For five to ten minutes. To release slowly, roll to rest on your right side, then come up to a sitting position.

Benefits: This posture relaxes the entire body, rests the nervous system and quiets the mind. It purifies the heart and lungs, improves respiratory functions and develops concentration and awareness. Practiced before sleeping, this posture helps eliminate insomnia.

This supported relaxation posture opens the chest, enabling deeper breathing and deep relaxation.

Savasana III

SAVA—LIFELESS BODY

Positioning: Lie on your stomach and rest your forehead on the floor or turn your head to one side. Stretch your arms forward above your head and relax the muscles of your whole body.

Breathing: Breathe slowly through the nose.

Focus: Have your eyes closed and focus on the sound of your breath.

Hold: For ten minutes at the end of a session of *asanas* or for a few minutes in between yoga postures. To release, roll to rest on your right side, then slowly come up to a sitting position.

Benefits: *Savasana III* improves posture, extends the spine and helps to prevent slipped discs. It relieves tension in the spinal muscles and relaxes the mind.

This resting posture is good for sleeping. The stomach is gently soothed, the arms extend above the head and the spine gently stretches.

Supta Baddha Konasana

SUPTA—SUPINE: BADDHA—BOUND: KONA—ANGLE

Positioning: Place a bolster or two folded blankets horizontally. Sit on the floor with your lower back touching the bolster, bend your knees and bring the soles of your feet together. Lie back over the bolster, rest your head on the floor and tuck in your chin. Your knees will drop down and your hips will open. Rest the bent arms on the floor alongside your head. Feel your abdomen extending over the bolster. Close your eyes.

Breathing: Breathe slowly and evenly through your nose.

Focus: On the sound of your breath.

Hold: For five minutes. Inhale to release up out of the posture.

Variations: Place your arms down alongside your body, with your palms facing upward. If your back is stiff, lie over the bolster lengthways, supporting your head and neck. For a more intense opening in your hips, use a belt. From the sitting position place the middle of the belt around your sacrum and the two ends over your thighs, knees and shins. Tie the belt under your feet. Keep the belt low on your back, firmly but not too tightly, and lie back over the bolster.

Benefits: This posture relaxes the whole body, opens the chest and encourages healthy breathing. It loosens the hip muscles, massages the abdominal organs, stimulates blood to the reproductive and sexual organs, promotes a healthy menstrual cycle and relieves menstrual pain.

This deeply relaxing posture opens the chest and massages the internal organs. The hips lie open, increasing the supply of blood to the pelvic and reproductive organs.

Child Pose

Positioning: Sit with your buttocks on your heels. Rest your torso on your knees, and the backs of your arms alongside your legs with the palms facing upward. Rest your forehead on the floor, drop your shoulders and relax every muscle in your body. Feel your head and body sinking into deep relaxation.

Breathing: Breathe slowly and naturally.

Focus: Keep your eyes closed and rest your body.

Hold: For a few minutes between postures when the body needs resting. Inhale to release.

Variation: Rest your head on a bolster.

Benefits: This posture calms the mind, and slows the breath and heart rate, cooling the body.

Symbolic of a curled-up child, warm and protected from the outside world, this posture offers a nurturing and restful space.

Knee Hug

Positioning: Lie on your back. Hug your knees to your chest, while you keep your head, neck and shoulders relaxed and on the floor.

Breathing: Use normal breathing.

Focus: Close your eyes or gaze beyond your knees and relax your back muscles.

Hold: For as long as it feels good. Practice this posture after backbends to release the muscles.

Benefits: This posture releases the muscles of the lower back and relaxes the body.

This simple posture softens the back. Hug the knees into the chest to release and relax tight, spasming lower back muscles.

Forward Rest

Positioning: Kneel on the floor. Bring your big toes together with the knees apart. Sit your buttocks back between your heels, onto the soles of your feet. Cup your fingers onto the floor in front, and inhale and lengthen out of your hips. Exhale and slowly release forward and down, walking your arms forward as you are extending and rest your forehead onto the floor. Keep your buttocks back to your heels and stretch your arms forward, spreading your fingers. Feel the two-way stretch of your spine: your shoulders and arms are stretching your upper back forward and your buttocks are working the lower back backward.

Breathing: Breathe deep, slow, full breaths through the nose.

Focus: Close your eyes, and focus your third eye (the point between your eyebrows), resting your body and mind and keeping your buttocks back toward your heels.

Hold: For as long as it is comfortable, and for a few minutes after a backbend to release tight muscles.

Variation: Turn your head to the side if your neck feels sore.

Benefits: This posture separates the vertebrae of the spine, promoting a supple healthy back. It also cools the body and relaxes the mind.

This is a gentle forward-resting *asana* that stretches, lengthens and straightens the spine. The forehead sinks to the floor, calming the activity of the mind.

Deep Relaxation

The following method of relaxation is designed to relax your body and mind, and release stress. It is a delicious technique that calms the mind and rejuvenates the soul. This kind of relaxation is a great way to wind down and return to your center after a busy day at work.

The process involves isolating each part of the body and consciously relaxing it. We move through the whole body, becoming more aware of tense areas. We release tension and hold in the muscles until the whole body is completely soft and relaxed.

Positioning: Choose a quiet environment away from any distractions. Take the phone off the hook and ask others not to disturb you.

Lie in *Savasana I* (page 110) and make sure you are warm and comfortable. You may like to use a pillow, blankets and eye bag for more comfort.

Become aware of your whole body lying on the floor. Starting on the right side, become aware of your right thumb. Relax it completely. Feel any tensions moving out of the thumb.

Now take your awareness to the second finger and relax it. Relax the third finger, fourth finger, then little finger. Relax all your fingers. Relax the palm of your hand, then the back of your hand. Feel your whole hand relaxed and soft, sinking into the floor.

Take your awareness to your wrist and release the muscles and joints in it. Then release your right forearm, elbow, upper arm and armpit. Relax your whole right arm completely.

Now move your awareness to your right foot. Relax your big toe, second toe, third toe, fourth toe and little toe. Relax the top of your foot, the ball and heel of your foot, then the inner arch. Relax your whole foot.

Relax your ankle, and then your lower leg. Relax the front of your knee, the back of your knee, the thigh, the back of your leg. Relax your whole right leg. Feel that the whole leg is soft and completely relaxed.

Now take your awareness to the right side of your torso. Relax your right hip, buttock, then the right side of your waist. Relax your chest, then your right shoulder.

Relax your whole torso. Relax your whole right side: arm, leg, torso.

Now repeat on your left side, starting with your hand, then leg and torso.

Then move your attention to your head and relax your whole head, neck and face into the floor.

Relax your scalp and every muscle in your face. Feel your skin falling away from the bone and your head sinking to the floor. Relax your eyes, nose, mouth; have your lips slightly parted. Relax your tongue, throat and jaw; then your cheek bones and your ears.

Feel that your head and your whole body is completely relaxed.

With your entire body relaxed, feel yourself sinking deeper and deeper into a state of complete relaxation. Ahhh ...

Breathing: Use normal, soft breathing through your nose.

Focus: Feel every muscle in the body relaxing, releasing tension in the muscles, and the whole body sinking. Whenever you find yourself thinking, return to the point of focus.

Hold: For as long as it is comfortable. Five to ten minutes is effective.

Benefits: This posture is extremely healing for stressed-out anxious minds. It calms the whole nervous system and relaxes the body and mind.

Meditation is yoga in its highest form. It is the experience of emptiness, a vacation for the mind.

Regular meditation, whether for five minutes or an hour, makes you more cheerful and positive. Your mind becomes clear and focused.

Meditation is about being totally in the moment. In practicing yoga, become aware of every breath and body movement. This itself is meditation.

The senses are withdrawn from the world and the mind focuses inward. Begin by focusing on the soft sound of your breath or reciting a mantra (a prayerful word or phrase). Then let all your thoughts and worries go. Give yourself the ultimate gift, time to relax.

Meditation can be practiced any time. The very early morning is ideal. It is also often easier after activities like dancing, walking or yoga when the body is relaxed and the mind has already been concentrating inwardly on the body and breath.

Meditation postures

Sukhasana Meditation

SUKHA—HAPPY

Positioning: Bend the forefinger of each hand and place it behind the nail of the thumb. Relax your other three fingers so they spread apart. (This hand posture is called *Jnana Mudra*. The nerve impulses of the forefinger turn inward and help to relax the body.) Sit on a neat pile of blankets and lightly cross the legs. Roll the shoulders down and back to open out the chest. Rest the backs of the hands on the tops of the knees.

Breathing: Use normal breathing.

Focus: Close your eyes. Find a point of focus you are comfortable with, such as the soft sound of your breath or the sensation of cool air moving in through your nostrils and warm air moving out. Whenever you lose focus, return your awareness to the focal point. Keep your head and back straight.

Hold: The longer the better. After a session of yoga, practice meditation for a few minutes before lying down into a version of *Savasana*.

Variations: Sit with your back against a wall for support if your back muscles are weak. Tie a cloth around your eyes to help draw your attention inward. Wrap a cloth firmly around your abdomen and lower back to draw the spine erect.

Benefits: Relaxing and meditating is known to promote clarity of thought and give you a more positive outlook on life. It helps you feel more rejuvenated and alive.

This is an easy position to sit in for meditation. The body is comfortable and the spine and head are aligned. Drawing the awareness inward comes effortlessly.

Half Lotus

Positioning: Sit in *Sukhasana*. Cross the left leg over the right. Raise the right foot out and place it on top of the left upper thigh. The right leg is now on top. The right knee sits over the left foot. Feel the hips opening. Sit the buttocks onto a neat pile of blankets if that is more comfortable. Rest the backs of your hands on your knees and bend your forefingers to rest behind the nails at the thumb. The other fingers relax completely. Close your eyes and bring your awareness to a quiet space within.

Breathing: Use normal breathing.

Hold: The longer the better. After a session of yoga, practice meditation for a few minutes before lying down into a version of *Savasana*.

Focus: Close your eyes and free your mind of thoughts. Focus on keeping your back upright.

Benefits: Sitting with the back straight promotes healthy posture and circulation. Time stands still as your focus is drawn inward.

When your **thoughts** wander, let them go and **return** your **focus** to the **soft** sound of your **breath**.

Virasana Meditation

Positioning: Sit with the knees bent and the buttocks resting back onto the heels. Keep the knees and feet together. Rest the backs of the hands on the knees. Bend the forefingers and rest the nails behind the thumb. Let the other fingers relax outward. Close the eyes and draw your awareness within.

Breathing: Use normal breathing.

Hold: For as long as you like. Practice meditation after a session of yoga before lying back into a version of *Savasana*.

Focus: Close your eyes. Find a point of focus you are comfortable with, such as the soft sound of your breath or the sensation of cool air moving in through your nostrils and warm air moving out. Whenever you find your thoughts wandering, return your awareness to the focal point. Keep your head and back straight.

Benefits: This deeply relaxing posture promotes clear thinking and rejuvenates the mind. You will feel alive and refreshed afterward.

Variations: Lean up against a wall if your back becomes tired. Keep lifting your torso upward.

When the body is still and the mind is free of thought, then there is an empty space to be at peace.

Simple sequences

Greeting the day, or *Surya Namaskar*, is an all-over yoga session in one simple sequence. *Surya Namaskar* is traditionally practiced at sunrise, a time of inspiration and abundant energy at the start of a new day. This is a dynamic practice in which the body warms up quickly after flowing through a sequence of postures with the breath. The circulation of body heat softens and opens the muscles. Toxins and wastes are released and excess body fat burnt off.

Practice the sequence at any time to refresh your body and mind, or to warm up your body before practicing other yoga postures. Keep the rhythm and flow of your breath even, inhaling and exhaling fully into and out of each posture.

With practice, the body will become more flexible and the rhythm of your breathing will improve to help the sequence flow.

Before beginning the sequence, take time to get in touch with your breathing. Stand with your feet together. Hold your hands in prayer position in front of your heart and relax your whole body. Breathe normally through the nose. Close your eyes and focus on your heart center. This posture aligns the body and develops concentration.

1

Stand in *Tadasana* (page 28) with your feet together and arms by your side. Look ahead at eye level.

2

Inhale and raise your arms above your head, bringing the palms together. Drop your head back to bring your eye focus up to your hands. The whole body extends upward. Lift your torso from the hips. Focus on the extension of your body. This posture stretches and elongates the body.

3

Exhale as you bend at the hips and release your torso down to your legs. As you come down, your arms extend out to the sides. Bring your fingers and hands to the floor, and, if possible, keep your legs straight. If your back is straining, bend your legs slightly. Bring your forehead to your knees. Your eye gaze moves down the body to the point between your navel and pubis. The posture activates the circulation of blood, stretches and tones the spine and spinal cord and stimulates the digestive and excretory systems. It also improves a sluggish stomach, cleanses the liver and kidneys and eliminates fat around the waist.

4

Inhale and look up. Extend your spine so your back straightens, raise your head and look forward. Keep your fingers cupped on the floor beside your feet. Keep your eyes focused ahead, bringing the internal focus to the heart center, lengthening your spine out of your hips and keeping your legs locked. This posture separates the vertebrae, and tones the spinal cord and nerves of the legs.

5

Exhale and step or lightly jump your feet back, releasing down into a plank position. Your arms bend and the elbows stay in close to your body, and your toes are curled under. If you have the strength, keep your body off the floor; if not, rest your body on the floor. Focus your eyes on the tip of your nose and your body in one straight line. This posture strengthens the muscles of the legs and arms.

6

7

As you inhale, roll onto the tops of your feet. Bring the front of your body up through the shoulders, straightening your arms. Drop your head back and arch your back. Keep your legs straight and squeeze your buttocks. Keep your whole body except your hands and feet off the floor, or rest the tops of your legs on the floor. Focus on your third eye, opening your chest, extending from your waist and on lengthening the front of your body. This posture softens and stretches the back, stimulates the spinal nerves and stimulates blood flow to the abdominal organs.

8

This posture is the resting pose in the sequence. It is held here for five deep, slow breaths. Exhale and lift up your buttocks and hips. Straighten your legs and work your heels back to the floor, with your feet hip width apart. Your hands face forward with the fingers spread wide apart, and your chest and head drop through your shoulders. Keep your eyes focused on a point between your feet on the floor. This posture counterbalances the backbending in the previous posture. The spine stretches and the muscles soften, and the arm and leg muscles stretch and open, stimulating blood flow through the body.

9) Inhale and lightly step or jump your feet to your hands. Look up as in position 5.

Exhale your head down toward your knees. This is the same as position 4.

10) Inhale and extend your arms out straight to the sides as you come up to a standing position. Extend your arms up as in position 3.

11) Exhale and release your arms down by the side of your torso. Return your eye focus to a point in front of you as in position 2. Repeat the sequence a few times and try experimenting with the pace.

This half-hour session relieves menstruation pains and restores energy levels whenever you feel exhausted.

For most women, menstruation means low energy levels and changing emotional states. We often have to work when all our body wants is time out and plenty of rest. Listen to what your body is asking for. Take time to restore your energy.

Inverted or strenuous postures are not suitable during menstruation. Practice gentle sitting postures that open the muscles around the hips and pelvis, relieving cramps, heat and tension. The Inverted Leg postures I, II and III on page 102 are safe resting postures since the hips are not raised.

If half an hour is too long, cut out a few postures or reduce the holding time. Always finish a practice with some time in *Savasana*.

Menstruation sequence

JANU SIRSASANA (page 68)
Practice this posture for one minute on each side. Rest your head on a pillow for variation.

TRIANG MUKHAIKAPADA
PASCIMOTTANASANA (page 70)
Practice this posture for one minute on each side. Rest your head on a pillow for variation.

Sit with your legs wide and rest forward with your forehead and arms on a chair for three minutes. This gets the blood circulating, releasing tight hip and pelvic muscles.

3

Sit with the soles of your feet together and rest forward with your forehead and arms on a chair for three minutes. Feel the hips softening and the body cooling.

4

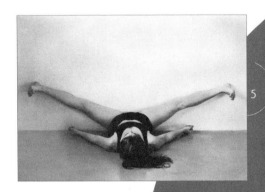

5

INVERTED LEGS II AND III (page 102)
Hold each variation of Inverted Legs for three
minutes. These postures are cleansing and
rejuvenating. Tired legs and feet are relieved of
aches and cramps while the rest of the body
relaxes on the floor. The body's systems slow
down and help to release stress and anxiety.
Feel your energy levels being restored.

6

SUPTA BADDHA KONASANA (page 116)

Hold this posture for five minutes.

VIRASANA II (page 74)

Hold *Virasana I* for three minutes. This posture opens up tight hips and relaxes the body forward and down.

SAVASANA I (page 110)

Lie in *Savasana I* for five to ten minutes. Make sure you are free from distractions. Use an eye bag if you wish to relax more deeply.

This sequence of postures keeps the body and mind healthy and supple during pregnancy and helps you prepare for childbirth. The muscles soften and loosen, keeping the body relaxed and flexible. The back is strengthened and aching legs and feet are relieved of tiredness and cramps.

Get in touch with the breath, breathing deep, full breaths throughout the practice. Make sure your yoga teacher is aware you are pregnant and always advise your medical professional or midwife of the yoga you are practicing. Do not practice any postures that cause strain, discomfort or tiredness. Keep the abdomen unconstricted at all times. Do not practice yoga during weeks eleven, twelve or thirteen of your pregnancy and do not exhaust your body in any way.

yoga during pregnancy

JANU SIRSASANA (page 68)

Use a belt to keep the lower back and abdomen lifting. This strengthens the back muscles that support the increasing weight of the baby. Hold for a minute on each side.

TRIANG MUKHAIKAPADA PASCIMOTTANASANA (page 70)

Keep the back and abdomen lifted and sit the buttock of the outside leg on a blanket for balance. Use a belt or strap. Hold for a minute on each side.

PASCIMOTTANASANA

Sit with the legs outstretched and the back straight. Hold onto a belt and keep the abdomen lifted and unconstricted. Straighten out and stretch the legs. Hold for a few minutes.

4a

4b

CAT ROLL

This gentle motion of rolling the back down and up gently rocks the baby and relieves lower back pain. First, sit on all fours with the knees hip width apart. Inhale and look up as you lift the buttocks and gently arch the back. (Do not arch the back in the last three months of pregnancy.) With the exhalation, tuck the chin in and under, looking down. Roll the spine up and drop the buttocks. Feel your baby gently rocking and your spine opening and stretching. Move back and forth with the breath. Repeat this motion five times or as much as it is comfortable.

PELVIC SQUAT

Squat down with the feet and knees wide apart. Do not squash the abdomen. Spread the knees wide. Bring the palms together and press the elbows into the knees. The pelvic muscles are activated and strengthened in preparation for the baby's birth. The hips are loosened and stretched. Practice deep, full breathing through the nose. Hold for five to ten breaths.

INVERTED LEGS I, II AND III (page 102)

Practice each posture for about three minutes. Use a bolster to support the head, neck, shoulders and back. Practice Inverted Legs II and III if lying with the buttocks against the wall is uncomfortable. In Inverted Legs III, the legs are spread apart. In Inverted Legs III, the knees are bent and the feet rest against the wall. These postures stimulate blood flow to the hips and pelvis and stretch the inner leg muscles.

SUPTA BADDHA KONASANA (page 116)

Use a bolster or a pillow for this posture. Do not use a belt. Gently place the feet together and let the knees fall open. Relax here for three to five minutes.

SITTING WITH THE BREATH (page 22)

Lean your back up against a wall for support if it becomes tired. Keep your legs outstretched if sitting cross-legged is uncomfortable. Practice deep, full, relaxed breathing through the nose.

Lie in *Savasana II* for ten minutes, relaxing the whole body deeply. The chest opens to assist in deep, full breathing. The abdomen opens and is supported. Use a blanket to keep warm and an eye bag if you wish to relax more deeply. Practice this posture in a quiet, warm environment free from distractions.

11

Yoga postures can help you find peace and relief from certain common ailments and conditions. Their therapeutic benefits help to relieve the body and mind of discomfort and anxiety.

The following remedial programs combine particular yoga postures in sequences that will help you with complaints such as backache and tiredness. A qualified yoga teacher will be able to help you further with individual problems. If your condition is serious, seek medical advice before practicing.

Try each of the courses so you get to know the sequences that work for you. Always conclude with a version of *Savasana*. If any posture feels wrong or causes strain, slowly release out of the posture. Each course has twelve postures and takes about twenty-five to thirty minutes.

Remedial courses

Relieving stress and anxiety

This sequence helps

to **eliminate** excess

mind energy, **restore**

the nervous system

and **calm** the body

and mind. Any

stress or anxiety will

melt away, leaving

you feeling **centered**

and **clear.**

1. Greeting the day: three times, page 138

2. Inverted Legs I, page 102

3. *Virasana I,* page 72

4. *Virasana II,* page 74

5. *Janu Sirsasana:* head resting on bolster, page 68

6. Child Pose, page 118

Relieving tiredness

Practice this sequence

when your body is

exhausted from a

hard day's work.

The **therapeutic**

relaxation postures

will **relieve**

tiredness and

restore your

energy levels.

1. *Supta Baddha Konasana,*
page 116

2. Inverted Legs I,
page 102

3. Inverted Legs III,
page 102

4. Knee Hug,
page 120

5. *Uttanasana,*
page 48

6. *Virasana II,*
page 74

Rejuvenation

If you are feeling

sluggish and want

a **pep-up**, practice

this sequence to

activate all the

body's systems. The

postures **stimulate**

circulation, **remove**

wastes and toxins and

leave you feeling

energized.

1. Greeting the day: three times, page 138

2. *Trikonasana*, page 32

3. *Urdhva Mukha Svanasana*, page 92

4. *Salabhasana*, page 94

5. Mini Backbend, page 96

6. Knee Hug, page 120

Focus and balance

Practice this sequence

when you are finding it

difficult to stay

focused. The

postures will **balance**

out the left and right

sides of your body

and help develop

concentration

and willpower.

Relieving backache

A **painful** back can

gently be relieved

with simple stretches

that **loosen,**

straighten and

strengthen the

spinal muscles. This

sequence will **soften**

and **relax** a tight,

aching back.

Abdominal toning

A **strong** stomach

helps to **support**

the back and

promotes good

posture. This

sequence also **tones**

the internal organs,

stimulating good

digestion and

bodily functions.

1. *Virasana I,*
page 72

2. *Virasana II,*
page 74

3. Greeting the day: three times,
page 138

4. *Trikonasana,*
page 32

5. *Janu Sirsasana,*
page 68

6. *Navasana:* three times,
page 78

Toning the reproductive system

Healthy sexual organs, muscles and glands **resist** disease and help **balance** hormone levels in the body. Practice this sequence to keep the reproductive system **functioning** well.

Relieving menopause

These **relaxing**

postures relieve

agitation or

stress experienced

during menopause.

The postures are

designed to **cool**

the body and

calm the mind.

1. Inverted Legs I,
page 102

2. Inverted Legs II,
page 102

3. Inverted Legs III,
page 102

4. Greeting the day: once,
page 138

5. *Urdhva Mukha Svanasana*,
page 92

6. *Janu Sirsasana*: with head on bolster,
page 68

Evening wind-down

If your day has been

exhausting

physically, mentally or

emotionally, spending

even a few minutes

to come back to

yourself will

help you **enjoy** the

evening and prepare

you for a restful **sleep.**

Relieving headache

Headache can be

caused by many

factors, such as

stress, fear, tiredness

or menstruation.

This sequence will

gently **stimulate**

circulation and **relax**

the body and mind,

helping to **relieve**

an aching head.

1. *Savasana II*,
page 112

2. *Supta Baddha Konasana*,
page 116

3. Forward Rest,
page 122

4. *Janu Sirsasana*:
with head resting on pillow, page 68

5. *Tri' Mukh' Pasc'*:
with head resting on pillow, page 70

6. *Bharadvajrasana*,
page 82

The following beginner's courses are made up of a sequence of postures from this book, combining standing, sitting, twisting, backbending, inverted and relaxation *asanas*. Some courses have a certain focus. For example, standing postures teach balance and twisting postures release toxins and soften the spine. All of the courses include standing and sitting postures and conclude with relaxation. Always finish with a version of *Savasana* or another relaxation posture for at least five minutes.

These sessions are your own private yoga classes and are a great way to explore the yoga postures. Each course is designed to be about thirty minutes long.

It is ideal to practice yoga every day for a healthy mind and body. However, three sessions a week is sufficient to keep your body toned and flexible throughout the week.

General yoga courses

Course One

Course Two

Course Three

Course Four

Course Five

Course Six

Course Seven

Course Eight

Course Nine

Course Ten

Course Eleven

Course Twelve

Course Thirteen

Course Fourteen

Course Fifteen

Course Sixteen

Course Seventeen

Course Eighteen

Index

About the author

Jessie first discovered yoga in 1991 and was instantly hooked. The positive effects it had on her mental and emotional state as well as her body inspired her to continue practicing. In yoga, she discovered a key to overcoming limiting beliefs and lifestyle habits, freeing her spirit and getting in touch with her highest potential in life.

Jessie explored many different styles of yoga and in 1997 completed the Yoga Arts Teacher Training Course in Byron Bay, Australia; she has been teaching ever since. She aims to inspire those new to yoga through the beauty of the poses, the simplicity of their practice and their inspiring benefits.

A freelance journalist, Jessie is author of *Yoga Sequences for Your Body, Mind & Soul*. She teaches yoga classes and retreats in Bali and Australia. For more information on retreats, classes and books, visit her website at www.intoyoga.com.

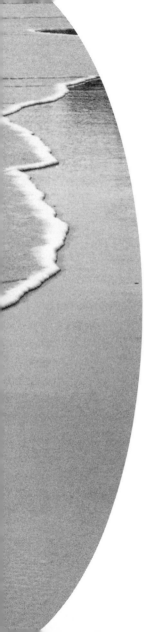

About the photographer

Dhyan first discovered the joy of photography twenty years ago, while traveling through South America. His "no fear," light-hearted and humorous approach to life has taken him to some unusual and beautiful places, enriching his life experiences, deepening his spiritual connection within, and making him an enjoyable photographer to model for. Based in Bali and Byron Bay, Australia, Dhyan builds Indonesian-influenced houses; surfs; swims with dolphins; hangs out with his gorgeous nine-year-old son Kai; and travels.

Acknowledgments

Making this book has been an exciting journey, especially when working with yoga models. Their patience when modeling postures in wet sand and in freezing temperatures wearing very little was extraordinary. Thanks so much to them all: Rachel Hull, Louisa Sear, Mathew James, Peter Watkins, Ronit Robbaz Franco (the beautiful pregnancy model) and Aloka.

Special thanks to Dhyan for all the time and energy he put into creating the gorgeous photographs that capture the essence of the postures.

Thanks to my mother Carole and sister Judy for their inspiration and support.

Thanks also to all the yoga teachers I have learned from, who have contributed their unique gifts and enhanced my experience of yoga, and to Mark Surman for his contribution with the photography.

Finally, I wish to thank the HarperCollins team: my editor Helen Littleton for sharing my vision; Katie Mitchell for her stunning design and layout of the book; and Jane Morrow and Wendy Blaxland for their wonderful word work.

Further reading

If you want to further your understanding of yoga postures, relaxation and meditation, try the following books:

T.K.V. Desikachar, *The Heart of Yoga: Developing a Personal Practice*, 1999, Inner Traditions Intl. Ltd.

B.K.S. Iyengar, *The Art of Yoga* (out of print — try your local library or a second-hand bookshop).

B.K.S. Iyengar and Yeudi Menuhin, *Light on Yoga: Yoga Dipika*, 1995, Schocken Books.

Annie Jones, *Yoga: A Step-by-Step Guide*, 1998, Element.

Silva Mehta, Mira Mehta and Shyam Mehta, *Yoga: The Iyengar Way*, 1990, Knopf.

Mary Stewart and Maxine Tobias, *The Yoga Book*, 1986, Pan.

Selvarajan Yesudian, *Yoga Week by Week* (out of print — try your local library or a second-hand bookshop).

Other books by Ulysses Press

HOW TO MEDITATE: AN ILLUSTRATED GUIDE
TO CALMING THE MIND AND RELAXING THE BODY
Paul Roland, $16.95
Offers a friendly approach to calming the mind and raising consciousness through various techniques, including meditation, visualization, body scanning for tension and mantras.

THE JOSEPH H. PILATES METHOD AT HOME:
A BALANCE, SHAPE, STRENGTH & FITNESS PROGRAM
Eleanor McKenzie, $16.95
This handbook describes and details Pilates, a mental and physical program that combines elements of yoga and classical dance.

PILATES PERSONAL TRAINER POWERHOUSE ABS WORKOUT:
ILLUSTRATED STEP-BY-STEP MATWORK ROUTINE
Michael King, $9.95
Designed for those who want to flatten and shape their abs, this book explains each Pilates exercise in an easy-to-follow manner. The key element is the series of two-page, step-by-step photo sequences that illustrate and demonstrate each exercise.

PILATES PERSONAL TRAINER THIGHS & BUTT WORKOUT:
ILLUSTRATED STEP-BY-STEP MATWORK ROUTINE
Michael King, $9.95
Instead of paying $100-plus per hour for private Pilates sessions, those looking to get the same kind of targeted workout to shape and slim their thighs and buttocks can find it in this book.

PILATES WORKBOOK:
ILLUSTRATED STEP-BY-STEP GUIDE TO MATWORK TECHNIQUES
Michael King, $12.95
Illustrates the core matwork movements exactly as Joseph Pilates intended them to be performed; readers learn each movement by following the photographic sequences and explanatory captions.